Support Your Local Vampire Kitty-Cat

Other books by the author

Fiction

The Hollywood Unmurders
Crimes and dangerous times in La La Land for Patch,
the vampire kitty-cat, and his partner, Meg.

The Summer Boy
A murder mystery wrapped around a coming-of-age story
set in Texas in the 60s.

Gundown
A speculative thriller that explores a real-world solution
for gun violence.

Final Fjire
A speculative thriller—a madman creates a
plague to wipe out humanity.

Nonfiction
Mastering the Craft of Compelling Storytelling
Coaching on fiction craft and narrative technique
for writers of all levels.

Support Your Local Vampire Kitty-Cat

THE VAMPIRE KITTY-CAT CHRONICLES

RAY RHAMEY

Ashland, Oregon

 The platypus breaks all the rules—it's the only mammal that lays eggs, is venomous, has a duck bill, a beaver tail, and otter feet—and it does just fine, thank you very much.

It can be the same for novels that don't slip tidily into genre pigeonholes. Platypus takes readers on unique paths to entertainment, truth, and enjoyable reads.

ISBN 978-0-9909282-6-3

Book cover and design by Ray Rhamey

For Sarah, Abby, Molly, Becky, Dan, Julia, Beth,
and the cats we have loved.

Bob
Alex
Sally
Isaac
Olive
Casey
Oscar
Rocky
Rugby
Skunk
Fraidy
Gracie
Peanut
Pepper
Xerxes
Floppy
Frisbee
Mittens
Wrigley
Lancelot
Sylvester
Alabama
Guinevere
Strawberry
Ryder Parsnips Revenge

1: Spot

Now that the blush of sunset has dissolved into the pale night of a full moon, it's romantic rendezvous time for this tomcat. I check myself in the tall mirror by the front door—fur is clean and groomed and calico colors are looking good, especially the orange bits.

I give a parting meow to my associate Amy, who as usual is reading a book in the living room. She waves goodbye, and out the pet door I go.

A cool September breeze, spiced with an earthy hint of fall, fluffs my fur as I bound down the steps of Amy's condominium and head for a shortcut through the neighborhood cemetery. It's a tidy place, grass mowed short and easy on the paws, silent tombstones and flat footstones gray in the moonlight.

The only sound in the midst of the graves is me, happily purring with visions of a certain svelte Siamese pussycat coming to my near future. If cats could skip, I would.

A murmur of voices slithers into my sweet little scenario. They chant, but softly, like loud whispers, "Death ... Death ... "

Death? Okay, that's scary. I lower myself to the grass and try to locate the death people.

Then they say, "Death to vampires."

Wait, vampires? Unreal. Literally. Give me a break.

The chant moves closer. "Death ..."

Four people, three of them men, come into view, more than just shadows in the bright moonlight. They walk in a line, an arm's length from each other. Each one has a flashlight, and they examine every grave as the line moves toward me.

One of them pumps a fist in the air to the rhythm of the chant, and my kitty-cat night vision picks up a stake in his hand, maybe a foot long, tapered to a knife-sharp point.

"Death ... Death to vampires ..."

They're hunting a make-believe monster? You ask me, the rationality of humans is considerably overrated and completely unreliable. The delusionary vampire hunters are coming my way, though, and while I'm not a vampire, I don't want to mix it up with a handful of nuts armed with pointy stakes. So I flatten myself in the narrow shadow behind a footstone that's high enough to conceal me and low enough that I can see them. If they notice me, I'm outta here quicker than they can say death to vampires.

"Dea—"

"Stop!" The woman halts, holds up a hand, and with the other aims her flashlight in front of her at raw soil that looks like the mound of a fresh grave. The others circle around, aiming their lights at the dirt.

A hand bursts out of the ground, startling the woman back a pace. Another hand follows, and then a man sits up, dirt spilling off of him.

The guy with the stake cries, "Gotcha!" and drives it into the chest of the man in the hole.

His victim falls back and writhes, his body spasming and twisting. The four chant, "Death to vampires!" There's a note of glee in their voices.

The shortest man claps the stake-wielder on the back. "I knew we'd find one sooner or later." He digs into a pocket and then there's a flash. And another one.

Selfies.

The writhing man in the hole stiffens, falls back into the hole, and lies still.

The woman points at him. "Looky that. Is he ... is he *melting*?"

The guy standing next to her turns away and pukes.

That's enough for me. I stay low and put a few gravestones between me and the horror show, and then I shift into high gear.

Just as I'm reaching my top speed, closing in on thirty miles per hour, a back paw catches on something and I tumble through the air, tail over teakettle. I land on my back but instantly flip to my paws.

The tripster is a hand sticking out of a mound of freshly turned dirt.

Ewww.

The fingers are slender, fingernails polished red. A woman's hand.

The pinky finger twitches.

Twice.

I don't hear the vampire hunters anymore so, curiosity being a thing with cats, I'm compelled to give the hand a sniff. It doesn't smell like meat past its use-by date. Doesn't smell alive, either, though there is a metallic nuance that reminds me of something ...

Never mind, a lovely pussycat awaits me and I'm not all *that* curious, so I turn to—

The woman's head pokes out of the earth in front of me and she sits up, loose dirt spilling off her.

Exactly like that guy who just got stuck with a stake.

By a vampire hunter.

Shock freezes me just long enough for her to grab my tail and hoist me into the air.

I twist to go for her with my claws, but then her other hand seizes the scruff of my neck. I go limp with the kitten reflex, just like when I was a baby and my mom picked me up.

My attacker holds me out in front of her. I figure I'm about to kiss my furry butt goodbye.

And I'm right.

Sort of.

She looks to be twentysomething in human years. Dirty blond hair—with dirt, that is. Her bulging blue eyes are scary, but I forget all about them when she leans in and bites my neck. Whoa, it hurts, but, held fast by instinct and the pull on my tail, I just hang there while she gets her teeth into my skin. Something warm and liquid oozes down my neck. The red scent of fresh blood fills the air.

My blood.

Where are the vampire hunters when you need them?

Or a cop. A cop would be good. There are laws against cruelty to animals, and I'm pretty sure this qualifies.

As she sucks and slurps, strength drains out of me along with the sweet sauce of life.

I don't even have enough energy to regret things I've done in my short life. Not that I have any regrets, seeing as how cats don't do that kind of thing. I flash back to when I peed on Amy's bed for switching cat food without checking with me. A petty thing to do to my associate, perhaps. But nothing to regret—she clearly deserved it.

Soon I'm spacey, just floating. The woman stops noshing and lays me on the dirt in front of her. Her eyes aren't scary anymore. Things are dim and it's hard to focus—but her expression seems sorrowful. Then she turns her head and, *patooie*, spits out a mouthful of fur.

Serves her right.

She turns sad eyes at me and says, "I'm awful sorry, kitty-cat. But the pain hurt so bad ..." She trails off and licks my blood from her fingers like she's just had some Kentucky Fried Kitty.

A prickly-tingly sensation starts on my neck where the woman bit me, like when your paw goes to sleep and then wakes up. I twist and twitch and wriggle as pinpricks spread all through me, head to toes and deep down into my gut. Then that stops and everything aches. Then the ache fades and it's over.

I can only lie there like a sack of cat meat.

As though handling something precious, she shifts me to the grass beside her hole and then climbs out. After brushing dirt from her clothes, she lowers me into the hole she's left in the dirt and lays me on my back, legs spread-eagled, a most undignified pose. And then she strokes my belly—humiliation on top of indignity.

She says, "Oh, I hate this so much."

Tell me about it.

She pushes dirt over me.

Too weak to move, I wait to die.

My heart slows and slows.

...

Goodbye, Amy.

...

It stops.

2: Meg

With Meg's cemetery hidey-hole six blocks behind her and reanimated by her kitty-cat snack, she crosses the street to the 7-Eleven on Fifteenth Avenue, the only nearby business open this time of night. It's her one hope of getting enough money for an Uber to take her to safety in her apartment before the sun comes up and she has to, ugh, go underground again to escape the burning of the sun.

She'd be home right now if the bitch who did this to her hadn't stolen her purse and left her unconscious. Who'd have thought researching graveyards for a Halloween TV commercial she was writing would lead to this? She'd stepped on a fresh pile of dirt at a gravesite, and a small woman, her black hair in long pigtails, had sprung up from under the dirt and grabbed her.

With the strength of a professional wrestler, the woman slammed Meg to the ground on her back and leaped onto her. Teeth tore into Meg's neck. She flailed wildly, hitting wherever she could, but her attacker delivered a powerful blow to the side if her head and all went dark.

A burning sensation on her face had roused her to see the sun glimmering on the horizon. It was dawn. When she held a hand up to block the sunlight from her face, the pain dimmed there but intensified on the side of her hand struck by sunshine. The only place she could see that might be a way to escape the burn was the hole her attacker had left in the loose soil. She lay down in it and scooped dirt over herself the best she could. When dirt covered her face, the pain stopped. She'd worried about breathing—but she learned, disturbingly, that she had no need to breathe.

She'd spent the day buried, wrapped in panic and terror, *what's happening to me* whirring over and over in her mind. She'd writhed in agony toward the end, craving blood as the pain of all pains burned throughout her body.

Meg was lucky to have had fresh blood waiting for her after the sun went down. But it hadn't been lucky for that poor innocent kitty. She hates herself for killing him, but there literally wasn't anything else she could do. A desire ... no, a *hunger* for blood had driven her, irresistibly. She'd had to ... *had* to ... She shoves the thought away. What she has to do now is survive, to get home before the sun is back and she has to bury herself again.

When she reaches the store, Meg peers at her reflection in the window and touches where the woman bit her neck. There's no wound; it's as if the bite never happened. She frowns at the black soil under her fingernails from raking dirt over herself. She still doesn't understand how she can be walking around without breathing. Wait a minute. If she's not breathing ... She places her fingertips on the underside of her wrist. Nothing. She guesses it makes sense to not need to breathe if she doesn't have a pulse.

The word *vampire* whispers in her thoughts. But that's crazy. She can't be a vampire because she can see her reflection and vampires can't do that, right? And they have fangs, too. She bares her teeth and checks her image. Yep, fang-free. Though fangs would have been useful when she attacked the kitty-cat. If she is a vampire, the myths are full of holes. No reflection, fangs ... what else do the stories have screwed up?

But maybe this is all going to turn out to be just a weird nightmare. She takes her cell phone from her back pocket, hoping that it has somehow miraculously built up enough of a charge to call her parents for a ride to her place. No, it's still dead. And she hates the idea of calling her parents anyway. She's a grown woman.

Who has a boyfriend. Well, a sort-of boyfriend; they haven't been dating that long. But to call Clive fresh out of a grave and dump whatever this is on him ... better to find another way home.

She brushes dirt off her jeans and straightens her tank top, slips her denim overshirt off and shakes it out. Inspecting her reflection, Meg decides she doesn't look too bad. She runs her fingers through her dirty hair, puts her shirt back on, steps inside the store, and heads for the Women's to do something about her hands.

The lights are lower than she expects in a convenience store, but even so, when she walks in, her exposed skin prickles in an unpleasant way, like tiny pins poking her everywhere. The clerk is helping a scruffy-looking woman with a six-pack of beer and pays no attention to Meg as she scurries to the restroom.

Once she's dug the dirt from under her fingernails and washed up, Meg meanders over to the magazine rack and pretends to be absorbed in the cover of *Vogue*, a magazine she's never actually read. She's more the *Good Housekeeping* type.

Deep in her gut, a twinge of blood hunger pulses. Though the cat was good-sized, apparently she hadn't gotten a fill-up. Oh, please, let the agony hold off. She doesn't want to hurt any of the people in the store.

When the woman with the beer passes her on the way out, a warm scent that makes Meg think of blood calls to her, and the craving for it kicks up a notch. Resisting a desire to sink her teeth into the shopper, she picks up a *Reader's Digest* that, ironically, has a cover story titled "The Scourge of the Undead" and waits until the woman is gone.

She sidles to the guy behind the counter. Her gut tightens at having to talk to a stranger, the curse of being an introvert. She hopes she won't be tempted to bite him. He looks up at her, and she takes a deep breath. When she woke in the graveyard and tried to scream, no sound had come out until she'd purposely filled her lungs with air. Not that screaming had done any good. "Excuse me, are you the manager?"

The clerk is a big guy. A head like a pumpkin above a narrow chest that spreads downward to a fat waist overhanging his belt. He takes a breath and then says, "That's me. George."

She gives George a smile that she hopes he sees as sincere. "Hi. My name's Meg. I, uh, do you have any work I could do? Tonight?"

George shakes his head. "Nope. You can apply down at the main office. But there aren't any openings at this store 'cause I'm it at night. Maybe there's something on the day shift."

She tries to keep her smile going, but the thought of another night under dirt wilts it. "I need work that's, er, at night. Tonight. Please, isn't there anything I could do? Just a few hours? Mop floors? Take out the trash?" She glances around the store. "Put your magazines in alphabetical order?"

George leans forward, his eyes narrowing. "I hear there're openings down at the unemployment office. Jobs a lot better than here."

"Ah, it's only open during the day."

He just stares at her.

"I'm ... I can't go out in daylight. I have photophobia."

"Big word."

"Big problem. I'm a good worker. I have a job at an ad agency." She slumps. There's no way she can go to work anymore. "I had a job at an ad agency. And now I haven't been able to get back to my apartment since this ... *condition* hit me. I was robbed, and my phone is dead." She never carries money in her pockets, and she'd had no way to pay for a cab or Uber after she was attacked. She glances out the plate glass storefront. Oh, God, please don't send me back out there.

She brushes at a splotch of dirt on her shirt. "I'm so embarrassed. I'm homeless, and I don't know what to do."

George smiles. He *smiles*? What an ass, taking pleasure in her distress. Then he says, "Welcome to the Night Shift."

She smiles for real. "I can do some work?"

He shakes his head. "'Night Shift' is just a handle for people like us."

She gazes out at the dark. She has to find a way to—

Wait a minute.

3: Spot

Silence.

...

Amazing how utterly quiet it is, lying here in total darkness. I've never thought about my heart beating, but now that it has stopped its constant lub-dubbing, I miss it.

I think, *Well, that's it.*

I wish I could give Amy a parting purr. I've been with her since kittenhood, maybe four years. We loved to sit in front of the fireplace in the wintertime, me curled in her lap, her with a philosophy book.

I enjoyed the times her college students came over. When one kid tried to argue that I was just a concept, I countered with reality by unsheathing my claws and climbing up his leg.

Ah, the intellectual life.

...

Silence.

...

And then I think, *I'm still thinking.*

I focus on my innards. No heartbeat. And I'm not breathing. Probably a good thing, with me having a snootful of dirt.

I push up with a front paw. The dirt is loose. I push harder and my paw breaks through. I turn over and crawl out of the hole. I'm alive.

And I'm not.

A light sweeps across me, and a woman says, "Something moved over there." It's the vampire huntress.

The light comes back and settles on me.

It sounds like the short guy who says, "It's a cat. Cats aren't vampires."

"I see a hole. Maybe the ones who come out of graves are."

I belly-crawl in the dirt, away from the light, and roll behind a tombstone.

The woman says, "Aww, it's gone."

The chant rises. "Death to vampires."

I peer into the darkness, but the woman who attacked me from her grave is gone.

"Death to vampires."

She's lucky to escape. I'm not feeling so lucky, and the voices are coming closer.

Home with Amy, warm and safe, is all I can think of. I stagger away, heading back to Amy's townhouse. I'll be okay there.

The three steps on the front stoop of Amy's townhouse loom like Mount Everest, and I'm way more than half dead, with an ache in my gut that makes it hard to think. One paw at a time, I crawl onto the bottom step. But when I stand to reach up for the next step, my back legs give out and I topple backward to the sidewalk. I don't see how I'll ever get there.

The ache in my stomach flares into flames of pain that shoot through me. I try to yowl, but nothing comes out of my open mouth.

I struggle to my feet and I can think of only one thing.

Blood.

Red. Meaty. Warm.

As the pain pounds hotter and hotter, beating like the pulse I don't have, new strength washes through me.

Blood-blood-blood-blood-blood.

A scuttle of rat paws comes from the side of the stoop, where a small lawn area is occupied by a trio of bushes. I creep until I can peek around the edge of the bottom step. The rat faces away from me, burrowing into the turf.

The pain is so ENORMOUS that it takes every bit of willpower to crouch and spring. Even though I've just had a whole lot of blood drained out of me, I feel superstrong. I belly flop right on top of the rat.

Its head wobbles when I flip it onto its back; I've broken its neck, and ratso is dead. Unlike me. Sort of.

The PAIN raging through me screams for BLOOD!

I couldn't stop now even if I wanted to. My mind says *ewww* when rat stink hits my nostrils, but my body steamrollers over that. Steamrollers? More like a tsunami, a fifty-foot wave of irresistible gotta-have-it driven by escalating pain. I'd go through a brick wall to get BLOOD. Crazily, I think I'm strong enough to do just that.

Mortifyingly, I go into a frenzy. Utter loss of control, totally uncatlike. I rip open the rat's throat and lap up the blood that spills out.

Relief is instant. My heart begins beating just like old times and most of the pain dies away. I bet it will be back.

Home is a mighty siren call, and I answer it, leaving the rat corpse, leaping up the steps, and pushing through the pet door.

Once I'm inside, the light stabs me in the eyes. It's the normal lamplight Amy always has on at night, but now it stings.

Squinting, I find her still in the living room. She doesn't notice me because, as usual, she's absorbed in a book. I have my usual answer for that—a leap into her lap, which always results in a friendly greeting and a good scratch behind my ears. Here I come, Amy.

Blood. I stop as the need rises in me. The rat didn't donate very much to the cause. The closer I get to Amy, the more ... *delicious* she smells. The pain swells. *Blood-blood.*

I want to bury my fangs in her leg and lap up her BLOOD!

I can't do that, not to my associate. I turn away seconds before launching an attack. My control is losing ground like a dog chasing a Corvette. Luckily, her scent grows fainter as I head back to the door, but still I want her BLOOD.

It's a drumbeat in my mind.

Blood-blood-blood ...

No-no-no.

She calls out, "Spot?"

Amy thinks calling me Spot is funny because of the patches of color in my calico fur. There are some things you just have to live with.

"Here, kitty-kitty."

Keeping going is one of the hardest things I've ever done. I want her to hold me, to comfort me. I also want her BLOOD! NO.

I push out through the pet door and hurry down the steps. When I reach the bottom, the door opens above me. I slip into the darkness at the side of the stoop so she can't see me.

"Spot?" she calls. "Come here, sweetie. Here, kitty-kitty."

I need her embrace, her love, and I want to meow for her to come get me. But that takes breathing, which is no longer part of my operating system.

She calls again a couple of times, and then I hear the door shut. She's safe. I sit there for a while.

My life with Amy is over.

I miss her already, which is unexpected. I've always thought of myself as totally independent. I'm a cat, after all, one of the deadliest predators on the planet. I have no need for anyone, especially a human.

Well, except for opening doors. And cans of cat food.

Damn the woman who ripped me from the arms of my associate, who had become my friend as well as the provider of never-ending gourmet dining and clean cat litter.

The cat thing to do is revenge—although peeing on my killer's grave seems like inadequate retaliation for what she's done to me. And, considering my current state of being, I suspect that it's not physically possible anymore.

Now what?

The graveyard. To track down my murderer. Vengeance will be mine.

It's good to have a mission; I don't want to think about what being dead will do to my life.

4: Meg

Meg squints at George. Had she heard right? *"Us?"*

George nods, then reaches out and touches the side of her neck. She flinches back. He holds up his finger—there's a red spot of blood on it that she'd missed on her clean-up. "Had a little bit of leftover breakfast there." He licks his fingertip.

Meg is a little freaked. Even though she figures she must now be a vampire, she doesn't feel all that comfy being around one. "I think ... maybe I'd better ..." She starts backing toward the door.

George holds his hands up in appeal. "Hey, hold on. I can tell you're new, and I'm sure you're scared, but you just got lucky."

Now, that is stupid. She shakes her head. "Dead people don't have luck." Except for the bad kind.

George ambles out from behind the counter. She retreats a couple more steps. He stops and smiles at her. "Hey, it's *un*dead people. There's no death certificate for you, right?"

As far as anyone knows, she's still counted as among the living. It's only been a day, an eternally long day. She nods.

"No funeral, no mourning, no grave, right? You can call up people and they'll think you're the same as ever."

He has a point. She isn't exactly a corpse.

George aims a forefinger at her. "If you were able to keep your job, you'd still be paying taxes, right?"

She guesses she would. Nothing stops the IRS, not even the Grim Reaper. "You mean that, even though I'm not alive, I have a life?"

He snorts a laugh. "You could put it that-a-way. We vees still need a place to sleep during the day and blood to drink, and those things take money, so we gotta work." George waves at the store. "Trouble is, lotta night jobs are pretty crummy. I have a PhD in history, but here I am."

It's just too much. She sags at the knees. George takes her arm, leads her around behind the counter, and sits her on a tall stool. Then he pulls a phone from his pants pocket and hits a button.

"Hey, Sammy, George here. Got a newbie." He listens, nods. "The usual, lookin' for night work." He examines her. "By the looks of her, the local cemetery."

Her gaze drops to the floor. She would blush if she weren't dead. Make that undead.

He listens, then says, "Name's Meg. Worked for a ad agency—"

Her internal editor blurts, "That's *an* ad agency. Dewey, Fakem, and Howe. I'm a writer."

"A writer." More listening. He grins. "Yeah?" He looks to her. "You want a job?"

She tries not to let hope rise, but it does anyway. "Oh, yes."

George nods. "She says yes." He ends the call and pockets the phone. "Sammy'll be over in a minute. He's with the American Vampire Association."

There's an association? The place is crawling with vampires.

She says, "Do you mean he has a j—"

George holds up his hand to silence her and stares at the front door. In the quiet, voices murmur. "Mumble ... mumble ... vampires!"

They come closer.

5: Spot

The hole in the graveyard where those crazy people killed a man—a vampire—is now filled with a pile of bones, a skull, and patches of red, meaty-looking stuff. Looks to me like what the woman said is true—the guy sort of melted, all except his bones.

I crank up every sense I have, but can't detect the killers. No chanting, no odors other than blood from the remains. There's just silence as I make my way to the hole Dirt Woman came out of.

The smell of her includes the normal human reek of animal and chemical, plus dirt-smell and a coppery undertone, like blood. I hurry along the trail of her scent; I don't want to lose her and my chance for payback.

I'm forced to entertain the wacky notion that I am now—it sounds silly—a vampire. I mean, I was dead, but here I am, walking around with no pulse. Okay, so what do I know about vampires? The story goes that they have fangs. I explore my mouth with my tongue. I have fangs.

But I've always had fangs.

My attacker had regular old blunt human teeth with those pitiful excuses for canines. She managed to do damage, all right, but she hadn't been properly vampiric. So she's not a regulation vampire? Fang challenged?

What else is there about them? No daylight or you're cooked. That one shouldn't be a problem. I can see in the dark, so the up-all-night thing is cool. And nobody'll think twice about a cat sleeping all day, while human vampires have to hide. Maybe that was what Dirt Woman was doing. How revolting is that? Imagine the mess when it rains. And when winter hits, you'd be a corpsicle. Come to think of it, cats are a whole lot better equipped to be vampires than people.

But right now, retaliation is in order. I'll track Dirt Woman down and then ... well, it's too bad a wooden stake is out of the question, my paws lacking opposable digits and me lacking a wooden stake. But I'll come up with something.

Leaving the cemetery, I pause at a street and look both ways. Even though I'm probably past any danger of being roadkill, why risk it? Voices chant, "Death to vampires" in the darkness. It's them again.

Why me, Lord?

Dirt Woman's trail goes toward a little store across the street. The four vampire hunters emerge from darkness on the far sidewalk. Flashlights aglow, they head for the store's front door.

"Death to vampires."

I follow Dirt Woman's scent trail across the street and toward the store. I sneak up to the vampire vigilantes and tuck in close behind them. The vampire in that store is *my* vampire, and they can't have her.

I shift into stealth mode, ready to follow them inside.

6: Meg

The door to the store opens and the chant becomes clear. "Death to vampires."

Meg cringes. As if this night weren't bad enough.

A woman leads three men into the store. They wear sheaths attached to their belts that hold something long and tapered to a sharp point. Their matching blood-red T-shirts sport a logo on the chest made of the letters *D, V,* and *L.* The chanters stop their chant.

George reaches under his counter and pulls out a metal baseball bat. "Get out."

What? She turns to George. "But I—"

"Not you."

He steps out from the counter and stands in front of it, bat in hand. Meg leaves the stool and stands behind him. She peeks around to watch the people who came in. George says again, "Get out."

The woman says, "What's your problem?"

"No gangs allowed in the store."

She laughs. "We're just a ... a club doing a service for our community." The others chuckle and grin.

A skinny guy puffs out his chest and taps the logo on his shirt. He says, "We're the Death to Vampires League." He grins. "Some call us the Devils."

"I'm calling you gone. There isn't any service I need that has to do with death. Go away."

A short guy pulls a stiletto-like stake from the sheath on his belt. "Hey, man, we don't mean you any trouble. In fact, we're here to protect you from vampires."

George lifts the bat. "Who's going to protect you from me?" He advances on them.

The woman holds up her hands. "Okay, listen. We're nonviolent."

"Looking at that stake, not when it comes to vampires."

Short Guy shrugs. "Hey, they're already dea—"

George shifts into a batter's stance, lifting the bat high.

Nobody moves. Then the short guy points at Meg. "Anybody seen that woman breathe since we got here?"

She takes a quick breath, but it's too late.

His grin is nasty. "Looks like our lucky night, mister. You better step aside—that's a vampire behind you."

Meg steps up beside George. She focuses on the lessons her Krav Maga instructor taught her about defending a grab 'n stab attack. She spreads her feet for good balance and readies a universal block to avoid a stabber's weapon arm if they charge her.

The woman says, "The guy's not exactly inhaling and exhaling, either."

George says, "What is there about 'get out' that you don't understand?"

She takes a stake from her sheath. "Looks like we got a twofer here."

They spread out into a semicircle as the other two pull out stakes.

7: Spot

Oh no you don't! She's mine! I lunge from beneath a potato chip display and leap for the nearest guy. When I sink my claws into the backs of his legs, he screams. I climb up his back to the top of his head.

He grabs me and pulls, but my claws are sunk deep. He yells and lets go. "Help!"

From my perch, the nearest Devil sports a mop of curly hair. It's the woman, and my next target. My captive screams again.

She whirls toward me and shrieks, "It's the cat that came out of that grave! Don't let it bite you!"

I launch myself at her, but she ducks and runs for the door. I connect with Short Guy's shirt instead, my claws catching the cloth, and I fall, my claws shredding his shirt.

He dashes out the door, and the remaining Devils jam into each other in their scramble to get out.

Good. I turn and face the guy with a bat. Dirt Woman smiles at me, a smile I'm going to make her regret. She says, "Hey, it's the kitty-cat."

I crouch and ready myself to attack.

8: Meg

She hadn't killed the cat!

It glares at her, does that wriggle thing cats do when they're about to pounce, and then bares its fangs in what looks like a silent hiss. Well, she can't blame it for being pissed at her.

The cat charges; it leaps straight at her. She flinches back in the face of the cat's fury.

George swings his bat and catches the cat in the midsection. He hits a line drive right into a display loaded with candy bars. The cat falls to the floor, and Snickers bars avalanche down on him.

George dashes toward the cat, the bat raised high over his head to deliver the coup de grâce.

Meg yells, "Stop!" George pulls up, and she runs to the cat, sweeps candy bars off him, and picks him up. He glares at her and unsheathes his claws, but she holds him tight to her front and grips his front paws with one hand.

George looms over the cat and Meg. "It's a cat. In my store."

She grabs the end of the bat with one hand. The cat looks at her hand on the bat and then up at her. Meg pushes the bat away—the poor kitty wouldn't be in this situation if it weren't for her. "It's *my* cat."

George points his bat at the door. "It could be God's cat for all I care, it's outta here."

"But those ... Devils are out there."

"It's three strikes for your cat. It's out. Now."

9: Patch nee Spot

Outside the store, the Devils are gone. Dirt Woman squeezes me tight to her as she peers around. George follows her out, still wielding his bat. Considering the weirdos that now lurk out here, I'm not unhappy about that.

She meets my gaze. I give her the stink-eye with both barrels.

George bends low and sniffs me. "I'll be darned." He straightens and relaxes.

He says, "So what's its name? Breakfast?"

Funny guy. She doesn't laugh. Good for her.

She takes another deep breath. "Actually, we haven't known each other long enough for me to give him a name. But I will, just so I can introduce you."

Dirt Woman sure is a heavy breather. Then I think about it. I focus on my chest and imagine taking a breath. My chest expands and air comes in. I breathe it out with a soft little "Mrrr."

If I'd known I could do this, would I have answered Amy when she called me? And then gone into a feeding frenzy when she picked me up and cuddled me? The pain had been so bad that I don't think I could have resisted. No, I *know* I couldn't have.

Back to my assassin. I take advantage of my newfound breathing ability to let loose a low growl.

The woman's eyebrows lift in an expression of surprise—that's a thing cats envy people, the ability to create expressions with your face. That and the thumbs.

Then she smiles again, as if she's glad to see me.

I flex my claws, ready to scratch and scramble.

As for a name, the woman is wasting her breath. Cats don't do names. I'm Me, and that's it.

Dirt Woman sets me down on the sidewalk and looks me over. I doubt she knows she's dealing with a rare creature. Not that calico cats are unusual—you can see my mixture of orange, black, and white all over town—but we guy calicos are few and far between. For every one of me there are about three thousand calico pussycats, and all us guys are sterile. It's a dead-end genetic profile that now seems extremely ironic.

But apparently, she just has to give me a moniker. She says, "Let's see ... patches of color ... How about Patchie?"

Ewww. Even worse than Spot. I stick out my tongue. Maybe she is sharper than the average vampire, because she shakes her head. "Naw, too cutesy for a big, fierce guy like you."

It's possible that I push my chest out a little.

"How about Patch?"

Not bad. At least it has something to do with me. Seeing as how she stopped George from batting practice à la kitty-cat, I decide not to hold my grudge anymore. We're sort of even. To let her know my opinion, I rub against her leg. Just once, though. I'm not a gushy cat.

Then I look up at her and do the eye-contact thing. "Mrrr."

She grins. "Patch it is."

George says, "It doesn't matter he's got a name or that he's yours, no animals allowed in the store. I can't afford to lose this job."

Headlights sweep across us, and a banged-up rounded lump with wheels, an old-style Volkswagen Bug, pulls up. George says, "It's Sammy." He heads for the car.

Dirt Woman scoops me up. I don't object; she knows how to hold a cat, too, with an arm under my hindquarters, none of that one end or the other left hanging.

The undertone scent of copper from her is strong, and I got the same thing from George. I must smell the same way. Is that what clued George that I'd been the woman's latest meal? The smell of blood—the scent of vampires?

A scrawny, sunken-chested little guy with squinty eyes gets out of the car. He sports a fulsome mustache that covers his mouth. His eyes widen when he sees Meg. He smiles—I can't tell if there are fangs underneath his mustache—and his bass voice seems impossibly deep for such a pipsqueak when he says, "Welcome to the A.V.A."

His gaze drops to me. "Now, that's curious. Cats usually hate to be around us."

He has that right. This whole vampire scene is definitely creepy. But it's not like it's my idea to be here.

George chuckles. "Yeah, but this cat *is* us."

Dirt Woman steps forward and sticks out a hand to shake, still cradling me quite comfortably with her other arm. "My name's Meg, and this is Patch."

We all flinch as bright headlights swing into the parking lot. George lifts his bat. "I hope that's not those Devils coming back."

Sammy shields his eyes from the light and asks George, "The Devils? Here?"

"Four of 'em." He waves his bat. "I ran them off."

Meg clears her throat and nods at me. George says, "Well, the cat helped. A little."

I aim a growl at George. He backs up a step.

She says, "A little. As in, he chased them away."

An old hearse, long and black with fishtail fins on the rear fenders and black curtains on the windows, pulls up next to the Bug. Sammy says, "Crap. It's Lester. He's been following me around, pestering people about 'living the true vampire life' instead of going with the A.V.A." He glares at the hearse. "You ask me, I think he's lonely."

Lester climbs out of the hearse. Unfolds, actually—he has to be seven feet tall. Black is his thing, with one exception—when he rounds the front of the hearse on his way to us, his black cape flares and reveals a silky crimson lining.

He smiles. Big fangs. Sharp ones that touch his bottom lip. He looks like the real deal. Now that I think of it, George doesn't have fangs, and I'm guessing that Sammy doesn't have any underneath that mustache either.

Lester gloms onto Meg right away and strides closer to tower over us. "My dear, let me welcome you to the underworld. My name is Lestat."

Sammy turns to Meg. "Lester is into Anne Rice these days." He shakes his head. "Note the fake fangs. Caps."

Oh.

Lester/Lestat glares down at Sammy. "You're such an insect. You and the rest of your breather wannabes." He spreads his arms wide, flaring his cape and showing the red lining, and smiles down at Meg and me. Actually, I don't think he's noticed me.

"I live the legend of the vampire, free, a law unto myself." He raises a fist into the air. "I am Lestat, the beast that feasts in night's darkest deeps."

Where does this guy get his dialogue? Maybe he spends his daylight hours in a theater dedicated to showing movies that were nominated for the Golden Raspberry Award, the annual celebration of godawful films.

Sammy says, "So, Meg, George tells me you're looking for work."

Lester steps between Sammy and Meg and me. "Work? Why work? If you need to feed"—he waves a really long arm at the night—"your dining pleasure awaits you, ready for the taking."

Sammy steps out from behind Lester. "Yeah, if you don't get caught. Most breathers don't like being chewed on. You can get hurt."

Lester puffs up. "Ha! Maybe you mice fear breathers, but those true to the Dark Path do not."

So now he's Darth Lester?

Meg says, "I don't think it's right to attack innocent people. That's what happened to me." She puts a hand to her neck, and her voice gets harder. "Thanks to that bitch, I have no job and no life. And had to sleep in the dirt, for God's sake."

Lester strikes a pose, chest out, hands on his hips, cape swirling, legs spread. I half expect him to break into "Yo ho ho, fifteen men on a dead man's chest."

He says, "You're mistaken, little woman."

Meg stiffens and tightens her grip on me. Her face looks like a snarl.

"You should praise that woman for setting you free, just as a munificent monster once did me. And you don't have to sleep in dirt." He points at his hearse. "When the sun comes, I just park, draw the curtains, relax in my coffin, and doze. I have a little TV, too."

He grips Meg's arm and pulls her to him, squishing me between them, his belt buckle poking me in the eye. It hurts, but not as much as I would expect. My senses are dulled down. Not numb, but close.

"Come with me, Megan. I know where to get a coffin just your size. There's plenty of room in my ride, and together we can enjoy the life eternal."

Sammy laughs. "The life of a petty criminal, you mean. With no job and no money, how do you think he feeds that gas hog of his?"

Meg pushes at Lester's chest with her free arm and creates a little space between us. It's a relief to get that belt buckle out of my eye. It's shaped like a bat.

I look up, and I don't like Lester's smirk. With the fangs and all, he looks a little on the evil side to me. Make that a *lot* on the evil side.

Lester says, "I have money, all I need. My dinners, er, donors gladly give me their worldly goods." He leers. "Well, perhaps it isn't gladly."

He yanks on Meg's arm to pull her back to him and crunches me again. That pisses me off, and I whip out my claws and plunge them into the back of his hand. He jerks it away, and my claws tug as they rip through his skin. What a sweet sensation.

Lester jumps back a couple of feet. "Foul beast!" He holds his hand out so the light from the neon sign shows the damage. Four nicely done furrows cross the top of his hand. In the greenish light they look black against his pale skin, and they don't bleed.

George says, "Uh-oh."

Lester stabs out with one of those four-foot arms, wraps his fingers around my middle, and tears me away from Meg. He lifts me high above his head and turns toward the brick wall of the store. I twist and slash, but all my claws catch is air. Dead or not, I don't think that wall will do me any good if Lester smashes me against it. He draws his arm back like a pitcher about to deliver a fastball.

10: Meg

Meg cries, "Call the police!"

Sammy shakes his head. "No, no, we can't."

"But that monster is going to hurt my kitty-cat!"

Lester lowers his arm and looks to Meg. "Monster?" He grins, displaying his fangs. "I like that. You really get me."

Holding his hands up to Meg, signaling a stop, Sammy says, "The last thing we need is to let anybody, especially the police, know that there are murderous, bloodsucking vampires in Bloomsburg."

Meg says, "But I'm just a regular person."

"Not anymore. You want to take a chance they won't round us up and throw us in jail?"

Lester says, "Cops, schmops. Who cares?" He shifts his gaze to Patch, still dangling from his big hand. "Where was I?" His fangs show. "Oh, yeah." He raises his arm.

Meg shouts, "Let him go! I have a Green Belt in Krav Maga, but I don't want to have to hurt you."

Lester eyes her and chuckles. "I had one of those for a midnight snack last week." He rears his hand back to throw Patch. Meg jumps up and grabs his arm. It stops his throw, but she just dangles there, her feet swinging in the air a couple of feet above the cement. Apparently Krav Maga isn't as effective as you would hope when you're dealing with a seven-foot vampire and you're only five two. "Let my cat go!"

Somehow, Lester doesn't seem troubled by her attack. He smiles down at her. No terror there.

He reaches across his body with the other arm and wraps his fingers around her neck. He rips her off of his arm and holds her out in front of him. Glad she doesn't need to breathe, she pounds on his arm. Tries kicks to his groin, but he just swings her out of reach. Suspended in midair by the neck, all her self-defense training is worthless.

He says, "Hey, spunky. I like spunky."

Then Sammy steps in front of Lester, his arm extended, his hand gripping a switchblade knife. The blade snicks open. He tiptoes and holds the knife against Lester's neck. "Let the lady down easy or you're going to have a nice, permanent hole from one side of your nasty neck to the other."

Lester releases Meg and she drops to the ground. Her knees buckle, and she sprawls in front of George. She looks up at him. "Stop him! He'll hurt Patch!"

"Not my fight." George backs away a couple of steps.

Still holding Patch, Lester grabs Sammy's wrist with his other hand and wrenches the knife away from his neck. The knife falls and clatters on the sidewalk a couple of feet from Meg. Then Lester grabs the little guy's neck and lifts him off the ground. "You do not cross Lestat, vermin."

Meg gets up and jumps for the arm holding Patch again, but Lester laughs, swings the arm that holds Patch and catches her in the head with his elbow, knocking her against Sammy's Volkswagen.

Lester looks at Patch, and then at Sammy, dangling by his neck, although he is in no danger of choking to death. "Which will it be? You first, Samuel, and a broken neck that will never heal?" He glares at her cat. "Or you, unnatural animal, with every bone smashed." He shows his fangs and chuckles. "Lestat likes the sound of that."

Who talks about himself in the third person?

George shuffles around in front of Lester. "Hey, uh, Les, could you take this somewhere else?" He looks left and right, worry all over his round face. "Night jobs aren't easy to get these days, and I can't afford trouble."

Her cat is about to be smashed and George is worried about his crummy job?

Lester laughs. "Move aside, numb-nuts, unless you want a faceful of cat."

George nods like a bobblehead doll. "Yessir. Right. Got it." He steps to the side. "Uh, could'ja make it quick, then? Maybe nobody'll see."

Meg hopes there is a special place in hell for George. If he ever gets there.

Patch sucks in air and starts hacking. Anyone who's ever had a cat knows the sound of a hairball barf and what it produces. One last hack and he hurls the mess straight at Lester's face.

Catches him right between the eyes. Woo-hoo!

Lester flings little Sammy into George, and they go down in a tangle. He screams into Patch's face, "Abominable creature!" Then his voice gets silky, which, along with the fangs and the sinister smile that appear, turns her woo-hoo into an uh-oh.

Lester glares at Patch. "First, I will break all of your legs into many pieces so you can't move. Then I will run over you with my hearse so your body is little more than a bag of ruptured organs and bone splinters. When morning comes and sunshine hits your flattened carcass, you'll writhe with the pain of the undead as your body is consumed." He smiles. "Maybe I'll record it with my phone. It would be fun to replay over and over."

11: Patch

Once again, I'm about to kiss my furry butt goodbye, but then Meg stoops, grabs the switchblade, and steps in front of Lester, the knife open in her hand. "Drop the cat!" She keeps her eyes on his, and he stares back, a smirk on his long face.

He says, "And why should I—"

His eyes widen when she puts the knife between his legs and lifts until the blade is tight against his crotch.

You go, girl.

Meg says, "Let go of my cat or you're going to live out the rest of your death missing a couple of parts."

Lester's voice squeaks. "You wouldn't—"

She adds her other hand to her grip on the knife and pulls up. Lester rises up on his tiptoes. "You're hurting my kitty."

"Stop!" He lowers Patch. "I'm putting it down."

I hate being called an "it." I try another swipe at Lester's arm with a claw when he lets go of me, but I have to twist to land on all fours. I know that we cats make that look easy, but it's not. Looking up at Lester, I decide that further infuriating a gigantic vampire is not strategically sound.

Bless little Meg, though. She steps back from Lester and kneels beside me. "Are you okay, Patch?"

I give her a little "Mrrr" of assurance. She runs a hand down my back and stands. I find myself wishing for more stroking.

Sammy and George have untangled, and Sammy steps next to Meg. He holds out a hand for his knife, and when she gives it to him, he says to Lester, "You can be sure this is going into a report at the A.V.A. And you can forget about ever becoming a member."

Lester sneers, which his fangs turn into a horrifically malicious expression. "As if I give a rat's ass." He looks down at me and then slices his finger across his neck in a throat-cutting gesture. It is a perfect time to give him the finger ... if only I had one. Giving him the toe doesn't have the same oomph.

He turns, swirling his cape, stalks to his hearse, and roars away with a squeal of spinning tires, leaving behind the stench of burning rubber.

Sammy puts away his knife and frowns at Meg, "I'm afraid you've made an enemy." Then he lightens up. "But you'll be safe with us."

"Who is 'us'?"

"The American Vampire Association. Our mission is to preserve and protect American vampire heritage and culture. Such as it is." He walks to his car and opens the passenger door. "Come with me to headquarters. We've got an opening for a good writer."

Meg looks down at me. "What do you think, partner?"

There's nothing a cat likes better than being given the respect he's naturally due. This vampire woman has potential for being a good associate, and besides, I am currently homeless.

Then a low burn glows like a coal in my belly, a glimmer of that gigantic pain that drove me to have a rat cocktail. It doesn't consume me in a rush like it did before, but I know the train is coming. I am going to need blood, and I'll do anything to avoid that pain.

Anything.

I look around. This is a convenience store, so there have to be, gag, rats out back by the garbage. But then my new associate picks me up, gets in the car, and settles me on her lap. "We're ready."

My gaze is drawn to her throat. Cats are realists. Practical, too. But there is no pulse beating there. And Lester didn't bleed when I scratched him. Is it possible to get blood from a vampire? The heat in my tummy cranks up another degree.

As Sammy drives, he points out places that are lit up in the night—convenience stores, a couple of gas stations, a burger joint, the emergency ward at a hospital—and says at each one, "We've got people there."

We come to a darkened four-story building, and he pulls into its underground garage, which does have lights on. "This is the local headquarters of the A.V.A."

We take an elevator to the top floor. The burn in my belly amps up, and I squirm in Meg's grip.

She runs a hand along my head and down my back. "Take it easy, Patch. I'll take care of you."

I don't want to bite the hand that pets me, but the blue veins on the underside of her wrist are inviting.

When the elevator doors open at the fourth floor, there are lights on inside the building, but they are blessedly dim. We step out to ranks of cubicles bordered by offices on the outside walls. The windows are covered with black curtains.

I once went to Amy's office when she wanted to show off her new kitten—like all cats, I never forget anything. Comes in handy for holding grudges. This place doesn't look much different than hers, except for the black curtains. People go from here to there, papers in hand. A phone rings now and then. Looks perfectly normal, and not anything like I imagine a vampire den should be. They ought to at least pipe in some creepy organ music. And where are the coffins?

A gray-haired woman shaped like a sack of doughnuts with legs cruises up. She looks like she should be home baking cookies for the grandkids, but she carries a bunch of file folders. "Sammy, I'm getting more reports of the Devils prowling around. And I heard a report on police radio of what has to be the remains of a vampire victim in the Fifteenth Avenue cemetery."

I bet that's the guy I saw get stabbed by those crazy people. The guy who melted.

He frowns. "That's the second one this week. Why don't they patrol the area?"

She shrugs a shoulder. "It's outside the city limits. Not the city cops' jurisdiction. And apparently the sheriff is too busy scouring the county for meth labs."

"What can we do? The cops can't know about us. We just need to be more careful, get the word out."

She inspects Meg and me. "I'd say welcome to you two, but to what?" She scratches me behind the ears. "Cute cat."

I hate "cute." Cats are cute only when we're kittens, and after that we're elegant or, in my case, handsome. On the other hand, I really like being scratched behind the ears. She is forgiven.

Sammy does introductions. "Meg, Patch, this is Vera. She runs Communications."

Vera the vampire? I bet she just loves that.

He says to Vera, "Meg's the writer George called me about."

Meg nods. "Advertising."

Vera gives her a closer look. "D'you think you can write nonfiction?"

"Advertising isn't fict—"

Vera cuts her off with a raise of her eyebrows.

Meg shrugs. "Sure."

"Come see me when you're settled. I need an assistant." She hands a folded paper to Sammy. "Here's tomorrow's newsletter. Let me know if you need any changes." She checks her wristwatch. "We've got an orientation class to do in five minutes." Vera hurries away and disappears into an outer office.

Meg clutches me and moans. I'm with her; my belly burns, and I wonder what I can do when the pain really hits. Attack a vampire? Doesn't sound promising.

Sammy babbles as he leads us down an aisle alongside a long wall decorated with photos of Bela Lugosi as Count Dracula. "A lot of our function is as an employment agency. And on the first floor we've set up temporary housing for new vampires until they get established." He glances at us. "We can help you there."

Meg says, "I have an apartment. If I can ever get to it."

"We can help with that, too."

We come to a doorway opening into a large room with chairs at long tables, vending machines, a refrigerator, and four microwave ovens on a counter. "This is our break room."

Meg whimpers. When Sammy turns to her with eyebrows lifted in a quizzical expression, she puts a hand on her stomach. "I'm sorry. It's starting to hurt. I'm—" She looks down at me and strokes my head. Mmmm. "We are going to need to go outside for a while." She pets me again. "My new friend Patch could only do so much for me."

What the hell, it wasn't my idea for her to suck my blood. And ratso didn't do a whole lot for me, either. Is a vampire rat out there, roaming the night? Naw. I'd broken its neck and it was totally dead before I dined.

The pain grows, and it is getting hard to think straight.

Sammy studies her. "Ah, the vampire hunger pain." He looks down at me. I inhale and give him a hiss.

He says, "You too, I'll bet. But you guys don't need to go outside. A little V1 juice will fix you up."

Juice does not sound appropriate for a vampire menu, considering the blood thing. It's time to start looking for an exit.

Digging into a pocket, Sammy crosses to a big red soft-drink machine. He feeds in a bill and punches a button. When a bottle thuds into the slot, he takes it out, gives the machine another bill, and punches another button. He doesn't pay much attention to which button he pushes as if only one thing is stocked. A second bottle arrives. He takes it out and walks to the microwave counter. The glass bottles look like V8 juice, and the label reads "V1," but the liquid inside is a brighter red than tomato juice.

"Some people take theirs cold, but I think it goes down a lot easier at body temperature." He uncaps the bottles and puts them in a microwave, but not before my sniffer picks up the scent of blood. He starts them heating and opens a cabinet door. "I'll get a bowl for Patch." He takes a bowl out and sets it on the counter.

The blood hunger fire spreads through me, and I have to move. I twist and flail my legs until Meg puts me on the floor. As the microwave hums, the scent of blood grows stronger. I pace to keep my mind off the pain.

A glance at Meg shows her biting her lip, her gaze locked on the microwave. She hunches over, gripping her belly with both hands. She groans long and low. "Are you sure juice will help?"

Sammy pulls out a chair for her. "Here, sit." The microwave dings and he takes the bottles out. The aroma of warm blood washes over me. Handing a bottle to Meg, he smiles. "V1 juice is our name for the animal blood we produce. With our own bottling company."

She grabs the bottle and gulps the stuff of life—and, apparently, death. Sammy pours half the other bottle into the bowl and sets it in front of me. I plunge my muzzle in and then lap as fast as I can. My heart starts up and the pain fades.

Sammy drinks the rest of that bottle. A feeling like the best scratch-behind-the-ears I've ever gotten expands through me. When I've licked my bowl clean, I just sit and purr, floating in a daze of well-being. Which, it strikes me, is an odd thing for a dead kitty-cat to be feeling. A few minutes pass, and then the euphoria wears off. I'd sigh if I were breathing. But that's okay, the pain is totally gone and I feel great.

Meg chugs the rest of her vampire juice and leans back, her gaze unfocused.

Our benefactor takes a chair. "You okay now?"

Meg manages a nod. I don't answer. Sammy tells us, "Some vees like the lassitude that V1 juice brings on so much that they sip all day long."

Meg sits up. "Wow. That's some feeling. Just as strong as the pain, but opposite." Meg leans close and scratches under my chin. "Feel better?"

Her touch, instead of being dulled, is supersweet. The blood has brought me back. I headbump her hand.

She gazes at the empty bottle and says to Sammy, "Thanks. I'm afraid I can't pay you for this yet, but if there's a job here ..."

"My treat. You get the next one."

Meg makes a sour face. "Have you got any gum? My sense of taste is back, and that blood ... Well, I was a vegetarian before I joined the club, so this whole blood thing is a tad repulsive."

Sammy contemplates her question. "Yeah, all your systems are restored after a good shot of blood. But it's short-term."

"Gum?"

"Don't have any gum. I wonder if it would work. Would your salivary glands start up? Would the vee bug care about a nasty taste?" He indicates the sink. "It might help to rinse your mouth with water. But don't swallow. It'll just sit in your belly."

I know how she feels about the taste of leftover blood. My muzzle reeks of it. I lick a paw and get to work washing my whiskers and fur. My mouth is dry for a moment, and then the insides of my cheeks tingle and moisture comes.

There's nothing better than licking, especially when I can reach a spot directly with my tongue instead of having to use my paws. It starts with a single spot of skin that sends out an itch of attention needed. Then, when I lick that spot, the pleasure begins, the itch moves on, and my licking follows, leaving behind a trail of happy skin.

Sammy says, "You should do our orientation class for new vees."

I'm a "vee"?

Meg says, "Orientation? For vampires?"

"We cover feeding, jobs, dangers, the cause of vampirism, the mission of the American Vampire Association, stuff like that."

"You mean I might get a clue about what's happened to me?" She leans down and pets my head. "To us?"

Sammy nods. "Yeah. Vera's good, and I chime in too." Sammy looks at his watch. "It's time." He points. "Two doors down," and leaves.

Meg picks me up. "Let's go, Patch."

I take a breath and give her a major hiss. She drops me like I was a bomb with a lit fuse. I'm not really angry, but proper cat protocol is to ask. We're not furry baggage you can just haul around. Humph.

She gazes down at me, her eyebrows high. "What's wrong?"

I glare up at her and shake my head. Actually, the orientation thing sounds like a good idea, but manners are important. I walk to the doorway, then stop and look back at her. Will she get the message?

Meg squats beside me. "I'd really like for us to stick together, Patch." She stretches a hand out to me, but makes no move to grab anything furry.

I like her intelligence. Maybe she's bright enough to become my new associate. I take in a little more air, say, "Mrrr," and then push my nose against her hand. I make no protest when she takes me and stands, cradling me. I believe that associates learn faster when you reward their efforts, so I provide a soft purr. She gives me a scratch behind the ears, and we go to a room set up like a classroom with rows of metal folding chairs.

Sammy and Vera stand next to a lectern, in front of a large whiteboard. They nod to us when we come in. My heart stops beating and the blood buzz has died down, no pun intended. At least I'm not hungry anymore. Meg goes to two empty chairs at the near end of the front row and sets me on one of them.

Three people sit facing the front of the room. In the row behind me, a grandmother type smiles at me, a twinkle in her eyes. How is it that a mostly dead person can twinkle? A round-shouldered, balding, middle-aged guy in an expensive-looking suit sits in the middle of that row. His gaze focuses on Meg. A tiny young Asian woman at the far end of our row glances at Meg. Her eyes widen, and she jerks her focus to the front of the room.

Meg scans the room. Then her eyes narrow, she clenches her fists, and she whispers, "That little bitch."

12: Meg

Meg stomps over to the Asian woman at the other end of the row and stands in front of her. She looks like a girl with pigtails, dressed in jeans and a T-shirt. The woman looks up at Meg and shrinks down in her chair.

Meg shouts, "It was you!" and stiff-arms the woman's shoulders with both hands, propelling her back. She falls and tumbles into the chairs behind her, and the people watching them wince at the clang and bang of metal as chairs collapse.

Meg moves toward the woman, her fists clenched, but Vera rushes to her and grabs her arms from behind. Meg pulls against Vera and fights to reach the girl. "She did this to me!"

The little woman struggles to her feet. She takes a deep breath and sobs, and her face twists as if she were crying, although no tears come out. "I'm so sorry. I couldn't help it. The pain, that awful pain ..."

"I understand about the pain, but you didn't have to rob me and leave me completely helpless."

The woman puts her hand out in denial. "I didn't ... I would never. Somebody else must have done that." She sobs again and lowers her head. "I'm so sorry."

When Meg hears that, she stops pulling against Vera's grip. She knows what that pain *makes* you do. And somebody else could have robbed her while she was unconscious. She glances at Patch. She hadn't been able to stop herself from feeding on him, and the woman is as much a victim as she is.

Vera says, "You going to calm down?"

Meg nods, "Yeah. I'm okay" and Vera releases her. Meg says to the little woman. "I know what that pain does to you." She looks at Patch again. He's watching, and he utters a soft "Mrow." Meg is as much a monster as the girl. Add a little more to her guilt pile.

Vera asks the girl, "What's your name, honey?"

After she answers "Seiko," Vera says, "Pick up those chairs, please, and we'll get started."

Meg helps set the chairs back in order and sits next to Patch while Vera returns to the front of the classroom. Meg strokes his back and whispers, "I'm sorry."

He gives her hand a soft headbutt. She likes this furry little guy.

Vera calls out to the class, "Does anybody here know the cause of vampirism?"

Literal dead silence. Sammy steps forward. "We'll get to that in a minute. But first, a little business."

What is this, bait and switch? Stick with the good stuff.

In that voice impossibly deep and big for such a sardine of a man, Sammy says, "I'm president of the local chapter of the American Vampire Association. There are nine hundred twelve members here in Bloomsburg and Mallan County, and nationwide we're the primary advocate for nearly five million vampire Americans, the nation's fastest-growing minority group."

Meg leans close to Patch and whispers out the side of her mouth, "And now a word from our sponsor."

Patch gives her a soft "Mrrr" and gets a scratch behind the ears in return.

Sammy says, "Our mission is to provide support for American vampires. To eliminate the need for ripping out throats in the night. To find jobs and shelter. To help vampire Americans with the adjustment to being undead."

That sounds good to her.

Vera chimes in. "You've not only lost your life, you've lost your living—your jobs, the places you lived, your friends—I mean, it's rude to dine on friends, so you can't be hanging out when the pain strikes. And what do you get in return for becoming undead? How many of you have noticed superpowers developing?"

Meg feels pretty much the same as before. She checks out the rest of the audience. Nobody raises a hand. She glances at Patch. Or a paw.

Vera says, "Well, don't hold your breath." She chuckles at her incredibly feeble joke. Nobody else does. Seiko draws a breath and lets out a sob. Nice work, Vera, bum us all out.

Vera shrugs. "You were only human before you were infected, and you're only human now. No more, no less. You are the same as you were before being infected." The audience sits up at that, and she nods. She's done this before. "That's right, infected. With a microparasite. If you've read vampire fiction, you know that a virus is often cited as the cause. Close, but no cigar."

Meg raises her hand. "Are we, like, contagious? I don't want to give this to anybody else."

"It's a body fluids thing. You can give it to someone with a bite. If you don't kill whatever you bite, they'll become a vampire. A kiss could do it. Maybe a sneeze, I guess, but vampires have no need to sneeze."

No kissing? Her boyfriend isn't going to like that. She doesn't either. Clive's a good kisser.

Is she going to have to be hands-off with everyone she knows? Mom and Dad?

Sammy adds, "If you interact with breathers, you are a danger to them. You could be overcome with blood hunger and nothing would stop you."

Not only hands-off, but out of sight. A lump of grief threatens to form in her throat. Vampire novels don't mention this. Being a vampire sucks. She frowns at the pun.

Vera walks to a long, narrow box high on the wall. "The storytellers muffed it on the cause, but they got the origin part right." She pulls a big map of the planet down like a window shade and points at a spot in Europe. "In the early 1700s, during a rabies epidemic among dogs and wolves in Hungary, the virus mutated."

Rabies? That's a nasty way to go ... except vees don't go, do they?

Meg blurts, "We're rabid?"

Vera shakes her head, then nods, and then shrugs. "Not exactly. Many of our symptoms are the same as rabies. Insomnia and night wandering are common with rabies. A quarter of victims are prone to biting. A rabies victim is supersensitive to all stimuli, including sunlight and strong odors such as garlic."

Meg frowns at her. "But this vee bug doesn't kill us, not totally, that is."

Vera nods. "Until the mutation, deadly viruses did just that—killed their host and then died. But this mutant rabies virus became a microscopic parasite that takes over a body cell by cell and keeps it working. It needs only blood for fuel. And you know how badly it needs that. No known vampire has been able to resist the unstoppable compulsion of the blood hunger."

Meg doesn't even want to think about the pain that comes when the hunger hits. So that's it. Tiny little bugs.

"What happens is that when you drink blood, it activates your stomach and then your heart in such a way that blood is pumped all through your body until the stomach is empty. Drink enough and it's usually a matter of hours before the hunger comes back. Typically, a quart of V1 juice will get you through a day."

Sammy takes over. "That's the reality. Storytellers blew it on the superpowers and the fangs part too, unless you glue some on. No shape-shifting into a bat. No flying. You can't eat garlic, but then, you can't eat anything else, either. We don't ordinarily have superstrength, although when the blood hunger hits, the parasite doubles its energy output and we're twice as strong until we either feed or dissolve when we can't get blood."

Dissolve? They can *dissolve*?

"The stories have it right about sunlight, though. Get hit with that and you're a pile of bones and ashes. Literally."

Meg raises her hand. "Could you go back to the dissolve thing? Really?"

Vera handles this one. "We don't understand the mechanism yet, but without a supply of blood, the virus consumes its host. You turn into something like raw meat, all but your bones."

How close had she just now come to dissolution?

The door bangs open and Lester sweeps in, his cape swinging behind him. He stops just inside the doorway and raises a hand. His other hand holds a leather strap that trails behind him and out the door. "Don't listen to those gutless wonders. Your deaths have opened up a grand new life for you, a life of darkness and freedom!"

Sammy groans. "Oh, Lester. Please."

"It's Lestat, and isn't this still a democracy? Don't I still have the right to be heard?"

Sammy says to the audience, "The A.V.A.'s policy is to provide shelter for any vampire, even the"—he shoots a look at Lester—"disagreeable ones."

Lester surveys the room and his gaze finds Patch and Meg, then focuses on Patch. He points with the hand Patch scratched; the wound looks exactly the same as when he did the deed. "Kitty-cat, I have something for you."

He steps in and pulls on the leather strap. "Come here, Nosferatu." In trots a burly black dog. A pit bull. She wonders if Lester has gone out and created a vampire doggie just for Patch. How special.

Although Patch's life is in no danger, since he doesn't have one, she doesn't want him chewed on. And Patch apparently agrees—he stands on his chair, inhales, and hisses.

She gets to her feet and faces Lester. "You leave Patch alone."

Lester says, "I'm not done with you, either."

The dog opens his mouth, bares his fangs, and looks as if he is trying to growl. Nothing comes out. He tries again. No luck. He flaps his muzzle as if he's barking. Of course, without taking in some air, nothing can come out.

Lester bends down and coaches. "Breathe, boy, breathe." Then he takes a breath and growls, as if the mutt can understand. The creature just stands there.

Lester scowls at Patch. And then he produces a slow-motion smile, letting his fangs show. The guy is very good at creepy. She suspects he practices. He holds eye contact with Patch while he leans down and unsnaps the dog's leash. He points at Patch and tells his doggie, "Kill him, Nosferatu."

13: Patch

Up until the part about "Kill him," I'd been enjoying Lester's attempt to coach his pooch on how to growl. Like Vera says, don't hold your breath. This is a dog.

But now Ol' Nasty goes into attack mode, and he's aimed at me. He stops his silent yapping and hunches his shoulders. He stalks toward me, his claws clicking on the linoleum. With no one breathing or talking, the sound echoes in the dead quiet (sorry, just couldn't resist that).

I'm thinking it's high time to get out of Dodge, and then I see scars on the dog's muzzle. Vertical rows of scars, both sides. Have to be from claws. A feline left a memento? I leap from my chair and land inches from Nasty's nose.

The son of a bitch flinches back a step. He gulps, too.

I do the bristle thing, the fur on my tail and back standing out, making me look larger.

Ol' Nasty glances up at Lester as if for reassurance. Lester makes pushing motions with his hands and says, "Go on. Rip him to undead pieces."

Nasty turns back to me and hunches his shoulders again.

I take a deep breath and let out a screeching caterwaul.

The dog's eyes widen. Another glance at Lester for more encouragement, then Nasty narrows his eyes and tries to growl again. If he wasn't so huge and dangerous, it would be laughable. I have a hunch those scars on his muzzle mean that he didn't come out on top in a close encounter of the kitty-cat kind.

So I suck in some more air and, bam, I rear up on my hind legs, front paws out with claws extended, and deliver a mighty hiss.

Nasty throws it into reverse, skids backward, and slams into Lester's legs. Lester reacts with a huge kick—a seven-foot vampire has a lot of leverage—and propels Nasty straight back at me.

Meg screeches, "Patch!"

Ha. I'm cool. I leap over Nasty's head, touch down on his back, and take a running jump up at Lester. I land on the big vampire's chest, and my claws dig through black cloth and into skin. Oh, boy. I climb his front, driving my claws into him like a mountain climber driving pitons.

I glance back and see Nasty skid to a halt, scramble around and reverse direction—and then Meg gives him a kick in the butt. He tumbles end over end for the doorway, bounces off the frame, then disappears.

As I say—losers.

I stop climbing when I'm at Lester's head, eye to eye, my front-paw pitons in the sides of his neck. His eyes have gone beyond bulging. If he had any blood pressure, he'd be about to blow a tire.

I give his nose a big, leisurely, rough lick.

Lester opens his mouth as if he's screaming, but, just like his canine crony, no gas, no go. He hits me with both hands and I fly back, my claws leaving artful furrows in his neck.

Meg snatches me out of the air and holds me to her chest. She shouts, "OUT!"

Lester fills his chest with air and lets out a scream. He extends his arms, his fingers form claws, and he takes a giant step toward me and Meg. He looks like Boris Karloff in that old Frankenstein movie.

A folding chair slams into his side and clatters to the floor. Seiko picks up another chair. "OUT!" She throws that chair, too.

The giant vampire dodges it.

Vera's voice is a shriek. "OUT!" She hurls a folding chair at Lester.

I gather myself, take a deep breath, and launch myself at him with a big-time yowl.

He spins and runs out the door, his cloak slapping me in the face as I arc down where he'd been standing.

I watch the doorway for a moment to make sure the creep is really gone, then turn back to Meg. The people in the room stare at me.

Then Meg grins, comes to me, squats down, and raises her hand for a high five. "Patch, my man!"

I can't resist. I raise a paw and give her the five. She wraps me up in a hug. Gasps of air intake sough around the room, and a moment later laughs and chuckles come our way.

Meg holds me close. I realize that her body isn't warming me, which is one of the nice things about having a human associate. She's room temperature. Come to think of it, so am I. Another strike against vampirism.

As the audience settles back into their chairs, Vera and Sammy come over to us. Vera rubs me under my chin—I lift it, close my eyes, and feel a purr coming on. But then, in a chilly voice, she says, "I know Lester. He's tough and dangerous. He's had to be to survive out there for two years. Kitty-cat, he's trouble."

Sammy says to Meg, "Lester was unmarked, too, and proud of it. You're new, so maybe you don't know—vampires don't heal. Some of the older ones are pretty beat up."

She puts her fingers to the side of her neck. "But the place I was bitten healed."

Sammy shrugs. "Yeah, the bite marks go away. After that, any other injury after you're undead is permanent. It's a mystery. A vampire scientist theorizes that the microparasite restores its host to what it was like before the bite. Once that happens, nothing changes and wounds don't heal."

Vera gives my chin a last scratch and then finishes with a pat on my head. "Yeah, Lester's going to be real pissed next time he looks into his rearview mirror. If you weren't already a dead kitty, I'd say you would be before too long."

14: Meg

Vera's words send a shiver through Meg. She hugs Patch a little tighter. No way is that guy going to hurt him. Although, now that she thinks of it, Patch is the one who keeps landing claws. But still ... "Maybe I should report this to the police. I mean, Lester's pretty hard to miss."

Sammy shakes his head. "Oh, no. No police. As far as they know, we don't exist. And we don't want them to."

What? "Why not call them? We're people, aren't we? We have rights, don't we?"

Heads turn in the audience, and all eyes focus on Meg. Seiko comes closer.

Vera shakes her head. "Think about it. Undead monsters running around attacking people and drinking their blood is not grounds for a good relationship with the law."

Meg scowls at that. "Hey, a bunch of those *people* attacked *me* tonight." She gazes at Patch. "And Patch here saved the day."

Patch lifts his head and she gives it a scratch right between his ears.

"The cops should be out there protecting us just as much as them."

Vera says, "They were people. We aren't."

Meg sets Patch down on a chair, scans the listeners, and then gets louder. "We are! We *are* people."

Vera says, "Are you crazy? We're *vampires*."

"George said that if I was still working, I'd be paying taxes. Is that right?"

Sammy shrugs. "Yeah, but—"

She waves a hand at the room. "Do you pay taxes on this building?"

"Sure, we have to."

"Your salary?"

He nods.

"But our existence has to be a secret? So we don't get police protection? So we can't go down to the unemployment office and apply for a job?"

"Well, you can't do that because the unemployment office is open only during the daytime."

Her voice rises another notch. "Exactly! At night I could just walk in and nobody would know I'm a vampire. We have a right to those services, don't we?" She looks at the audience. "C'mon, guys." But they just watch. "Our tax money pays for those things. They're *ours*. Including police protection from being murdered by a gang of wacko vampire hunters."

Seiko takes a breath, hesitates, and then nods. "Cops are supposed to serve and protect. Everybody. And we are, well, bodies." She types on her phone screen.

Meg says, "We can't live like this ... er ... you know what I mean." It's hard, keeping the whole undead thing straight.

Seiko looks up from scrolling on her phone. "Well, I've seen commercials for a cop running in the primary election for county sheriff. The old sheriff is retiring, and there's nobody else running. Why couldn't you?"

Meg has seen the commercials, too. Crazy idea. She starts to say good luck with that, and then the fist of anger in her that quieted after she shoved Seiko rises up. It has just waited for a better target. In this case, it's *Them*. The system that shuts her, Patch, and all of these people out. Then comes the thought that makes her smile. "Maybe we do need a vampire candidate."

Sammy snorts. "That's nuts."

Meg puts her hands on her hips, lifts her chin, and challenges him. "Is it? Because I'm a woman?"

Sammy hesitates too long before he says, "No. Because you're a vampire."

Little misogynist.

On the chair beside her, Patch stands and butts her hand with his head. "Mrrowf."

She gives him a smile and a skritch under his chin.

Everyone in the room stares at her, and the grandmother lady points a finger at her own head and twirls it around: *crazy*. Well, Meg has to agree that an undead person running for sheriff seems like a pretty weird idea. On the other hand, in Illinois, especially in Chicago, dead people have been known to vote. On another hand, people in Missouri once elected a dead guy to the US Senate.

Vera laughs. "So you want to out us?"

"There's no law against being dead, is there? They can't arrest us for just being us. That's un-American."

Vera sobers and looks at Sammy. "Another one bites the dust." She puts a hand on Meg's arm and talks to her as if she were a two-year-old. "Why don't you sit down, honey? This vampire thing is such a trauma, and we understand if you're, er, upset. Sometimes being undead really gets to people."

Meg shrugs Vera's hand away. "I'm not crazy."

Sammy says, "Of course you're not. We do, however, have a resident psychiatrist who helps vees adapt to their new lifestyle."

Meg turns to the people in the room. "What kind of *lifestyle* is this? Hiding all day. Cut off from everything we know and love, especially chocolate. And then vampire vigilantes kill us with nobody to stop them!"

The middle-aged guy stands. "It sucks." He's clean, with none of the dirt smudges the others sport. "I don't think she's crazy."

Sammy shakes his head and tells Vera, "We should call security."

Seiko steps next to Meg. "Maybe you should. You've got *two* crazy vampires on your hands."

The man adds, "Make that three."

Sammy walks to the front of the room and spreads his hands in a calming gesture. "You folks are new to this. You just don't understand the reality of it."

The man says, "I'm a lawyer—Tom Conway—and there's nothing illegal about being dead. Or undead."

Meg recognizes him from a TV commercial. In it, he talks about helping people who are hurt in an accident. She laughs. He turns to her, and she says, "Weird. A vampire ambulance chaser."

Tom shrugs. "It's a living."

Vera joins Sammy at the front of the room. "Maybe there aren't any laws about vampires yet, but there've been ripped throats and unexplained deaths. More breathers besides the Devils will come after us."

That creeps Meg out. "You're still drinking people's blood? But I thought the A.V.A.—"

Sammy says, "No, no, our members don't—we supply everyone with V1 juice. But there are still feral vees out there, ones like Lester who prefer doing it the way nature intended. We all get the blame."

Vera frowns at Meg. "Do you want to be locked in a cell when the pain hits? Or be dragged to a courtroom when the sun is up? You'd be dead ... uh, deader. Totally dead."

It's strange to think of something being lethal to dead people, but there it is.

Sammy scans the faces in the room. "Can you imagine what will happen if the Devils learn where we are? A mob will be outside, torches burning, just like that old Frankenstein movie, only it's us they'll be after."

That makes a certain amount of sense to Meg. "But who knows how people would really react? Vampires are all over the place in novels and TV shows and movies. There's one on *Sesame Street*. People love them. Maybe they would love us, too ... or at least tolerate us." She turns to Seiko. "Do you know if candidates can still enter the primary?"

She checks her phone. "The deadline is five o'clock tomorrow."

Sammy laughs. "This is nuts. Besides, you aren't qualified. You're not a cop, or even a lawyer."

Looking up from his phone, Tom says, "I just checked, and the only qualifications are being a citizen, living in this county, having a high-school education at the minimum, and not being a felon. The guy who's retiring was a plumber." He smiles and looks at Meg. "It doesn't say you have to be alive, either."

Meg grins. "Plus, I have years and years of watching *Law & Order*."

Sammy takes a cell phone from his pocket and makes a call. "Bruce? Come to the classroom. We need to, er, calm down some new vees. And bring restraints." He glances at Meg and Seiko and tells the phone, "They're prone to violence."

Meg says, "Restraints? You can't do that. We've got rights."

Sammy puts his phone away. "Around here, I'm the one who decides who has rights and who doesn't." Sammy looks as though he's strutting in place. "We've got a good thing going here, and you're not going to screw it up by exposing us."

His beady eyes shift—funny, she hadn't noticed before that they are beady—to peer behind her. She turns, and a man who resembles a two-legged building squeezes through the classroom doorway.

Sammy says, "Bruce. Please come in."

Chains clink when Bruce steps into the room. One humongous hand dangles several pairs of handcuffs.

Sammy points at Meg. "This one first. Poor soul, she's really confused. Lock her up until we can get treatment for her."

15: Patch

Meg glances down at me, then leans close and whispers, "I'm sorry it ended up this way, Patch." She faces the brute, her little fists clenched. "You leave us alone."

I decide that I won't end up the way Meg is thinking. I try to reassure her with a "Mrrr," and she gives me a small smile. Then I leap from my chair and run for the door.

Meg shouts, "Go, Patch, go!"

Bruce lifts a thick-soled motorcycle boot to stomp me, but I dodge with ease and flash past him and out the door. I pause there, hoping Meg will be right behind me.

Sammy's voice comes after me. "Forget the cat—he'll be easy to catch when the pain hits him. Take the two women."

Lawyer Tom points at Bruce. "This is not legal."

"So sue me." Sammy chortles at his riposte. The witless are so easily amused by themselves.

Okay, I'm free. Now what?

I don't see how I can help Meg, so I might as well exercise the art of escape. I trot past a row of cubicles, getting looks from office vampires, but no one tries to catch me. The scent of warm blood draws me into the break room, but no one is there, so I continue on. At the elevator, I try leaping for the Down button. I miss and fall hard. Thinking of what Sammy said about permanent wounds, I don't want to break a leg that will never heal. Enough leaping. The buildings that people make are not cat-friendly, and I resent that now more than ever.

I headbutt a door marked "Exit," but it doesn't budge. I hate it when I need human help to do things. Especially when escaping from crazed vampires. Not that that comes up often, but still.

Maybe it's just as well. I don't feel right about leaving Meg to face the brute squad alone. She saved me from being crunched by Lester.

I trot back to the classroom and find Meg and Seiko backed into a corner by Bruce. Sammy fidgets behind him. "Just grab one of them."

He turns to the others in the room and holds his arms wide. "Sorry about this, folks. Sometimes new vees are a little unhinged by the experience. PTSD is, in fact, a common reaction."

Meg says, "I'd like to unhinge you."

Feisty. I like that in an associate.

Tom takes a step forward. "I protest. They are clearly not violent."

Bruce grabs for Meg's wrist, but she clasps her hands behind her and presses her back against the wall. Seiko does the same.

Sammy aims a finger at Seiko. "That one was throwing chairs."

"Only to stop a true madman who was trying to kill a kitty-cat."

Bruce looks around until he spots me. His eyebrows rise. And he smiles, just a little bit. Happy to see me? Happy to squash me like an ant under his thumb?

Tom calls to Meg. "Miss, do you want legal representation?"

Sammy says, "Shut up or you're next."

Cats have a built-in resistance to orders—you may have noticed that we don't take them well. Why should we? We can just walk away and live off the land.

If, that is, somebody opens the door for us.

I need to get Bruce away from Meg, but he isn't going to move.

Unless Sammy tells him to.

I loose a fighting yowl and charge straight at Sammy.

Sammy's eyes bulge. I guess he doesn't want permanent scratches like I left on Lester because he scrambles backward, circling the lectern. I pursue at top speed, but I skid on the linoleum floor and slide into the wall. Bouncing off, I hurl myself in Sammy's direction.

He climbs up onto a folding chair, which promptly folds, and he falls to the floor on his back. "Get the cat! Get the cat!"

Bruce wheels around and stutters, "K-K-K-K!"

Perfect. Bruce lumbers after me. I leap over Sammy—well, not exactly over. I just happen to plant a paw on his nose on the way. He squeals.

I run under chairs and Bruce follows, plowing through them like an icebreaker at the North Pole.

Throwing a quick glance back, I see that Meg still stands in the corner. I double back and run in her direction. Bruce tries to follow in a wide turn that has him slamming into a wall.

Meg holds her arms out for me, but I run behind her and butt her leg.

Bruce rights himself and rushes us.

She says, "I get it." With a "Come on" to Seiko, she runs toward Bruce. I flash past her and run toward Sammy again.

Sammy, now perched on top of the lectern, screeches, "Get the cat!"

I throw a fake to the left, Bruce lunges, I zig to the right, he falls on his belly, and I zag past him. I glance back and see Meg plant a foot on his butt and leap over him. Seiko does the same, and Tom follows on the run. He shouts, "My car's in basement parking!"

I stop outside the doorway and Meg runs down the corridor toward the elevators, followed by Seiko and the lawyer. Sammy's screech continues, "Get the cat!" I have seriously upset the little feller.

Bruce bursts out of the room, wildly scanning the office. Figuring Meg could use a diversion, I take a breath and hiss. Luckily, Bruce has a couple of brain cells to rub together. He locates the sound—not difficult, I'm only five feet away—and lurches in my direction.

Then I run into the cubicle maze, darting left and right, from one aisle to another. The big guy does his best, but he isn't equipped for quick pursuit and sharp turns. I hear a crash followed by a curse from a woman. "You broke my damn cubicle!"

Using my infallible sense of direction, I run for the elevator, only to see the doors close. Going to the stairwell exit door, I shove with everything I have. Doesn't budge.

Footsteps sound behind me and I spin, but it's just a vampire worker. I breathe in and mew plaintively and point myself at the door. How humiliating to have to beg for help. But the worker obliges and opens the door for me. I plunge down the stairs, heading for the parking level under the building.

The big metal door at the bottom of the stairs is shut, of course. I let out a plaintive cry. Meg's voice comes. "Patch?"

Footsteps sound on concrete, and then the door opens and I run into the parking garage. About twenty feet ahead, a big black SUV idles, and Lester's hearse is parked a couple of spaces over. The gassy smell of exhaust mingles with the garage's atmosphere of damp concrete.

The SUV's windows are so dark they're almost black. The two doors on my side are open. Tom is at the wheel and Seiko is in the back seat, peering out. Meg goes to the SUV and gives me a big smile. "C'mon, buddy, let's go."

Lester gets out of his hearse and starts my way.

I trot toward Meg. Leaving is good. I gotta tell you, I'm getting a little weary of the constant chase scene.

And then somebody growls.

Lester steps between me and Meg, Nasty the dog at his side. He growls again.

Lester, that is, not the dog.

The raw, red-black claw slashes on both sides of Lester's neck look pretty gruesome. Perhaps I was a little too aggressive in dealing with him. Now I have to escape again, but I worry that he's seen my best moves. I let him know my irritation with a snarl.

Lester flashes his fangs in a smile. "Good kitty."

What? I check behind me to see if some other cat is here. But it's just me. I turn back to Lester and give him a low growl.

He looks down at Nasty. His voice dripping with derision, he says, "See that, Nosferatu? If a cat can do that, why can't you?"

Nasty hangs his head. Although I doubt he understands the words, even a dog can't miss the tone. Personally, I think it's about time a cat is held up as an example to a dog.

The towering vampire takes a step toward me. I back away, and he stops. "Don't be afraid, kitty-cat. I've changed my mind about you."

Meg calls from beside the SUV. "Lester, leave him alone."

He ignores her and takes another step toward me. I hold my ground, although it hurts my neck to look up at him. He says, "I've realized that I asked the wrong one to join me when I first met you and that female. You're the bold one. You're the one to be at my side, stalking hapless victims and plunging our fangs into soft flesh." Lester stretches his arm out, his black cape flashing its crimson lining, and points to his hearse. "Come with me and know the joy of striking terror in the night."

Where *does* he get his dialogue? I have to admit, though, that the idea of striking terror in the night has appeal. When you're less than a foot tall and weigh only fifteen pounds, you feel like there's a target painted on you for your whole life. I've had more than one kick aimed at me, and a few that connected. The idea of creating fear instead of feeling it is tempting. But then I'd have to listen to Lester yammer about the Dark Path.

I detect a little bit of whine in his voice when he says, "I can't help it if other vees don't want to hang with me because I make them feel so inferior, and rightly so. But you ... you're a superior vampire too."

Meg comes to us, though she goes wide of Lester and Nasty by a few yards. Nasty turns his head and opens his yap as if to growl. Nothing. Dogs.

She says, "Patch, Tom wants us to come with him to his townhouse. We'll be safe there."

What need does a bold beast such as I, a terror of the night, have for safety?

Egads, I'm beginning to sound like Lester.

Meg says, "He has plenty of room, and we would be comfortable. No hiding in the dirt."

On the other paw, comfort is a major thing with cats, mainly because we sleep so much. I start toward her.

"Please, er, Patch." Lester glances at his empty hearse. "To be honest, it gets kinda lonely out there in the dark."

He moves to cut me off. Meg reaches out to me and says, "Let's go."

Give old Lester credit, he's determined. He surprises me by lunging at Meg instead of me. He wraps an arm around her neck—he has to stoop over to do it. "I'm tired of your interference." He grins at Meg. "I wonder how your kitty-cat will feel about seeing you with a broken neck, your head flopping around like a rag doll. Forever."

Darned if he isn't threatening me with harm to Meg. Lester has unsuspected depths; very few people get how much we cats really understand what they say. Despite that, what he's doing decides me against going with him. It's not good to be around someone that large who has anger management issues. But what to do?

Tom gets out of the car and approaches Lester. "You're opening yourself up to a big lawsuit. And I'll warn you, I win all of my cases."

Lester laughs. "In what court do you sue a vampire? And for what?"

Tom's face falls, and then he takes out a cell phone. "I'll call the police."

"Go ahead. I'll just snap her neck and leave. Then you can explain to them what happened. I'm sure they'll love it when you start babbling about vampires."

Tom pockets his phone.

Okay, it's up to me. I don't want him hurting Meg—I like her, and she has potential to make a good associate. Figuring it won't be all that hard to escape from Lester at some point, I walk toward his hearse. Lester follows me, hauling Meg with him, his arm still around her neck.

When we get to the hearse, he steps forward and opens the passenger door for me.

Nasty moves toward the door, but Lester sticks a foot out to block him. "Our friend Patch first." The look Nasty gives me as I approach suggests that escaping sooner rather than later is a fine idea.

I jump up onto the front seat, sit, and look up at Lester. But he doesn't release Meg.

He clamps his huge hands on the sides of her head like a vise. She grabs his wrists and pulls. He laughs. She tries to kick his shins, but he just lifts her clear of the ground and her legs flail. He says to her, "You've been rude to me ever since we met, you stiff-necked little bitch. I'd like to see how you act when your cervical vertebrae are fragments and the only thing you'll ever look directly at again are your toes."

The bastard! I spring toward him, hoping to hook into one of his arms. Maybe Meg can break free. But Lester anticipates me; he lifts a foot the size of a litter box and I smack into it in midair. I slam back into the hearse, and he kicks the door shut.

Paws on the window, I watch Lester brace to twist Meg's neck. I scratch at the glass, hoping to distract him, anything to stop him.

The stairwell door bursts open, crashes into the wall with a booming clang, and Bruce rushes out. He pulls up short when he sees what's going on, then stumbles forward when Sammy slams into him from behind. Sammy shouts, "Where's the cat? Get the cat!" Excitable little guy.

I jump to the driver's seat and throw myself against the horn. It honks and I run back to the window.

Bruce, bless his two active brain cells, points at me. "K-K-K-K—"

Sammy yells, "Get him!" Bruce takes off in a run toward the hearse.

Lester tosses Meg at Bruce, which is like throwing a balloon at a locomotive. She rebounds off him and hurtles toward the hearse to flatten against the passenger door, eye-to-eye with me.

She wrenches the door open. I jump out, and Lester rushes at me from one side, arms outstretched, and Bruce does the same from the other. I slow, just a little ... They're close ... I slow ... They dive for me ... I shoot forward.

I look back to see a wonderful collision. The two enormous vampires topple and then grapple on the concrete floor. Meg runs toward the SUV, where Tom stands by the open back door, urging her on. She cries, "Patch!"

Then a hand catches me by the tail and lifts. Hanging several feet off the floor, I rotate around and find myself face-to-face with Sammy.

He grins. "Gotcha."

Sammy pulls out his switchblade, clicks it open, and holds the blade against the base of my tail. "I think this would make a nice souvenir to remember you by."

"Helpless" gives only the palest hint of how it feels to be dangled in the air by your tail. Having it cut off will avoid that problem in the future, but I hope a less radical solution will present itself. Soon. Make that immediately.

Meg calls out, "Say cheese."

Sammy and I look her way. She holds a cell phone.

She strides toward us. "Hold it right there." Stopping a few feet away, she aims the phone at us. "I said, say cheese." I'm not inclined to smile in this circumstance, but I do look right at the phone. She taps the screen and examines it. "That ought to do it."

She holds the phone up. "This little snapshot, friend Sammy, will soon be emailed to the Bloomsburg Humane Society and the police department. The email will include your name and the address of the A.V.A."

Sammy yells, "Bruce!"

Bruce's voice is smothered because he has Lester's forearm in his mouth as Lester tries to choke him from behind. Bruce says, "Mmmmmmph!"

Meg turns and tosses the phone to Tom. She turns back to Sammy. "I believe it's time you let my friend Patch go."

Sammy gazes into my eyes; the man exudes a hot fog of hate. He tightens his grip on my tail.

"Tom, email that picture."

Sammy's eyes shift. I rotate to see the lawyer pressing keys on the phone.

Sammy says to her, "I'd probably get vampire fleas from it anyway." He drops me, and I land on all four feet. I turn to face him, and he points his knife down at me. He takes a step back. "I let him go, but I won't be responsible for what happens if he attacks me."

Behind him, Bruce and Lester disentangle, roll apart, and lumber to their feet. Lester surveys us. "Bah!" He aims a long forefinger at Meg. "You will live to ... er, come to regret crossing the Vampire Lestat. I have eternity to collect my revenge."

He tosses Nasty into his hearse, gets in and slams the door, then guns the engine and backs toward Meg, who scoots out of the way. She gives his rear fender a kick, and he peels out.

I go to Meg and rub against her leg to thank her for saving me from mutilation. She leans down and runs a hand over my back. "I owed you one, Patch." She gestures at Tom's car. "Shall we?"

I run ahead and leap into the back seat, next to Seiko. She smiles at me, and Tom says from the driver's seat, "Patch, you may not have nine lives anymore, but you do pretty well."

Sammy screeches at Bruce, waving his arms as if he wants to take flight. Meg sits beside me and closes the door. "Now what, Tom? I think I've worn out my welcome at the American Vampire Association."

"To my place. I think it's time for a midnight snack."

He holds up the phone. "Would you show me how to see the picture you took? I can't find one here."

"Oh, I faked it. It was all I could think of to do."

Continued possession of my tail had been riding on a bluff? My new associate has some moxie.

Now that I'm no longer threatened with dismemberment, I notice that the burn in my gut has reignited. Imagine the sensation of being ravenous with a consuming hunger that fills your stomach like a gas. Now set fire to it. A snack is a great idea. I don't want to—what was it Sammy said would happen if we don't feed? Dissolve?

16: Meg

The burn in Meg's belly fires up, not yet ravenous, but a consuming hunger is on the way. She doesn't want to dissolve.

She calls to Tom. "Starting to get hungry in here."

Tom turns into a driveway to a ground-floor townhouse garage. "We're there." The garage door opens and they cruise in.

Tom leads them to a kitchen the size of her apartment—she assumes she still has an apartment; her rent is paid to the end of the month. Every surface, empty, gleams. Of course, with vampires there is little use for a kitchen. Like at the A.V.A. headquarters, the windows are covered with heavy black curtains.

Tom takes four bottles of V1 from a case in a pantry and heats them in a microwave. This time Patch gets a whole bottle in a bowl, and his pink tongue is soon a blur of high-speed lapping. She takes a big sip from her bottle. What a rush. Seiko lifts her bottle in Patch's direction. "Here's to Patch."

Meg joins the toast to her mighty little fighter, then chugs the rest of her bottle. Patch sprawls on the floor, and lethargy washes over Meg like a wave of lazy. She sits in a kitchen chair, relaxes, and enjoys it. For a couple of minutes, the only sound in the room is Patch's purr.

Then she examines her empty bottle. Pretty creepy, having bottled blood in your pantry. "Uh, Tom, this blood ... just animals, right?"

"Right. The A.V.A. works with slaughterhouses all over the country."

She checks the ingredients on the label and, sure enough, it reads "100% AB bovine blood." That's okay. "I can live with that. Not much different from a rare hamburger."

Her heart is still beating and Patch is still purring when she picks him up, cradles him in her arms, and follows the lawyer to a den with a big oak desk, book-lined walls, and leather-covered furniture. Seiko goes to the bookshelves, and Meg sits in an armchair with Patch in her lap.

"Thank you, Tom, for feeding us. I'll pay you back as soon as I can find a job. I suspect I blew the one at the A.V.A."

"Maybe there's something else for you. I've been thinking about your idea of running for sheriff. I think you'd make a fine candidate."

Meg's eyebrows make a move to meet up with her hairline.

Tom adds, "You were serious, right? Tell the world about vampires here and now?"

The villager mob scene from the old Frankenstein movie comes to mind, the whole town storming the castle with torches in the foggy night.

Patch looks up at her and hisses.

Apparently, Patch doesn't like the idea of her running for sheriff, but she does. "I was dead serious." Lordy, how is she going to avoid puns like that? Her condition seems to attract them like monkeys to bananas. "But it does mean outing vampires."

Seiko says, "Do it, Meg. You were right. We have rights. We're citizens."

"But how? I mean, there's this little problem of the sun coming up every day."

Tom says, "We can work around that. I have a paralegal surrogate—a breather—who does things for me in the daytime. He can register you. We can use radio and television to get the word out, and you can have rallies after dark."

He checks his watch. "It isn't all that late, so let's get started." He sits at the desk, reaches for the phone, dials a number, and wakes up his computer.

Tom says to the phone, "Can you come over? We've got some work to do." He hangs up and tells Meg, "He's on his way."

Patch naps in her lap while the lawyer gets papers out and they discuss plans. Meg borrows a legal pad and makes notes. Now that she's thought about it, there is so much to do in a political campaign. She begins to wonder if she's taken on a hill too steep.

A doorbell rings, and Tom leaves his desk to answer it. He returns with a short Black man. "Meg, Seiko, this is Archie Slovinski."

Archie's smile is bright white and warm. "Pleased to meet you." His gaze settles on Patch. "Hey, a kitty-cat."

Patch rouses and gazes at Archie, so Meg gives him a head scratch. "Patch, meet Archie."

Archie comes to them, extends a hand toward Patch, and then pauses, his fingers poised within sniffing distance of Patch's nose. He says to Meg, "Can I pet him?"

"It's up to him."

Meg suspects that Patch never turns down petting. He gives Archie full eye contact. Archie gets the message and does a few gentle runs on Patch's back.

Tom says, "Can you get our friend Meg here registered as a candidate in the primary for sheriff?"

Archie's eyebrows climb up his forehead. He steps away and studies her. "Nice looking, professional, young. But isn't she ... isn't she a—"

Meg frowns. "Vampire. I'm so beginning to hate that word." She has to hand it to Archie. Here he is, in a roomful of people who have an occasional uncontrollable need to drink blood, and he's cool.

Seiko raises a hand. "Not to pour water on your fire, Meg, but we need to be realistic. Isn't it a problem that people think vampires are bloodthirsty, murderous monsters that turn into bats and sleep in coffins?"

Meg laughs. "Listen, the way media spin machines convince voters that politicians are on their side, getting votes for a vampire should be a day at the beach." She holds up the pad with her notes. "Give me a decent media budget and I can do it."

Shaking her head, Seiko says, "You really think people will vote for a dead person?"

"That's undead. We're not corpses. A dead person would just lie there. I can walk and talk."

"Still, it's a problem. How far can you get with the necrophilia vote?"

She's right, and the wind in Meg's sails drops to a breeze. "Yeah, I know." She straightens and lifts her chin. "But we'll get all the vampire votes. And the outcasts—we could be big with the homeless."

Archie waves a hand. "All the ostracized. You'll get a bunch of LGBTQ votes, too."

Tom says, "Maybe so, but I think we also need to do something to humanize her."

Meg crosses her arms and gives him a scowl. "I am human."

"That may be debatable but, okay then, we need to unmonsterize you." He snaps his fingers. "Yes! Maybe if you had a lovable running mate."

Archie claps his hands. "Brilliant!"

Seiko turns to Tom. "Since when are two vampires better than one?"

"Since when one of them is a sweet kitty-cat."

Patch's head comes up at that. Meg gets up and sets him on her chair. She likes to pace when wrestling with a creative problem. She studies Patch as he gazes at her, inscrutable as ever. Yet he does have a sweet face, and she knows about his courage. Yeah, this could work. "I like it. With Patch, we'll get cat-lovers, too."

She goes back to Patch, who eyes her as she kneels beside him and strokes his head. "I can see the commercial now. I'm sitting in front of a fireplace, flames crackling behind me, Patch curled up in my lap, and I talk passionately about freedom from tyranny and protection of *all* citizens."

Seiko chimes in. "Don't wear red."

Little sensualist that he is, Patch lifts his chin for a scratch. She obliges. "Patch, you'll help us change the image of vampires from bats, which are basically rats with wings, to warm and furry cats."

Archie says to Meg, "I'll register you first thing in the morning." He grins. "You're on your way."

Tom holds up a hand. "If there are going to be commercials, we're going to need money." He shakes his head and turns to Meg. "I'm near broke. Business has been crappy since I haven't been able to go to court during daytime."

Meg says, "I'm paycheck to paycheck. And I don't think I have a job anymore."

Seiko shrugs. "Well, that was a short campaign."

17: Patch

I'm just getting my head around not being a candidate just after I was one when Tom grins and snaps his fingers. "Papa. I'll call him."

Archie says, "You sure you want to involve him? There are rumors about the company he keeps."

"Hearsay isn't admissible with me. I think it'll be perfectly safe." He takes out his phone.

Last time I heard someone say, "It'll be perfectly safe" was in a horror movie that nearly turned my fur white when the character who said it was ... well, let's just say "done in."

Meg says to me, "Isn't that great? They can call on family for support. This is going to work!"

I look up at Meg. Terrific. Now I'm going to be the poster pet for bloodsucking fiends. What would my mother have said?

But maybe it's not all bad. I imagine a throng of happy voters at a vampire rally. They are dancing and chanting, "Patch. Patch. Patch. And Meg."

Then the picture darkens and morphs into the crazed villagers from the Frankenstein movie chanting, "Burn. Burn. Burn. And kill."

Tom ends his call. "He's coming over."

He gets papers out and tosses ideas around with Meg, their talk bouncing back and forth like ping-pong balls. Meg writes on a pad of paper, but I'm content to doze. People lucky enough to be a cat's associate know that we don't sleep deeply; they're not called cat*naps* for nothing. We relax almost totally, but there's a little part of our minds that stays alert even though we look like we're sleeping, tuning our ears to sounds like furry sonar scanners.

Then Meg says, "I've roughed out a commercial. Patch, listen to this."

At the sound of my name, I come to full attention. If it's about me, I want to hear it.

"We open with clips of police officers helping people. My voiceover says, 'Our police promise to serve and protect us.' Then we cut to footage of the Black Lives Matter protest. I say, 'But for too long, that didn't apply to some minorities.'"

Seiko says, "Wow, you don't mess around. That's going to raise some hackles."

"I say, 'It's been a struggle—here we show footage of that police chief kneeling with a Black person after the big protest—and I continue, 'Things are getting better—there's progress.'

"Then we dissolve to a shot of Patch, and I say, 'But not for this new minority that's being failed by the police.'"

I tune in to her at that point and sit up on my chair. I wonder if I will get fan letters.

Seiko says, "But cats aren't a minority."

Archie chuckles. "I just read that there are fifty-eight million cats in the US."

I hate it when reality puts the brakes on.

Meg comes to me. "This handsome guy is part of a new minority." Putting her pad on the lamp table beside the chair, she picks me up, sits in my chair, and cuddles me on her lap, stroking my back. "We show Patch and I say, 'He, too, is denied the rights others enjoy.' We pull back and reveal that Patch is in my lap."

Papers rustle as Tom stirs. "I like it so far, but wouldn't it be more leader-like for you to stand?"

"Maybe later, but I think seated is less threatening when we get to the vampire part."

"Good point."

"Then I say, 'There are Bloomsburg citizens who, through no fault of their own, because of a tragic illness can't count on protection from violence.'"

Seiko claps. "Going for the sympathy vote, too."

"Hey, it's all true. Then the camera goes in for a close-up of Patch and I say, 'You see, Patch is a vampire kitty-cat.'"

I think about which is my best side. They're both perfect. Will I need makeup? Maybe touch up my orange spots a little? I'm going to have to do some serious licking before I get in front of the cameras.

Meg says, "Then the shot cuts to me and I say, 'Afflicted by the same tragic disease, I have lost everything. I can't work at my day job. I can't even go to the unemployment office because it's open only during the day. I'm a vampire, you see, and Patch and I are prisoners of the night."

"Wow, you managed to use *tragic* twice," Tom says. "If I could cry, I'd be sobbing by now."

Meg glances at her script. When is she going to get back to me? She reads, "Worse than losing my job, and maybe my home, I'm afraid of the night because there are lawless vigilantes out there hunting ... and killing ... vampires." There's a catch in her voice. "And the police are doing nothing to protect us." She raises a fist in the air "We are citizens too!"

Lowering her voice, she says, "Police all over America swear to protect and serve. Where is our protection?" Her expression hardens, her lips thin and tight. "Your life is important; undead lives are important, too."

Tom shakes his head. "Strong stuff. I don't know ..."

Meg rests her hand on me and strokes my back. Mmmmm. A little to the left ... ahhh.

Then she says, "That's why I want your vote for sheriff. With me"—she looks down at me—"and my kitty-cat partner on your side, *all* minorities will have the law covering their backs."

Being a very small minority of one, that sounds like a good thing to me.

She sits straight and hugs me to her chest. "Here's the finish." She smiles and looks straight ahead as if at an imaginary camera. "A vote for Meg and Patch—" she glances down at me and scratches behind my ears "—is a vote for equal protection for each and every one of us."

Mom, apple pie, kitty-cats, equality, vampires, and the American way—it's enough to make you meow. I do my best to smile for the imaginary camera, which means I don't really have to do anything since we cats have natural smiles. I don't open my mouth, of course, because when you're coming out as a vampire, it's probably not a good idea to show fangs.

Seiko sits with her mouth open. She snaps out of her fascination and says to Meg, "You're good. I hardly felt manipulated at all." She steps close and scratches the top of my head. Good spot selection. "You've got my vote."

Hey, you've got to hand it to kitty-cat power.

Archie stands and stretches. "I think it's amazing." He looks at his watch. "Goodness, it's almost dawn. I've got to catch a little sleep so I can get things going when the courthouse opens. And I'll call the TV stations and the newspaper." He gives Tom a salute and sashays out the door.

Stimulated by runaway fantasies about being the powerful associate of a powerful sheriff, I ease myself out of Meg's lap to check this place out, something I should have done long ago. As I sniff here and sniff there, I eye the black curtains over the windows. Are the stories about the effect of sunlight true? The black curtains in the room suggest that they are.

But cats are born investigators. I head for the window. It has been a while since I've seen the night sky, and I have a need for a glimpse. At the window I stand, put my paws on the windowsill, and poke my head under the curtain.

The moon is out, and stars are faint because of city lights, but it's good to see them. Movement in front of the house attracts my gaze—Archie, getting into his car. After he drives away, something tall and dark steps from the shrubbery by the front walk. The figure turns toward the window, and Lester's pale face looks my way. I don't think he sees me, which makes it even creepier when he smiles in my direction, his fangs almost luminescent in the moonlight.

That's more creepiness than I'm ready to handle, so I drop down from the window and leave Lester to the deep dark whatever.

Meg puts down her pad and paper on Tom's desk. She stretches and says, "I'm done."

Tom stands. "Me, too. I have plenty of room upstairs, so please make yourselves at home."

She starts for me, then stops and digs her phone out of her pocket. "Got a charger I can use? I'm dead." She laughs. "Sort of."

"There's one in the kitchen. We need another hit of V1 to get through the day anyway."

The lawyer serves up another helping of V1 juice, then takes us upstairs to guest rooms, one for Seiko and one for Meg and me.

His condo is more like a "manso," with an office, four bedrooms, and accompanying baths. Chasing ambulances must pay well. Tom hurries into a bedroom and returns with large T-shirts for Seiko and Meg. Since Seiko is tiny and Meg is small, they'll make fine nightshirts. Meg's shirt has a Grateful Dead logo on it, and Seiko's is a Black Sabbath shirt.

Ha.

The showers are a big hit with the ladies, and Meg comes out smiling after hers. With the windows covered by black curtains, I can't tell when the sun actually comes up, but my eyes and the skin on my nose itch when I pass by the window. Tom warns us. "Don't open the curtain unless you're sure it's dark. I peeked on my first day as a vampire, and it took me two nights to get over the shock."

So Meg curls up in the center of a king-sized bed, and I do the same on a well-padded chair. I like to sleep with my associates, but I've found that it's a good idea to first learn whether or not they toss and turn. I settle and get in a good lick—after a fresh shot of blood, my skin seems as sensitive as it was before I became a vee, and I have a fine time.

Night has come again by the time the blood hunger starts up in my belly and burns its way through an enjoyable dream about that little Siamese I'd been on the way to visit when Meg grabbed me. Meg is moaning. I leap onto the bed and nudge her hand with my nose. Somebody has to open the door and then a bottle of vampire juice. Right now would be good.

Her eyes open and then the corners crinkle when she gives me a grin. "Hey, Patch." She reaches to stroke me, but I give her a short "Mrrrf," hop to the floor, go to the door, and look back at her.

She sits up, and then frowns and puts a hand to her stomach. "Ouch." She scrambles out of the bed and leads the way down to the kitchen, her bare legs flashing and the T-shirt billowing. I have to scamper to keep up.

Tom is up and dressed, but Seiko isn't there yet. After a bowl of blood gets my heart to pumping a steady pulse and my purr to humming, I lounge on a rug while they plan their day—er, night.

After a first gulp, Meg takes her time, sipping her blood from a coffee mug. She tells the lawyer, "I dreamed about making a speech, and then this mob came after me with torches. It was like the villagers in that old Frankenstein movie."

A shiver runs down my spine, all the way to the tip of my tail.

She frowns. "Am I crazy to do this?"

Tom says, "Not to worry, this is a civilized country. I mean, we're in Illinois, surrounded by cornfields. Archie emailed me. We've got a press conference here at eight-thirty tonight with the newspaper and KTBC, which should get us good exposure for the ten o'clock news.

"And," he adds, a gleeful look on his face, "we'll own tomorrow morning's newspaper. I'm sure vampires being in Bloomsburg will be the buzz for a few days. Half of getting elected is name recognition. Meg, you and Patch will be all over the place."

Meg's eyes widen and she puts a hand to her heart. "Oh, no. My parents! They can't learn about me being a vampire from the news." She looks to the lawyer. "I have to go see them."

"Sure. Take one of my cars." He points to the door that leads from the kitchen to the garage. Three sets of keys hang on hooks beside it. "Try the Porsche."

She looks down at her T-shirt. "I only have the clothes I came in, and I've been wearing them for days, including in and out of the ground."

"You haven't been home?"

"I was robbed and my phone died. I had no way to get home until the A.V.A. came along."

"You should top off with a little V1 juice so the hunger doesn't hit you. Here ... "He opens a drawer and takes out two small cylinders wrapped in red paper. He hands them to her. "Carry these with you in case you get stuck out there."

She examines the wrapper. "Death Savers?" She opens one and takes out a little red ring and then laughs. "Blood candy?"

"Pure and simple," Tom says. "If you'd like to stay here, bring your things back with you."

"I think I will for a night or so. I kinda need to know I'm safe and won't have to go hunting something to feed on." She looks to me. "Hey, Patch, want to go for a ride?"

What the heck, lying here listening to a lawyer talk politics is as stimulating as a conversation with a dog.

And Meg seems happy about going out, so I might as well share the wealth. I'm due for some peace and quiet.

18: Meg

Meg drives to the brick courtyard building where her apartment is. She doesn't want to be separated from Patch, so she gathers him up and goes to the manager's apartment. Mr. Hermph answers the doorbell and scowls at her. His gaze drops to Patch. "No pets."

"He's not a pet."

"Sure looks like a pet."

"Patch is more of an ... associate."

"Call it what you want, no pets, especially cats."

"He's just visiting."

"Let me be clear. No visiting cat associates."

Patch takes a little breath and she feels more than hears a low growl. "Okay, I'll put him in the car. But I need a key to my apartment. I ... lost mine."

"Gonna cost you ten bucks."

"Can I pay you later?"

His leaden stare makes her wonder if he's sensing her current status as an animated corpse. She takes a breath, just in case.

"No later than tomorrow." He adds a glare. "And I don't like to be disturbed after dark."

She gets a key and then puts Patch in the Porsche and locks its doors. Satisfied that he'll be okay, she collects her mail and goes to her apartment.

She grabs her phone charger and then her laptop so she can go online to get her bank card and credit cards replaced, waters her plants, and shakes her head at all the food in the refrigerator that she can't eat.

Well, there's no sense in wasting it, so she fills a grocery bag with stuff her parents can use. As she puts clothes into a backpack, she frets about the proper outfit for telling your parents that you're a vampire. She settles on a tan pleated skirt and a forest green cotton sweater.

On the way out, she pauses just to feel the love and pride she has in having her own place. Her glow is dimmed by the thought that she might lose it. Who knows what life has in store for a newbie undead person?

At her parents' home, a tidy brick colonial in a quiet, tree-filled neighborhood, she takes the bag of groceries with one hand, holds Patch with the other, and heads for the front door.

Patch squirms. "Mrow." She realizes that she's squeezing him awfully hard and lets up. "Sorry, partner. This isn't easy."

She rings the doorbell, and soon the porch light flicks on.

"Oh, Patch, this is going to kill them."

When Mom answers the door, she gives Meg a big smile. "Sweetheart!" she says, and opens the door. Meg has an urge to throw herself into that embrace and cry "Mommy," but she needs to keep her distance. Instead, she hands the grocery bag to her. "I had some leftover food I thought you could use."

Her mom's expression is quizzical, but she says, "How thoughtful." Then she pats Meg's hand. "My, you're cool." She steps back and lowers her gaze to Patch. "Who's your handsome friend?"

Meg gazes down at Patch and gets the sense that he is ... preening. Well, he is a cat, of course he is. "This is Patch. We've kind of teamed up."

"How nice." Mom leads them to the living room where Dad is reading a newspaper in his recliner. It's good to be home. Plenty of comfy, familiar furniture to curl up on, and they have a fire going in the fireplace.

Mom says, "Look who's here, dear." She lifts the grocery bag and says to Meg, "I'll just put these things away."

Dad sets his paper on a side table, boosts himself out of his recliner, and comes to hug Meg. After the obligatory introduction of her cat—all Patch gets from Dad is a nod—he says, "Glass of wine?"

Meg's heart is full. She'd thought she'd never see them again.

"Nothing, thanks, Dad." She settles onto a love seat, Patch in her lap. "I've, er, cut back. And I can't stay long."

Mom returns from the kitchen and sits next to her while Dad returns to his chair. Mom says, "We've called several times. All we get is voicemail."

Her voice is soft, but it drips with accusation. Mom isn't all sweetness.

Meg lets that go and just shrugs. "I've been busy. And then my phone died."

Dad frowns. "You work too hard at that advertising agency."

"Not anymore. I'm into something ... new."

Oh, how to tell them? They wait, and she now understands what is meant by a pregnant pause. She fears what this one will give birth to.

She stops petting Patch and grips his fur in her fist, then lets go to wring her hands. "I'm a ... I've become ..." She can't say it.

They lean forward. Mom says, "What is it, dear?"

Come on, girl, spit it out.

"I'm ... I'm going to run for sheriff."

That is not exactly cutting to the chase, is it?

Their brows furrow. Mom says, "Ah, that's a long way from being a copywriter."

Dad adds, "I know I've always told you that you can do anything, but ... sheriff? Why, forevermore?"

"There are problems ... well, crimes ... happening in our county, and I think I have unique insights into how to deal with them." She strokes Patch, his soft furriness somehow reassuring. "There's going to be a press conference tonight. I'll probably be on the ten o'clock news."

"Oh, gosh!" Mom says. "Our little girl on television. We should call the neighbors, maybe have them over, serve some wine and cheese—"

"I don't think that would be a good idea."

"But why not, Sugar? They like wine and cheese."

Meg goes back to clenching Patch's fur. It's a good thing a cat's skin is nice and loose or she'd be strangling him. He looks up at her, but doesn't protest. Who'd have thought a cat could be understanding? "I'm going to be talking about a different issue. Uh, protection of minorities."

Mom smiles. "That's nice, dear. Is it any particular minority?"

"Well, yes—"

Dad says, "I thought we had all our minorities pretty well taken care of. I mean, we've got civil rights all over the place. And now the gays can live like regular people."

Thank goodness there's more to her dad than archaic attitudes. "There are a lot of people who still aren't treated equally, including LGBTQ people, and now there are—"

"Oh God!" Dad puts his hand over his eyes. "You're gay?"

Mom and Meg say at once, "What?"

He stands and paces. "It's all clear now." He gets louder. "I mean, here you are in your twenties and not married, and you haven't brought a man around for months."

Mom's voice escalates, too, but she aims it at him. "Maybe it's because you glare at them and grill them about how much they—"

"I'm a vampire." Her cry stops Dad, er, dead.

"You're not a lesbian?"

"No, although there's nothing wrong with that. And I have a boyfriend." *Maybe* she has a boyfriend. "His name is Clive."

He collapses back into his recliner. "Thank God." He squints at her. "Clive? What kind of name is that?"

Mom studies her. "I thought you looked a little pale."

Meg strokes Patch. "So is Patch. A vampire, that is. And we're going to campaign for sheriff to protect us from vampire hunters."

Apparently, it still takes Dad a while to let things to sink in. He's smart enough, but she suspects he has a low-capacity processor. "A vampire? Like in the movies?" He peers at her. "I don't see fangs. And you don't look dead. I mean, you're talking."

"Technically, I think it's undead. I'm mostly the same as I ever was." She holds her arm out to him, the underside of her wrist up. "See for yourself. No pulse."

Dad leans close and places his fingertips over her wrist. "Cold." He looks up at her. "No pulse, either."

Mom scoots a little away from her. "Ewww. Do you drink blood?"

Meg stiffens at that, and then holds Patch to her chest and stands. "I'd rather not get into the gory details. I just wanted to tell you before you saw it on the news or maybe heard it from the neighbors."

Now Mom covers her eyes. "The neighbors! What will Steve and Betty say?"

Meg smiles, but her eyes feel sad. She touches Mom on the shoulder. "I'm sure you'll find a way to deal with it."

Dad leans forward in his chair and frowns. "Wait a minute. You're not one of those defund-the-police liberals, are you?"

Mom whips an equally powerful frown at him. "I hope she is! We need to get money where it helps people, not buy more and bigger guns for cops."

Dad stands and confronts Mom. His face flushes. "We should have tanks ready to roll. Who knows what's going to happen next?" He glances at Meg. "Especially with vampires skulking around in the night."

Mom stands and pokes his chest with a finger. "No. Nonononono!"

Meg slips out the front door.

Back at the lawyer's condo, Meg carries Patch into the kitchen from the garage. Seiko is there, rinsing out empty V1 bottles and putting them into a recycling bin. "How did it go?"

Meg puts Patch down on the kitchen floor and heads for the stairs. She can't avoid a tremor in her voice. "Okay."

Seiko isn't buying it. "You want to talk?"

Shaking her head, Meg says, "I think I'll just go up and rest for a while, maybe work on what I'll say at the press conference. Call me when the reporters get here."

"But—"

"I'm *fine!*"

19: Patch

I watch Meg head up the stairs, her shoulders slumped as if she hurts.

Seiko glances at me. "Pretty rough, huh?"

Well, it wasn't like her parents kicked her. At least not physically. And what does she have to be so sad about? Here she is, about to embark on an exciting new career in law enforcement. Gotta be better than advertising. What do I have to look forward to? Sammy probably has the entire American Vampire Association out looking for me so he can finish cutting my tail off. And what is that wacky Lester up to, skulking around outside?

Come to think of it, I'm feeling a little depressed, too. Well, it's an associate's job to lend aid and comfort, so I trot upstairs and go to the room Meg and I share to get a little comfort-petting from her.

She hasn't turned any lights on, and she's curled up on the bed. I hear an intake of breath. I hop up and walk to her.

Then she sobs, so softly that no one but me could have heard. Maybe the idea of being a vampire sheriff isn't all that exciting. She looks at me. "Oh, Patch. I feel so alone. So lost."

Stepping carefully, I lie next to her. Being room temperature, I can't warm her like I want to. But I can at least purr. So I do.

She sobs again.

Death sucks ...

Then she hugs me to her.

... but not all the time.

Her sobs go away, and I think about things. There hasn't been much time to think. Cats don't normally need to do a lot of thinking. Why should we? We live in the moment, and we know all we need to know from the get-go. How to hunt. How to play. How to purr. How to take a bath. The necessary stuff.

But there isn't anything in my genetic database about being undead. What Meg says about loneliness is disturbing. In our case—"our" being us vees—it's bigger than being lonely. "Untouchable" is more like it. I mean, even her mother said "Ewww."

Am I doomed to be repulsive for the rest of my death? Maybe I need to get out and see if I can locate that little Siamese and find out if my sex life is as moribund as the rest of me. Although a wrong move could turn her into a vampire. Better leave that question unanswered.

I do a mental survey. I feel all right. No aches or pains. There's an uneasiness in my belly that I recognize as the beginnings of the blood hunger. Meg stirs beside me. Probably feeling the same thing.

A murmur of voices from downstairs crawls into the room. Riding on top is Sammy's big boom. Well, he's on my turf now. I stand and check Meg. Her eyes are closed, so I decide to leave her in peace.

Downstairs, I pause in the doorway to Tom's book-lined study. Sammy, with Bruce looming behind him, faces Tom while Seiko watches the confrontation. Behind Sammy and Bruce, a pale-faced guy scribbles in a notepad. Sammy says,

"You can't expose us. Vampires all over Bloomsburg will be hunted down."

"As it is, with the Devils out there, they already are," Tom says. "If Meg succeeds, maybe we'll all be liberated from the repression of discrimination. Maybe we'll have the protection of an honest sheriff."

"Why take the chance? The A.V.A. has a good thing going, but that will end when there's nothing left but our rotting bodies and the rubble of our building." The little guy looks pretty desperate. "Look, we took you in and saved you from having to roam the night."

Seiko says, "Yeah, and then you wanted to handcuff us."

Meg's voice comes from behind me. "And then you wanted to cut off my cat's tail."

She scratches the top of my head. I'm glad she's feeling better. I walk into the study, Meg beside me.

Sammy steps behind Bruce and points at me. "Keep that mangy corpse away from me."

Mangy? I arch my back and bristle.

Meg picks me up, and I relax in her arms. "I think you owe Patch an apology."

"To a cat? Look, I admit I might have gotten a little carried away, but that thing attacked me."

A woman's voice calls from the front of the house. "Hello?"

Tom looks out the front window and then tells us, "It's KTBC."

Sammy's eyebrows shoot up. "You've got the TV guys here too?"

"Not just any old TV guys. It's Ginger Grant."

Ginger Grant? Queen of Bloomsburg TV news? I bet Amy'll see me. How cool is that?

Meg moves to stand beside Tom and says to Sammy, "We need to get the word out about my campaign."

The guy with the notebook says, "Are you a Democrat or a Republican?"

Sammy tells her, "Jerry here is on the newspaper's night shift, and he's one of us."

Jerry gives Meg a little wave. She says, "I'm an Independent."

A slender, sharp-faced woman, a ferret without the fur, strides into the study and fires a barrage of questions. "Who's in charge here? Where's this new candidate? What's this nonsense about vampires?"

Meg steps forward. "I'm the candidate. Meg Murrow. And, unfortunately, it's not nonsense." She sticks out her hand. "I'm a fan. Pleased to meet you, Ms. Grant."

The woman ignores her hand. "Yeah." She turns toward the front door and calls, "In here." In troops a bulky bearded guy wearing a bandanna on his head over curly hair. He carries a camera and pulls a cart with lights on it.

Sammy eyes the lights, and his mouth turns down in a smug "gotcha" expression. "Yeah, you're gonna be sorry. C'mon, Bruce." He leaves, Bruce tagging along. Jerry the vampire reporter finds a corner and watches, making a note now and then.

After the equipment is set up, Ginger Grant positions Meg in front of a bookcase. Meg calls to me. "C'mon, Patch. You're in this too."

Grant scowls. "We don't need your pet for this."

"Oh, yes we do. I wouldn't be here if it weren't for Patch, and we're in this together as co-candidates."

Grant arches an eyebrow. "A cat candidate? For sheriff? What's he going to do, track down mice?" She shrugs. "Whatever."

I trot over to Meg. She picks me up and holds me to her chest. I wonder if my fur is smooth. Maybe I should give myself a licking. And what about makeup?

Grant holds a microphone to her mouth. "Testing, testing. We good?"

She swivels to the cameraman, who now has headphones on his head and his eye to a camera eyepiece. "Sound is good, we've got focus. Want to start on you and widen out?"

"Yeah." She faces the camera. "Let's go."

He turns on the lights—

SCREAMS ...

PAIN-N-N-N ...

MY EYES ...

I clamp my eyes shut and the pain cuts down to merely excruciating. My nose and ears where the fur is thin burn as if someone is holding matches to me. The rest of my skin itches like crazy, but doesn't hurt.

Above my head, Meg wails and drops me.

Tom screams, "Turn off the lights!"

Having in my mind an image of exactly where I am, I race for the open front door. The instant I pass through it and out of the light, the pain and itching vanish, and I open my eyes. The reflected glow of light from behind me makes them water, but I can see. Behind me, the light in the study shuts off. The screams whimper down.

I stop on the front lawn in the deliciously pain-free night. A van with a satellite dish on top and "KTBC" written on the side is parked at the curb, the sliding door open and the interior light on. Sammy, with Bruce behind him, stands on the sidewalk and peers into the interior.

Inside the van, a guy stares at a monitor. He says, "Jeez, look at that."

I trot to the van to see what they're watching, but stay out of Sammy's line of sight.

Sammy chuckles. "I told 'em they'd be sorry." Then he scowls. "If they keep this election crap up, I'm gonna make 'em a whole lot sorrier." When he turns to go, he spots me. "You. I'm sharpening my knife."

20: Meg

Meg scans the room, searches behind furniture, under the desk. No Patch.

Grant goes to Meg. "Wow. That was weird." Turning to her cameraman, she says, "No more lights. Do the best you can with the room lighting. It should be good enough. We can brighten it back at the studio."

Meg asks the reporter, "Did you see my cat?"

Grant shakes her head. Meg goes to the front door and calls out. "Patch? Here, kitty."

She steps outside, and the stinging in her skin fades in the darkness and cool air. Before those lights had gone on, she would have said she couldn't imagine a pain greater than the one that comes with blood hunger. She'd have been dead wrong. It had been like being dropped into boiling water.

"Patch? Kitty-kitty?" She smiles when Patch emerges from the darkness by the street and trots up to her, apparently all right. She lifts him up and pets him. He snuggles a little, a first. Maybe they're really connecting. There hasn't been time enough for much of a relationship.

On the other hand, he'd had her back when Bruce attacked, and after their encounters with Lester there was a bond, at least one from her to Patch. It feels like he belongs with her. She wants him to be a part of her ... life?

Ginger Grant's voice comes from behind her. "Miss Murrow? Are you all right?"

Grant stands on the front porch. Meg goes to her. "I needed to find my cat."

"Is that important?" The cameraman joins her and aims his camera at Meg, the porch light illuminating her and Patch. Grant uses her microphone. "What does finding a cat have to do with vampires running for sheriff?" She aims the mike at Meg.

Good question.

"He's important to me. And he's my co-candidate."

Grant gestures inside. "You still want to do this interview?"

They need it to start their campaign, so she nods and follows the reporter into Tom's study.

Grant positions Meg and Patch in front of the bookshelves again and then stands beside her. Grant eyes the distance between them and takes a step back.

Meg says, "We're not contagious." Well, not exactly.

"Good to know." Grant says to the cameraman, "We'll do this as a two-shot." Patch gives her a nasty meow. "Okay, a three-shot." The cameraman plugs his camera into a small monitor he puts on Tom's desk. Meg can see what the camera sees. Tom and Seiko watch from off-camera.

With a nod from Grant, the monitor image zooms in to a close-up of the reporter, cutting Meg and Patch out of the shot. The cameraman says, "Rolling."

Grant addresses the camera, "Ginger Grant here, reporting on a most unusual new candidate for county sheriff—a self-professed vampire."

The picture widens to include Meg and Patch as Grant turns to Meg and continues. "Meg Murrow, are you the real thing?" She extends the microphone to catch Meg's words.

Meg nods. "Yes, I"—she shifts Patch so he's facing the camera—"*we* are candidates who want to serve the county and work for the protection of Bloomsburg's minorities."

"No, I mean are you real, bloodsucking vampires?"

Meg drops her gaze and swallows, but then looks the camera in the eye. "We don't, er, suck blood. But all my hopes and dreams were instantly ripped away by this terrible disease."

"Disease?"

"Yes, what else would you call it? But I'm going to fight to get my life back."

"Life? Aren't you the undead?"

"Exactly. *UN*-dead. And there are hundreds like me in Bloomsburg who suffer from this monstrous disease, including my co-candidate, Patch."

"Is someone touting a cat as a candidate for sheriff actually serious about what she's doing?"

Serious? "Dead serious." Meg gives Grant her best scowl. "Answer me this, Miss Grant. If you were physically assaulted, would you expect law enforcement to do something about it?"

Grant scoffs. "Sure. So would anyone."

"A vampire was killed this week, and the sheriff is doing nothing about it. We all need the law to protect us."

Grant shrugs. "I'm not worried. I'm alive and important. They'll protect me."

Meg takes a step toward Grant. Grant's eyes widen and she backs up a pace. Meg says, "Are you dead certain nothing can go wrong to cause you to lose your protection?"

"Absolutely."

"Are you sure? I was just a writer doing my job, and a vampire bit me." She takes a step toward Grant, who hops back. "What if I were to bite you?"

As Grant's eyes widen, Meg says, "Are you sure now that nothing can go wrong for you? Like it did for me?

"What would you do if you could go out only at night and there was a vigilante organization looking to kill people just like you?"

Grant's expression shows confusion, and then she gets it. "You mean if I was a ... was a ..."

"Vampire. Yeah. Like me and my cat. It wouldn't take more than two seconds to turn you into one." I lick my lips, feeling a little guilty at faking a threat.

Grant casts her gaze around the room as if looking for a way out. She looks back to Meg. "I ... I don't ..."

"How about if a 'club' of vigilantes was out to kill you and the sheriff acted as if they didn't exist?"

Grant has no answer.

Meg gazes at the audience beyond the camera. "This started with me and my troubles, but this is about more than just me. A vote for me"—she strokes Patch's head—"and my co-candidate, Patch, is a vote for equal protection under the law for each and every one of us."

Grant scowls at that. "Your cat is really your co-candidate? Aren't you concerned that people will dismiss you as a kook?" The corners of her mouth turn down, and her sour look suggests that she is ready to do just that.

"Patch is an innocent victim of vampirism, and he represents all of us who have suffered the same fate. Besides, anybody who knows cats will understand what it's like to have an independent thinker to talk to."

She strokes him. "More than that, cats are genius hunters, especially in the dark, and that's where the vigilantes operate."

Grant's expression changes to that of an attack ferret. "You haven't really answered my question. Are you a vampire?"

Meg sighs. "Yes, but through no choice of my own."

Grant shoves the mike at her. "Show us your fangs."

What? "I don't have fangs."

"If you're a vampire, you have to have fangs. Everybody knows that." Grant turns to the camera. Her laugh is nasty. "Or do they come out only when you turn into a bat."

"We don't ... can't do that! That's a myth. I'm a human being!"

Grant sneers. "Yes, now it's clear that's *exactly* what you are. A fake. And what you are not—a vampire." She hands the mike to the cameraman. "I think it's a wrap, Ernie. This was a waste of time."

Ernie sounds surprised. "Seems like a vampire story oughta be good."

"Yeah, if she was a real vampire. But her? A nice young woman worried about her cat? No fangs? She's utterly normal. Except maybe wacko—what sane person would want to claim to be a vampire? No way."

Ernie says, "What about the thing with the lights? Looked pretty harsh to me."

"Faked." She glances at Tom. "I've seen this guy on TV. He'll do anything for publicity. You seen any bodies lying around with fang holes in their necks?"

Tom shakes his head. "So you're not going to do the story?"

Grant narrows her eyes at the lawyer, and then at Meg. "This is all a hoax, isn't it?"

Meg says, "Hoax? You think this ... this ... horror is—"

"A PR stunt. Right over there is a blatant ambulance chaser who stops at nothing to get his face on television. And there's you, apparently out of a job but *not* the vampire you claim to be."

Her smile is vicious. "Actually, I think I do have a story. A vampire hoax is a scoop I'm happy to make." She strides out of the house, Ernie tagging along behind her.

Meg says, "What just happened? A hoax? What do I have to do, bite somebody?" She sends a glare after the departing TV reporter. "Maybe that's not a bad idea."

Tom shrugs. "You heard her. Without a bloodthirsty fanged killer to show, it looks like we might be a wrap."

He takes out his phone and makes a call. "Archie? Can you join us? Our press conference didn't go as well as we would have liked." He nods, then ends the call.

Meg goes to the front door and watches as the KTBC van leaves. *My campaign is over? Just like that?*

21: Patch

I'm happy to see Archie arrive. He seems to be the sane one around here—if you don't count the fact that he's willing to hang out with vampires who are prone to the sudden onset of bloody munchies. After Tom tells him how the interview went sour, Archie says, his voice musical in a way I like, "We don't need Grant if we can run some ads." He shakes his head. "But that takes money, and your practice isn't exactly thriving these nights."

Tom says, "We have an angel on the way." The doorbell rings and he checks his watch. "Right on time."

When Archie opens the door, a big guy who reminds me of Bruce shoulders his way in, one hand tucked inside his suit coat. I've seen gangster movies with guys just like that doing the same thing. Generally, they sooner or later pull out a gat and blow somebody away.

Big Guy takes a quick look into the study and adjoining rooms, then goes back to the door. To someone outside, he says, "Clear, Boss."

Big Guy steps aside and in comes a bald-headed man with the short-legged, stocky body and the jutting lower jaw and jowls of a bulldog. He surveys the room with an attitude that suggests ownership. My hackles want to rise, but I calm myself.

Tom says, "Welcome, welcome." He turns to us. "Folks, meet Papa Gambino, the conservative who makes the right wing look like Communists."

Papa stops in the middle of the study and examines us. "That would be me." He pulls out a cigar and lights it. His easygoing drawl sounds more like Georgia than the Midwest. "Hi, y'all."

Tom says, "Uh, this is a nonsmoking household, sir." I think it's interesting how he calls the man *sir*.

Papa shrugs. "You vampires don't breathe, right? So there's no problem with secondhand smoke."

Archie comes into the room. "It's a problem with me." Big Guy follows him in, then stands in the doorway. "I'm a breather."

Meg says to Papa, "I know you're most of the money and power in Bloomsburg, Mr. Gambino, but being rude isn't going to get you anywhere here. And we have to breathe in order to speak, so your smoke is hurting all of us. Including you."

Papa shakes his head, then holds the cigar out. "Giles." The big guy rushes forward to take it, and then grinds it out on his palm and puts the butt in his coat pocket. Doesn't even flinch. Papa says, "Oh, for the good old days when everybody had the freedom to smoke wherever they wanted to. All this legal nonsense about smoke has robbed us of our liberty."

Meg frowns at him. "And we're running to enforce that 'nonsense.' Do you have a problem with that?"

Papa studies her. "You're the one running for sheriff."

"Yes."

He swings his gaze to the lawyer. "And you're asking me to support her campaign?"

He gets a nod from Tom.

Meg, her tone pugnacious, says, "So?"

"I think I can help y'all out." He snaps his fingers and Giles steps forward, reaching inside his coat.

I brace for a leap, ready to escape.

Giles pulls out two thick bundles of money with rubber bands around them. He hands them to Papa Gambino, who holds them up. "How about a little campaign financing?"

Tom licks his lips and says, "Pretty."

"Twenty-five thousand." He tosses the money to Tom, but his throw goes high.

Like an outfielder on the New York Yankees, Tom's gaze never leaves the cash, and he makes a great leaping catch from a sitting position, snaring a bundle with each hand. He cuddles the money, his gaze moist with love. He croons, "Ooo, hundred-dollar bills" as if whispering sweet nothings to a lover.

Papa chuckles, "This is under the table, of course. It's how I like to make all my political donations. Just a little help between friends."

Meg says, "We have to be friends?"

His face settles into a scowl, which makes him look even more like a bulldog. Then he shrugs. "Y'all got a problem with friendship?"

"No, but that's not what you're after. Cut to the chase. What do you want?"

He raises his eyebrows and spreads his hands as if wrongfully accused. "Just to help you creatures—"

"People," Meg says. "We're people."

"Sure you are. I want you to be free to enjoy your, er, lives, just like you say."

"Because ..."

He studies her. "Okay, have it your way. You guys stay up all night, right?"

Meg nods.

"And there are a bunch of you?"

"Close to a thousand in Bloomsburg alone."

He rubs his hands together. "Perfect. Your, er, people are what I need to expand my toxic waste processing plant to twenty-four-hour production. I need a night shift, and you need jobs. If you're elected, me and your constituency get what we want." He shrugs. "I won't have to pay for medical insurance, and I won't have to worry about them getting sick and dying."

"That doesn't tell me why you're supporting us for sheriff."

Papa bares his teeth in what seems to be intended as a comradely smile. "Seems like there might be county laws against the way I need to run my plant to be, er, efficient. Maybe a new sheriff could help with that."

Tom finishes counting the money. "Yep, twenty-five thousand. Nice." There may be a bit of drool at one corner of his mouth.

Papa says, "So we got a deal?"

Meg stands, picking me up and cradling me in her arms. Papa focuses on me and backs up a couple of steps. She says, "You want a sheriff who looks the other way?"

"Hey, I'm helping to clean up the environment and offering you and your, er, people a good deal." He sneezes. "There is one thing I definitely want. Get rid of the cat. I'm allergic." He sneezes again.

I'm starting to feel allergic to him. Like any cat, I don't like pushy people. We like to be asked and, whenever possible, coaxed. Pleading is even better. Seems to me cats have the better system for getting things done. And if anybody is going to be pushy, it's us.

Meg shakes her head. "No deal. Patch and I are partners, and he's been announced as part of the team." She turns to Tom. "Give him his money back."

Tom doesn't move. Archie sighs and goes to him, and then pries Tom's fingers off of the money. Archie says to Meg, "Tom doesn't mean anything. I think it's just a lawyer reflex."

Tom says, "My firm is low on cash, Meg, and I don't see how we can have any campaign at all without that money. Especially now that we won't be getting coverage from the press after Ginger Grant is done poisoning the airwaves about us."

Papa winks at Tom. "I'll throw all my legal work to you, too. Hell, with the environmental suits alone, you'll be rich."

Tom giggles. "Isn't that generous?" Then he recomposes his face into a serious expression. "So you think you can buy our loyalty?"

"Why should you be any different?"

Cynical guy. Or a realist.

Meg says, "Morals."

Ha! You go, girl.

Papa shakes his head. "You think I'm immoral for offering a little cash? Not from my point of view. In fact, paying well for services rendered seems to me to be high morality." He sneezes again. "All you gotta do is lose the cat."

I wriggle and Meg sets me down. She says, "No cat, no deal."

Archie holds the money out to Papa Gambino.

Papa waves him off. "All right, keep the damn cat. All I want is a little, uh, flexibility when it comes to a couple of unconstitutionally restrictive laws."

I look up at Meg's face. Her gaze cuts to the money and back to Papa. I've seen enough politicians on TV for the words *slippery slope* to come to mind.

Tom says, "You need it, Meg. And I need the business. Do I have to remind you how much I've helped you out?"

Wow. I have just heard money talking. Meg's eyes are wide. She stares at the money in Archie's hand, and she looks like she's been hypnotized. "I'm free to do what I think is right? Follow the law?"

Tom and Papa chorus, "Absolutely."

Archie opens his mouth as if to speak, but Tom clears his throat and Archie stifles his thought.

Meg takes a step toward Archie.

Papa Gambino grins and rubs his hands together.

She reaches for the money.

Oh, Meg ...

Meg's mouth tightens and she squints as if she's struggling, and then she takes the money from Archie. She examines it, and the smell of money drifts my way. The aroma is both sweet and soiled. Just like Meg is about to become. I take in a little air and give the wad of cash a low growl.

Seiko stands. "I don't think you should do this, Meg. I've got a little in a savings account I can get to through the ATM. And maybe Vera and the American Vampire Association can help."

Meg says, "What's the problem? Money is just money, and he says I can do whatever I want."

Like he's giving her permission. Which he can take back. That's enough for me. I jump from her arms and walk over to stand with Seiko. The thing is that being true to yourself is something you have to do all the time. Cats are built that way. Oh, we'll grovel for a good petting when we want it, but that's still the way we are. And we won't let you near us if we don't want you.

Meg says, "Patch? What's the matter?"

I saunter over to Papa and rub against his leg. He sneezes and lifts a foot as if he's going to kick me.

"Don't even think about it," Meg says to Papa. She squats down and holds a hand out to me. "Look, I'm just being practical. After all, the goal is to get elected. We can't do anything to stop those killers if we're not elected. That has to be our focus."

It seems to me the focus ought to be on doing things for cats.

Papa claps. "So, little girl, do we have a deal?"

Little girl? See, Meg? He thinks he's making a deal, not a donation. And he's sure he'll get something out of it—his pint of blood, as a vampire would say. I walk back to her and butt my head against her leg.

She gazes into my eyes. "Patch, stick with me here. I know what I'm doing. This is important. It's about protecting innocent people! We can do a lot of good if we're sheriff, but getting elected comes first."

Papa says, "Sure you can. We're right behind you."

Yeah. With your hands on the steering wheel. I turn and walk back toward Papa. His eyes widen and he backs up a step. I keep coming. He scoots around behind Giles.

"Keep that thing away from me." He sneezes, and then wipes his nose on Giles's coattail.

Giles slides his hand inside his coat again. I don't think he's reaching for another envelope of cash.

Meg raises her hands. "Please. No violence." She says to me, "These people aren't here to hurt us." She lifts the cash. "They're trying to help."

Papa Gambino, peeking around Giles, sticks his tongue out at me.

Okay, what to do? This is not fun. I'm not being petted or adored. Meg is ankle-deep in corruption, with Tom the lawyer eagerly panting at her side. I need some air. Well, not literally, but you know what I mean.

Exiting the room, I make sure to brush against Papa's leg on the way out. I'm rewarded with a trio of sneezes.

I go out the open front door and stand on the porch to consider my situation. I truly like Meg as my associate, but this is a matter of principle. The night is quiet.

Meg's voice comes from inside. "Patch?" I glance back. She stands in the foyer, the money in her hand. "Come on. We can do good."

Doing good doesn't interest me. Cats don't do good. Or bad, for that matter. With the occasional exception of peeing on a bed, but only if it's the right thing to do when an associate needs disciplining. Some people need lots of training.

I look back at Meg. I hate this. She's done her best for me. Maybe I should just go along.

But then I'd be corrupt too. This is no business for a cat. She'll have to go down the road to perdition all by herself.

I'm out of here. I'm free to hook up with that little Siamese—if I can. I head toward the sidewalk, on my way to being just an ordinary vampire kitty-cat.

When I pass a fat bush on the way to the sidewalk, I'm scooped up and lifted into the air and hang upside down, suspended in netting.

22: Patch

Lester's voice comes. "Well, if it isn't my old friend Patch. I thought you'd come along sooner or later." He strides away from the house, carrying me.

Let me tell you, bobbing upside down in a net hanging from the shoulder of a colossal vampire who once wanted to crush you into a sack of ruptured organs and bone splinters is a worrisome thing.

It doesn't help that his vampire doggie, Nasty, tags along behind, leaping up now and then and snapping his teeth perilously close to my belly.

When we get to Lester's hearse, he dumps me out of the net and into a coffin that's just my size. There are two other coffins, a really long one and another smallish one, but bigger than the one he puts me in. "This is yours now, Patch." He lowers the lid, and soon my body sways when the hearse goes into motion.

Time passes, I don't know how much, and the hearse stops. Like all cats, I have no sense of time. It's all "now" to me. But enough of now has passed for the burn of blood hunger in my belly to grow. It's starting to really hurt.

The lid lifts on my coffin. *My* coffin—a truly creepy thought. Lester's big hand envelops me before I can launch myself out of it. He holds me in front of him, face-to-face, far enough away so that my claws can't reach him.

Lester is not what he was when I first met him, primarily because of the open wounds on both sides of his neck, four claw tracks on each side. Not to mention the furrows on his hand. It looks like it's true that vampires don't heal. Makes sense, I guess. We're pretty much dead, after all.

Behind Lester is a park. Four people play tennis on a lighted court in the distance, there are people barbecuing in a gazebo, and others are strolling. There are lots of big trees and grass. I'm dizzy with pain, but I remember hunting here. Because it's a park where people picnic, the squirrels are especially plump.

Lester smiles at me. "I'm sure you're wondering why I brought you here."

I squirm. I don't give a meow why he brought me here, I need BLOOD. But he just has to have his say.

"You shall now know the bliss of striking terror in the night alongside the vampire Lestat. Once you have tasted blood spiced by fear, you will embrace the Way of the Vampire and never turn back."

Who talks like that? The blood hunger in me grows stronger. I kick to be free.

But Lester isn't through. He turns me to face the park. "In the kingdom of the wild, free vampire, this is our grocery store. I think of it as Lestat's Food Park. Other vampires have tried to shop here, but I dissuaded them." He holds me to face him again. "This place is for you and me, Patch." He glances down at the dog. "And my friend Nosferatu, of course."

He lowers me, but doesn't release me. "Go and feed, my beastly companion. I shall as well. I see a terrible backhand on the tennis court that the world will be better off without. Return here before dawn so I can protect you from the sun."

The hunger pain is so huge, pounding in my ears, that I hardly hear his last words. I give a twist, wrench myself from his hand, and hit the grass running. So crazed am I that I would sink my teeth into any living thing that came near, even a person. But there must be some of the cool that all cats have as standard equipment still functioning because I head for a big oak tree. I know from my last visit that a supply of squirrels lives there.

I won't go into the gruesome particulars. It's embarrassing to even think about the madness of blood hunger. But soon the world is minus one chubby squirrel, and I sprawl on the ground, purring. There wasn't any "spiced by fear" aspect to the blood as far as I can tell, but then, I'd killed that squirrel so fast there hadn't been a chance for it to be afraid.

Three people with tennis rackets run past me, screaming. I give myself a good licking to clean up blood spatters on my fur.

So this is my new life? Maybe I was hasty when I decided Meg was corrupt. After all, she hasn't done anything illegal. Yet.

I wonder how she's doing. And if I can find the lawyer's house. Having come here in a coffin, I don't have much in the way of clues. But still, my kitty-cat locator sense gives me a good idea of where it is. Once in the neighborhood, I can scout around until I find it.

I don't want to be done with Meg. She needs me, and maybe I need her. So I get up to leave the park.

I trot past Lester's hearse, but there's no sign of him. Unfortunately, Nasty is there, blood matting the fur on his muzzle. Dogs are such slobs. He positions himself in front of me and bares his teeth.

Okay, I'll just go around. But then a too-familiar giant hand snatches me. Lester says, "Good kitty. I knew you'd return." He opens up the rear of the hearse. Nasty jumps in, and Lester drops me inside. But he doesn't shut me in my coffin before he closes the door.

When Lester gets into the driver's seat, he says, "I know a great place for dessert, where the winos have a nice flavor. Then we'll park and get ready for dawn."

I'll pass on the winos. As he drives, I poke my nose between the side curtains to see which direction we're going. My locator sense tells me we're going farther and farther away from Meg. Oh, well. Easy come, easy go.

But I miss her.

23: Meg

Meg comes back into the office after yet one more look out the front door and a call of "Here, kitty, kitty, kitty."

Seiko says, "No luck, huh?"

"Where could he be? What if the blood hunger hits him and he needs some V1 and can't get any?"

Papa smiles.

Seiko says, "I'm a little worried about Lester, too. Not about not having blood; he takes that whenever he wants. But there are those Devil crazies out there. As big as he is, he can be outnumbered."

Papa taps the money Meg still holds. "So, if the cat's gone, are y'all still gonna run for sheriff?"

She studies the cash and then tightens her grip on it. "As long as there is still injustice for me and my people."

"People." He chuckles. "Yeah, *people.*" He looks to Tom. "We good here? Donation's okay? And don't forget, you'll be getting all my environmental business."

Tom salutes him. "Yessir. I look forward to working with you."

Papa goes to the front door. "Let's go, Giles, we got the deal we wanted here."

When they're gone, Tom plucks the cash from Meg's hands. "I'll look after this, okay?"

She frowns at it. "I wish we didn't have to ..." She gives him a smile. "Still, I'm glad you've got a new client."

"Business will be good."

But she's on her own. She takes out her phone and opens her bank app. There's enough to pay the rent for one more month, and maybe enough for V1 juice. "Maybe I can get my old job back until the election is over."

She sits at the dining room table and dials.

A man says, "Hello?"

Meg's voice is tight. "Mr. Swanson? I'm sorry to call you at home this late, but—"

"Meg? Is that you?"

She smiles with relief. "You remember me?"

"Who could forget my best copywriter? Especially when she just disappears."

"Well, I got, er, sick."

Mr. Swanson laughs. "I know all about it. I've been following the adventures of you and that cat. The bit with the cat is a nice touch."

"Patch is a lot more than a bit. He saved my life." She braces herself. "Speaking of my life, sir, is my job still there?"

"We've been getting by with freelancers."

A hopeful smile comes. "So I can come back? I can work remotely. And after dark. All night."

After a lengthy, uncomfortable silence, Swanson says, "Ah, we got a call from Papa Gambino."

Her smile dims. Here comes a bus. "But he's not one of our—I mean, your—clients."

"True. But he also made phone calls to all of our clientele." To give the man credit, his voice softens. "I'm truly sorry, Meg. I just can't. And I don't think you're going to find anything in Bloomsburg."

Meg puts on another smile, and it almost makes it into her voice. "I understand. Thanks. Anyway, I'm planning on being the new sheriff."

"Hey, you've got my vote. Love the cat."

"Thanks." For nothing. She ends the call and stares into space. *Oh, Patch, come back. I sure could use a good purr right about now.*

24: Patch

I don't know how long I napped after Lester terrorized a homeless camp, but it's pitch dark when I open my eyes. Just like when Meg buried me alive. Oh, yeah. I'm in Lester's cat-sized coffin. Although cats do like little cave-like places to curl up in, we want an escape route, too. When he put me in, I tried to push the lid open by arching my back, but then came the click of a latch being closed.

Lester had parked the hearse in the garage under the American Vampire Association building. Not a lot of risk there. Lester isn't quite as wild a vampire as his rant suggests. A crack of light appears above me, and the lid swings up. After the total darkness of the coffin, the parking garage lights stab like claws into my eyes. I climb out and stand in the rear of the hearse, blinking. Nasty's coffin is already open, and he sits behind the car, his tongue lolling.

At the rear of the hearse, Lester greets me with his fangy smile. "Well, Patch, how did you like your first night of wild freedom?"

I give the coffin a glare, but I don't think he gets it. As for the hunt in the park, I don't care for the whole crazed blood hunger scene. Highly uncivilized. Yeah, I know that I'm a carnivore and a predator, and I have no regrets about the squirrel. It's nature. But this is different. It's insane, and

I can tell you that rationality is high on the list of kitty-cat virtues. We like rational. We like civilized.

I stare up at Lester until he shrugs. I step forward, thinking maybe I can hop out and slip away, but Lester slams the rear door in my face.

Back in the car, he says, "I wonder if our little visit to the park made the news." Funny how people like to talk to cats. Would they do that if they knew we understand what they're saying? There's a click, and then a tinny voice announces, "Here's more from the Bloomsburg news beat."

When I go to the front seat, I discover that Lester has a small TV mounted below the dashboard. The picture is crummy, but I can make it out.

It's Meg and me being interviewed. The reporter keeps pressuring Meg about whether or not she's a bloodsucking monster, but Meg tries to focus on protecting citizens. And she makes sure to tell everybody that I'm her co-candidate. Now, that warms my heart.

Lester shakes his head. "Nay, wench, he'll never return to your political schemes. Patch has tasted the wild life."

Wench? Although I generally abhor violence, I wish Meg could hear him say that. It would be fun to see her dismantle him.

He turns to me. "Without you, her nights as a politician are over. And so are yours." He snorts. "It was a dumb idea anyway."

Taking away her campaign for sheriff will kill Meg. Okay, not really, but it'll be a close second. It's her hope for a new "life." Lester is turning out to be a bigger ass than I'd thought, and he was already huge.

But then the scene changes to Ginger Grant in the newsroom. She says, "We here at KTBC are dedicated to protecting you, our viewers, by exposing hoaxes like this one." A still shot of Meg's sweet face appears next to Grant's narrow, angry one. "Is this a vampire?" She laughs. "Not on your life." She sobers. "But there are strange things happening in the dark."

The picture changes to a daytime shot of a park. I recognize the oak tree my dinner lived in. "In a related story, tennis players at Prairie Park reported an attack by a giant vampire last night." A split screen shows Grant and a middle-aged guy made of sags—bags under his eyes sag, his cheeks sag into jowls, his head sags on his neck.

Lester slaps the steering wheel. "Here we are, Patch!"

Grant says, "Officer John McGregor, was there a killer in the park?"

Not me. Unless the cops are after the perp who did in a squirrel. Lester grins.

The officer shrugs. "Uh, we have not found anybody's body."

Lester chuckles. "Too dumb to look up. But that tree limb won't hold him forever."

Grant continues. "Do you think this could be a part of the vampire hoax being perpetrated by alleged bloodsucker Meg Murrow, the wackiest candidate for sheriff in Bloomsburg history?"

I cringe. Lester whacks the steering wheel and laughs.

The cop shrugs. "I dunno. It could be a Halloween trick."

"In September, Officer McGregor?"

"Nuts can come out of the shell any time of year."

Grant says, "Thank you, Officer McGregor." The picture cuts to a close-up of Grant. "This supposed appearance of vampires in our midst has provoked strong words from the Reverend Pat Bobson, head of the Righteous Hallelujah Church. We spoke with the Reverend Bobson at his church office."

The scene changes to a kindly looking, white-haired gent relaxing in a rocker in front of a fireplace, logs ablaze. A cat curls up on the hearth, a big Persian. Now, I generally say a cat is just a cat, we're all about the same, but I've never gotten along with Persians. They tend to be elitist and cranky.

Grant's question is voiceover. "Reverend Bobson, what do you have to say to reports of vampires right here in Bloomsburg?"

Bobson's sweet eyes widen, his kindly mouth opens, and he says, "Abominations!" His benevolent appearance is in such opposition to that word, I'm not sure I heard him right. But I did.

"These vampire creatures are abominations in the eyes of the Almighty!" Talk about cognitive dissonance: the tone of his voice and expression would fit words more like "Welcome to the loving arms of the Almighty." This guy could say anything and make it seem reasonable and inarguable.

"They should not be allowed to run for public office. No, they should have stakes driven through their foul hearts and then burn in the everlasting fires of hell."

Hey, how about a little brotherly love here?

Grant says, "But, Reverend Bobson, this so-called vampire claims that she and her cat are victims of a disease and can't help what they are. She says that they did not choose to become vampires at all."

"Ha! Evil is always a choice, and these perverse creatures have volunteered for the forces of Satan." He stands and raises a fist in the air. "The Almighty tells me to hunt them down, to destroy these godless vermin!"

Lester switches the television off. "Idiot." He looks at me, and then he smiles. "I think we should teach the good reverend a lesson."

The good reverend didn't strike me as being open to learning anything. What could Lester possibly teach him?

"I think I can help him come to understand the feral joy of eternal undeadness." He starts the hearse and backs up.

There's a bump and a crunch. Lester throws the hearse into Park. He gets out and shuts the door before I can leap for freedom.

He goes to the rear of the hearse and I run back to see. Lester stoops and then stands, holding his doggie in his arms. Nasty's tongue still lolls, but his face looks thinner to me.

Opening the rear door, Lester sits Nasty in the back of the hearse. "Poor little Nosferatu." Putting his thumbs in the dog's mouth, he pulls out until the mutt's muzzle pops back to its normal blunt shape. Lester examines his work. "There, you'll be fine."

Well, not totally. The dog's muzzle looks like it's making a left turn. Nasty doesn't appear to be happy.

Lester shuts the door and goes back to the driver's seat. We pull out, three little vampires on our way to see how the ungodly fare in the realm of righteous preachers. I wonder if the Reverend Pat has holy water, and what will happen if he throws it on a certain vampire kitty-cat.

25: Patch

We drive past Tom's condo on the way to Pat Bobson's church. There are two TV vans parked in front, but Grant's KTBC van is not in sight. Maybe twenty people mill around in the front yard. The lights are on in the house, and I glimpse Archie opening the front door and stepping out onto the porch. The reporters on the lawn swarm toward him like vultures after roadkill.

I keep track of streets and landmarks as we go. One of these days I'm going to get away. Although Lester hasn't mistreated me, he isn't my idea of an associate, especially with his vampire pooch hanging around glaring at me. Danger seems to be Lester's constant companion, too, and that's a kitty-cat no-no. You'll never see a cat looking for trouble, although we'll give you some if you invade our space.

There are more TV vans and an even bigger crowd at Pat Bobson's Righteous Hallelujah Church —one of the TV vans is the KTBC mobile studio. The low, wide building covers most of a block. The Rev himself is on the broad steps in front of the building.

Bobson faces a front line of reporters aiming microphones his direction and cameramen focusing on him. Ginger Grant and Ernie are closest to the preacher, mike and camera in his face.

A hundred or so men and women, mostly white, mostly middle-aged, back up the media. A couple of people in the crowd carry signs that declare "Undo the Undead."

Lester finds a parking spot where we can still see the front of the church and switches on his little television. Sure enough, there's live coverage of the goings-on in the land of the righteous.

Pat Bobson shakes a finger at the camera. His voice seems mild, but a vein in his forehead pulses, and it feels like he's yelling even though he isn't. "These vampires have an ungodly agenda. They want to get into our schools, violate our children, and invade our homes to turn all of us into abominations."

Lester snorts. "That would be dumb. Then we wouldn't have anybody to feed on."

Speaking of feeding, the blood hunger is warming up in my belly, getting ready to freak me out again. And here I am, shut inside a hearse with vampires. This undead business sure has its inconveniences.

The Rev raises a fist, and his voice rises from soft to ecstatic. "The Almighty has spoken to me, and He has given me a grand vision of my mission to eradicate these unnatural perversions from our fair city. I will lead a host against the unholy undead and stomp their filthy, twisted bodies back into the dirt where they belong!"

The man has a temper. In the crowd, fists shoot into the air, mouths open, and a roar roars. Having a hundred rabid vampire haters only a few car lengths away makes me a tad nervous, but Lester just watches with a grin on his face, his fake fangs glistening in the light from the television screen.

The Rev holds up his hands and the crowd quiets. "Brethren, heed my call. I go inside now to pray and prepare.

Return at midnight and we will begin our cleansing with the filthy corpse the vampires have chosen to campaign for sheriff. Bring wooden stakes and fire, the sacred tools of a holy purge."

The crowd goes nuts. "Undo the Undead" signs bob up and down. He raises his hands high, smiles, then turns and goes inside. The scene cuts to a close-up of Grant. "There you have it—"

Lester shuts off the television and starts his hearse. "Let's see if there's a back door."

He drives down an alley and parks next to a backyard behind the church. Not only does the building have a back door, but it has a cat-sized pet door. Lester lets Nasty out onto the pavement, but snatches me when I make my move to get out. He eyes me. "I don't know why, but I don't think you've answered the call of the wild life yet. However, I think I know just what will bring you over."

I hope it's a bowl of warm blood. The burn is growing in my tummy.

With me tucked under his arm, Lester tries the back door and finds it unlocked. A heavyset woman wields a mop in the wide hallway inside. Using a small smile that doesn't reveal his fangs, Lester goes to her. "Sister, would you be so kind as to tell me how to get to the reverend's office?"

She cocks a hip and puts a hand on it. "Sister? I ain't no sister of yours, I'm a good Baptist. I just work here." She gives him the vertical stare. "I gotta say, though, that's a fine cape you got there."

I can't help but think of how much blood flows through her big, round body. Lester's hold on me tightens. I suspect he's feeling the blood hunger too. But he keeps his voice cool.

"Uh, we're all brothers and sisters in the sight of the Lord. Please, the way to the reverend's office?"

She tells us and we trek upstairs to a set of oak double doors. There's another pet door in one of them. Lester walks right in. We find Pat Bobson at his desk, petting an obese Persian that lies on it in front of him; it's the cat we saw on Lester's TV.

Bobson looks up and gives us that warm, loving smile. "May I help you?"

Lester closes the door. "Oh, yes."

The Persian stands, arches its back, and hisses. Lester strokes my head. "Look, Patch. Dinner."

I don't think so. If I can avoid it, that is. It would be like, well, cannibalism. Come to think of it, isn't what Lester does a form of cannibalism? But if the blood hunger takes over, I don't know what I will do.

Actually, I do know—a feeding frenzy.

Bobson's face remains saintly. "What is it, my son?"

Lester says, "I heard your little rant about vampires, and I want to give you a new insight into them."

"I don't need a new insight. In fact, I haven't needed a new insight for decades." He holds up a black book for Lester to see. The title is *The Righteous Hallelujah Gospel*. By the Reverend Patrick J. Bobson. "Everything I need to know or think is in here."

Lester takes a couple of steps forward. "Really? I mean, vampires weren't around when you wrote that, were they?"

Bobson smiles. "Doesn't matter. My gospel tells me what to think about perverts and abominations like vampires and queers." He touches a fingertip to his temple. "And if it's not in the gospel, well, the Almighty lets me know directly."

Lester sets me down. "I think you need something new to chew on. Or, more to the point, *I* need something to chew on." He's at the reverend's side with three long strides. That Lester is a monster of action, all right. He grabs the Rev by the lapels, lifts him out of his chair, and has his fangs stabbing into Bobson's neck before the Rev can scream.

The cat leaps down and races past me, I figure heading for the pet door. Its blood calls to me, but I'm still in control. A crunch sounds behind me, and I turn to find Nasty's massive jaws gripping the cat's neck. Nasty drops the body and, with a quick rip of his canines, has the Persian's blood pooling on the floor. Nasty laps greedily.

I want some!

But it's a cat!

A groan accompanies slurping sounds from the reverend's desk. A quick glance shows Lester having a fine dining experience with the preacher, who squirms but doesn't break Lester's hold on him.

Lester looks at me. "Come here, my pet. A taste of this is what you need to feel the true power of the vampire!"

Intellectually, I'm not interested, but my body is ... The smell of blood is overpowering ...

I turn for the pet door, but Nasty steps in front of me. He opens his jaws for a silent growl—will the creature ever get it?—and blocks my way. Screw Nasty. I take a deep breath and charge straight at him, yowling. His eyes bulge and he stiffens. I duck low and run between his front legs and through. His claws rasp on the carpet behind me, so I put on speed.

In a flash I'm out the pet door and in the hallway. A crash sounds, and I turn to see Nasty's head in the pet door opening, but that's all that will be coming through. He's stuck.

I go back to him. Oh, the fun of watching him go nuts trying to scrootch another inch through the door to get me. I give him a quick lick on the nose. A yucky taste, but the silent howl he doesn't utter makes it worth it.

Blood hunger boils in me; I race down the hall, hoping I'll find the big woman, and hoping that I won't, too.

She's gone, thank goodness, so I run out the pet door at the back of the building. Maybe there's a rat out there. I slam into a skinny pair of human legs and fall onto my back. I look up. It's Ginger Grant, ace reporter. She points at me. "Hey, isn't that the alleged vampire cat?"

I spin and run, but bang into another pair of legs. Grant shouts, "Grab him, Ernie!"

It's the cameraman. Before I can get moving, he throws an open equipment bag over me and everything goes dark.

Grant tells Ernie, "Let's take him to my house."

You haven't known misery until you've been a vampire kitty-cat trapped inside a smelly leather bag with the pain of blood hunger blazing through every cell of your body. If it were possible, I would suck myself dry. The bag is picked up, zipped up, and then dropped. A lurch tells me I'm in a car, moving.

After too long a time, the zipper on the bag opens. *Light!* But indoor light, so I'm okay with that.

Sound. The yap-yap-yap of one of those yappy little dogs. Propelled by blood hunger, I leap out of the bag. Well, I intend to leap, but in my frenzy my hind legs catch on the bag, and I fall the rest of the way to land on my nose.

Laughter joins the yapping. I lie upside down on a black slate floor, staring up at Ginger Grant, laughing at me. I must be in her foyer. One of those bite-sized poodles stands between her feet, yapping so hard its spittle spots the floor. The thing is white, much of its hair shaved, and red ribbons decorate its ears. How can it stand the humiliation?

Answer: it's a dog.

Next to her stands the cameraman, the same bulky bearded guy with a greasy-looking bandanna on his head who'd been at the lawyer's house. He has his camera aimed at me, capturing my humiliation on video.

From experience, I know that the yappy's brain is the approximate size and horsepower of a BB. More importantly, the yappy is chock-full of BLOOD.

I get to my feet and charge, my claws scrabbling on the slick floor. Blood hunger provides a burst of strength—maybe *fury* would be a better word. I hit the yappy at full speed, knocking it back and out from under Grant.

Grant screeches. "Puffy!"

I rip Puffy's throat open and the dog lies twitching, then goes limp and very dead. While I lap up blood, Grant cries, "My God, it *is* a vampire."

The sound of clapping catches my attention. I glance up to see that the cameraman has lowered his camera to applaud.

Grant shoots him a hot look. "Ernie!"

Ernie shrugs. Then he raises his camera to video my action.

Grant reaches for me, but I turn and face her, draw a big breath, and hiss as hard as I can. I suspect that, along with my fangs dripping Puffy's blood, I make a pretty scary sight. She backs away a couple of feet.

With one hand, the cameraman offers her a microphone— the show must go on. She doesn't hesitate to grab it. I go back to lapping blood beside Puffy's body. The pleasure of relief is already spreading through me. Puffy is tasty.

Grant says into the microphone, "This is Ginger Grant with a KTBC exclusive, the first look humanity has had of a vampire feeding. And this kitty-cat vampire, if we are to believe the words of Meg Murrow, allegedly another murderous vampire, is a co-candidate for sheriff."

I don't attend to what she says next. I've lapped my fill of Puffy's blood and sit to let the pleasure course through me. I feel a purr coming on. But it dies in my throat. My body is languid, but my mind can't relax.

Meg is in danger from Pat Bobson's flock. I flash on the mob scene from the Frankenstein film again. Bobson's bunch looked like they were capable of the same kind of lunacy. And he told them to come back with torches. And stakes. At midnight. I look at the door. It's very shut, and I need to get out of here.

Grant continues. "Apparently, the creature has finished feeding off of my sweet puppy. What happens next? Does this cat turn into a bat?"

Good grief. I give her my best kitty-cat "Are you an idiot?" look, the one where we level our gaze at you with eyelids lowered. It shuts her up.

A clock in the foyer chimes. I can't read clocks, but I can count. Twelve. The feeding lethargy has worn off, so I get to my feet and walk to the door. Ernie the cameraman tracks with me, stepping back out of my way. I stop at the door and wait.

When nobody moves to open it for me, I decide to add a little motivation. I turn and slink toward Ginger Grant in hunting mode, my belly low to the ground, my gaze focused on her neck.

She says, "Oh, crap. It's coming after me!"

As she backs away, I swing wide and come in from an angle that will get her moving toward the door.

"Ernie, are you getting this?"

"Yep. Vampire kitty-cat attacks newswoman. Great stuff."

She reaches the door and backs into the knob. I think that's a great point at which to inhale and let out a long, low growl.

Grant gropes behind her for the doorknob. "There aren't going to be any attacks on this newswoman." She flings the door open and leaps aside. "Get out!"

I rise to my full height and stride out the door, chin high, tail waving.

Behind me, Grant whispers, "Get the bag."

A glance back shows Ernie grabbing that equipment bag and starting for me. I run for it and leave Ernie holding the bag.

Meg's face is all I need to turn on my directional sense, and I set out to find her. It'll be good to be with calm, rational people for a change.

Thanks to Puffy's contribution to my well-being, strength flows through me, and I have no trouble trotting all the way to the lawyer's condo. I don't know how I can alert Meg to the danger of Bobson's bunch, but I'm determined to find a way.

I stop beside a wall-tall hedge that separates the lawyer's condo from an apartment building next door. The gang of news vans and people still clusters in front of the condo, and now a cop directs traffic past the place. How should I approach? Then a low moan comes from the shadows by the hedge.

Slipping through a flower bed, I creep close. There stand Lester and Pat Bobson. Bobson is the one moaning. It sounds a lot like the moan that comes from Meg when the blood hunger is upon her. Bobson strains forward, toward the TV crews, and Lester holds him back with a grip on the back of his shirt.

Lester says, "Patience, Brother Pat. We don't want to be discovered."

Bobson's answer is a snarl.

A man's voice comes from the crowd. "Any place to take a leak around here? I'm about to drown."

Another male voice says, "That hedge over there works pretty good."

A female voice whines, "I hate it that guys can do that and I can't."

Moments later, the rustle of leaves signals the arrival of the guy who has to pee. He rounds the end of the hedge and bumps into the reverend, who grabs him by the shirt and throws him to the ground. Bobson dives onto the man and chews on his throat.

Lester says, "Go for it, bro."

And then a second man arrives. Bobson looks up at him, the blood covering his mouth and chin clearly visible in the light from a streetlamp. Extreme makeover, vampire-style.

The man says, "Reverend Bobson?"

Lester steps forward, and the man looks up and up to the seven-foot vampire's face. The man says, "Oh-h-h-h-h shi-i-i-i—"

Lester lunges at him, arms outstretched, but the guy spins and runs into the street, screaming for help.

I suspect that this will not do the vampire cause a lot of good.

Bobson is back to sucking on his now lifeless victim. Screaming Guy runs to the traffic cop. His screams turn into yells, and he points to where we are. Snatches of words come. "Blood! Body!"

A competing sound, a rising mumble of many voices, comes from another direction.

A mob of twenty or so people rounds the corner beyond the apartment building. Maybe ten of them carry torches.

The mumble resolves into a chant. "Undo the undead. Undo the undead." It's Bobson's bunch of dim bulbs.

The traffic cop, his gun drawn, stomps our way, a grim look on his face. Reporters and cameramen trail him, the reporters chattering at their microphones.

Lester grips Pat Bobson's shoulders and pulls him off the dead guy. "Enough. We have to go."

I am down with that. I take off running along the hedge, toward the rear of the apartment building. People stare out of windows at us.

A roar goes up from the Bobson bunch. I glance back. They are charging after me, holding torches and stakes high. From the other direction, the traffic cop bursts into a run, with the press fanned out behind him, on the heels of the Rev and Lester.

I reach the end of the hedge and sprint toward the back of Tom's condo. It's quiet in his backyard. Behind me, feet thud on the grass. Meg and Archie are visible through the kitchen window, so I run for the kitchen door at the back of the house.

There's no pet door. I'd knock, but furry paws don't do much more than produce a *puh, puh* sound, so I rear up and scratch. I glance back. No mob or cop yet, but Lester and the reverend run toward me.

I scratch harder.

The mob gets louder.

26: Meg

Meg turns to Archie. "What could have happened to Patch? What will happen to him when the blood hunger hits and there's no V1 juice?"

Seiko enters from the dining room, finishing a glass of V1. "Have you called 911?"

Meg shakes her head, takes out her cell phone, and dials.

A woman answers. "Nine-one-one, what is your emergency?"

"My cat is missing. He's a—

"Wait a minute. You're calling 911 for a cat? A *cat*?"

"Yes, well—"

"You wanna be busted for a nuisance call? Nine-one-one is for real emergencies."

A tear wells in Meg's eye and she wipes it away. Why can't they understand? "He's important to me, and I'm worried—"

"Not important to me."

"Wait ... wait ..." She hopes there's some humanity in the operator. "Are you there?"

No answer.

Silence. She ends the call.

Her phone rings. The screen shows *Clive*. Oh, no. But she has to. "Hello?"

Clive's voice says, "A vampire? Seriously? A vampire?"
He gets louder. "And you didn't *tell* me?"

"Well, it's been a little crazy—"

"Not so crazy you couldn't go on television and run for
sheriff!"

She heard an unsaid *What about me?* "I'm sorry. I didn't
do this on purp—"

"Do you drink—I can't believe I'm saying this—do you
drink *blood?*"

This conversation couldn't be more horrible. Was this the
way all her relationships were going to go?

He screeches. "You do, don't you!"

"But it's not—"

"Are you going to sink your fangs into my neck?"

"Clive, of course not, I don't even have fangs, but we will
have to be care—"

We?" His voice lowered at last. "I don't think there's any
more *we* to be had."

"Can't we talk this out?"

Silence.

"Clive?"

Silence.

Sorrow crushes her as she turns her phone off. She wants
to cry.

But how can you cry without tears?

Anger floods her. She glares at her silent phone. "I'll show
you, you, you lily-livered ... *LILY!*"

After her outburst, the silence seems loud. It only amplifies
the hollow feeling of loss.

Oh, Patch. Where are you?

The quiet is interrupted by scratching sounds from the
kitchen door. Meg goes to the door and opens it. Patch zooms

inside. "Patch!" Joy floods her as he skids to a stop on the tile floor and turns to her.

Meg shuts the door, squats, and holds out her arms. Patch trots to her, and she lifts him up and holds him tight. A wave of happy tightens her throat. "I was so worried."

Patch says, "Mrrrow."

There's pounding on the back door. Archie says, "Got it."

When he opens it, Lester lunges inside, pulling a man with him. He shouts, "Shut the door!"

Archie slams it shut. Meg stares at the man Lester holds by an arm. His mouth, chin, and the front of his shirt are red, and she's hit with the smell of fresh blood. "Lester, what ... ?"

Lester grins. "Meet the Reverend Pat Bobson, pastor of the Righteous Hallelujah Church and brand-new vampire." He frowns at the door. "Who, unfortunately, was unable to control his appetite."

More pounding on the kitchen door. Lester pulls Bobson out of the kitchen and into the dining room. They disappear from sight.

Archie opens the door and a cop stands there. Behind him, the backyard is crowded with a milling jumble of cameramen, reporters, and excited people carrying sharp wooden stakes and torches.

Archie remains calm. "Yes, officer?"

The cop starts forward, but Archie holds up a hand. The cop stops. "Let me in."

"And your reason?"

"To search for a murder suspect."

Archie glances back at Patch, Meg, and Seiko. Meg shrugs and strokes Patch's head. Archie says, "I don't see any murderers here." He turns back to the officer. "Do you?"

The cop studies each of them. Meg gives him her best girl-next-door smile, Seiko flutters her eyelids, and Patch offers a sweet meow. The cop says, "No, not them. That's why I want to search. I think he came this way. You could be in danger."

"I believe we would have noticed someone running through the room." Archie peers at the mob behind the cop. "And this is your posse?"

The officer looks back, then says, "No, that's a mob."

Meanwhile, the stake-holders chant, "Undo the undead. Undo the undead." One of them uses his torch to set fire to a chaise longue on the patio. Scores of rabid human beings with killing on what little there is of their minds make Meg uneasy. Or maybe *terrified* is a better word.

Archie, however, is the essence of calm. "I assure you that there are no murderers here. I'm not letting you in without a warrant." He points at the yard full of mob. "If you want to be helpful, how about arresting those trespassers?"

The cop glances behind him, then back to Archie, his mouth gaping. Archie says, "Thank you so kindly," and closes the door. He comes to Meg and Patch and gives her kitty-cat a scratch behind the ears. "Good to see you, kitty-cat." To her he says, "I think we'd better let Tom know what's going on."

Meg follows Archie into the dining room. Bobson huddles behind Lester, his eyes demented and his gaze darting here and there. He is, literally, a bloody mess.

Meg stops. "So, Lester, suddenly you've got religion?"

He smiles, fangs peeking out. "A taste of it."

Bobson pushes his hands at them as if to drive them away. "Begone, abominations, away from me!"

Lester laughs. "Abominations?" He grips Bobson's shoulders and turns him toward a mirror above a sideboard. "Who's the abomination?"

As Bobson stares at his bloody image, Archie reappears, followed by Tom. The lawyer says, "Hello, Lester. What's this about abominations?"

Archie says, "This is the Reverend Pat Bobson we saw on TV a little while ago."

"Of course." Tom goes to offer Bobson a hand. "I didn't recognize you with all the blood on your face. A new ritual in your church?"

Bobson shies back. "You're the abomination! All of you!"

Lester says, "Oh, I don't know, Rev. Who was recently slurping blood from a lifeless corpse?"

The reverend's eyes widen. The guy looks like he is about to explode. "But I couldn't help it."

Archie giggles. "Oh, sure you could. Why, didn't you say just a little while ago that 'evil is always a choice'?"

Meg didn't think it was possible, but the reverend's eyes get even wider. "But I didn't *decide* to do this! I couldn't help it."

This is too much for Meg. She snorts. "Oh, come on, Reverend Bobson. You know how all the perverted people, like gays and vampires and atheists, *choose* Satan. Right?"

"But-but-but-but ..."

Bobson's spot-on impression of a motorboat is interrupted by a wail of sirens from the front of the house. Tom says to Bobson, "I think that's for you."

Bobson sinks to his knees. He raises his hands toward the ceiling. "Almighty, save me from these godless heathens."

Archie says, "I resent that. I'm a good Episcopalian."

Tom adds, "And I'm Catholic."

Patch wriggles in Meg's arms and says, "Mrf." Which she interprets as "Cat," an unsectarian sect. She gives him a scritch.

Bobson stares at them, then goes back to heaven-gazing. "Oh, Almighty One, send me Your divine aid." The sirens wind down, and then there's pounding on the front door. The reverend looks that way, and then again beseeches the heavens. "Or at least a good lawyer."

Tom claps him on the shoulder, his hand avoiding splotches of blood. "Thank God He's brought you to me." Tom grins. "Temporary insanity! Irresistible urge! This could be big, defending vampires." He turns to Meg. "You've opened up an entire new field of law, Meg. I'll be forever grateful."

Considering that he can't die completely, that's a heck of a promise.

The Reverend Bobson says, "You're a lawyer?"

Tom laughs. "An abominable lawyer, by your definition. But who better to understand your, er, difficulty?"

An amplified voice attacks the front of the house. "You in there. Open up. We have a warrant."

Bobson dashes to the back door and flings it open. But the traffic cop and the mob wait there. Bobson slams the door in the cop's face. Quite a rude fellow, Meg thinks, calling people abominations and slamming doors in faces.

He turns to Tom. "All right. Represent me."

Tom grins. "Of course. But first, let's settle on a retainer." He gestures toward the study. "Do you have your checkbook with you? I also take credit cards, promissory notes, pinky swear ..." They disappear into the study.

Lester watches him go and then rubs his belly. When he goes into the kitchen, Meg follows with Patch.

The big vampire pushes a black curtain aside and peers out the window. "Still a mob out there. And I'm starting to feel the pain."

Seiko opens a cabinet and takes out a roll of Death Savers. She tosses it to Lester. "Try these."

"Oh, no. None of your manufactured blood food products for me." Then he winces and grabs his stomach. "Well, maybe this once." He opens the package and pops a couple of blood rings into his mouth. Within a few seconds his face relaxes and he smiles. If it weren't for the fangs, he would have a nice smile.

Meg laughs. "So you can be corrupted, eh, Lester?"

Seiko frowns. "Now, that's unkind."

She's defending Lester? Meg says, "You're right. He doesn't deserve that."

Lester grimaces and then sets the roll of Death Savers on the counter. "Not from you."

Archie comes to the door. "I thought I should warn you that Tom is going to let the cops in." He gazes at Lester. "From what I've heard, you're in the habit of avoiding them."

With a shrug, Lester says, "When I go out for dinner, sure. But they have nothing on me."

Meg says, "The Reverend Pat Bobson, vampire. I've gotta see this."

Archie leads the way. Meg glances back to see if Lester is coming, and he is. She notices that the Death Savers aren't on the counter anymore. So Lester is a hypocrite. Or maybe just an opportunist.

They go to the front door. Tom stands in the living room, beside Bobson. Someone hammers on the door again. "Open up in the name of the law!"

Archie says, "Have some patience in the name of my aunt Martha!" He opens the door, and a flood of light from the TV crews silhouettes two people who stand at the door. All of the vampires leap out of the light's path. Shielding his eyes with a hand, Archie calls out, "No lights." When the lights don't shut off, he shouts, "No press if the lights aren't turned off" and shuts the door.

A knock comes, and Archie opens the door a crack. The lights are off.

A guy with shoulders nearly as broad as the doorway holds out a badge. "Bloomsburg Police. Captain Cook, chief detective."

He looks familiar. Something on television ... It's the guy running for sheriff.

"Yes, officer?"

The cop hands Archie a folded piece of paper. "I have a warrant for the arrest of a murderer, and I have reason to believe he's in this house."

Tom calls out from the living room, "He's here, Captain. Please come in."

The captain tells the other cop, "You wait here." He glances out at the gang of reporters and cameramen. His shoulders lift and drop, and he gives a big sigh. "I guess we gotta let them in."

Tom says, "Sure. We've got nothing to hide." He turns to Meg and whispers, "And we need every bit of publicity we can find, and we've captured a murderer. Looks good on the resume of a candidate for sheriff, right?"

When Captain Cook enters and goes to the living room, reporters and TV crews swarm around the remaining cop at the door like ants going around a rock on the way to a picnic. The look on their faces makes Meg think of what she feels when the blood hunger hits her. It's unsettling to think that she has something in common with the press.

Tom says to the captain, "Officer, I'm Tom Conway, and I represent the Reverend Bobson. He is willingly surrendering himself to you." He turns to Bobson. "Now, Reverend, please don't say—"

Bobson raises his arms high and shouts, "I am innocent. I am pure." He points at Lester. "That creature contaminated me. I couldn't help myself. I had no choice."

Archie, standing next to Meg and Patch, whispers, "Funny how it's a good excuse for him and not for you."

Ginger Grant shoves her way to the front of the crowd, arm outstretched, holding a microphone, Ernie behind her with his camera held high. That woman surely does get around. "Reverend Bobson, did you do it? Did you suck a man's blood?"

Tom shakes his head. "Ms. Grant, you know better than that." He turns to Bobson. "Don't answer any questions."

She presses forward. "How does it feel to be an abomination, Reverend Bobson?" Meg suspects it will take a baseball bat between the eyes to stop her. She wishes for the one George had back at the 7-Eleven.

Bobson stands straight. "I'm not an abomination."

Grant whips a mirror out of her purse and holds it in front of him. "Then what is this?"

He stares, then touches the dried blood on his chin with a forefinger. He slumps. "Evil." He lifts his gaze and stares out at the crowd. "But how? What did I do to deserve this?"

Meg says, "Same as all of us. Got born."

Archie nods. "Amen to that, sister."

Captain Cook takes out a pair of handcuffs. "Mr. Bobson, you're under arrest for the murder of ..." He turns to the cop in the doorway. "What's the guy's name?"

Shrug. "All I know is that a guy went to pee behind the hedge."

Tom says, "Do we have to do the handcuffs, Captain?"

"Are you kidding? This guy ripped out the throat of The Guy Who Had to Pee."

The Guy Who Had to Pee. What a way to be remembered.

Bobson grimaces and offers his hands, and the cop puts the cuffs on. "You have the right to remain silent. Anything you say can and will be used against you in a court of law. You have the right to speak to an attorney, and to have an attorney present during any questioning. If you cannot afford a lawyer, one will be provided for you at government expense."

The captain leads the way outside, the newspeople retreating before him. Tom sticks by Bobson's side. He checks his watch. "We've got a few hours before dawn. I'll drive down and help you at the police station, Mr. Bobson." To the cop he says, "He needs a cell with no windows. And regular doses of blood."

Meg follows, carrying Patch. When they get outside, the lawn is full. The mob from the backyard, still carrying torches, has joined the media crowd. The Bobsians chant, "Undo the undead. Undo the undead."

The mob mutters down to silence. Then a big, bearded guy at the front holds his torch high and shouts, "Save Bobson. Save Bobson."

The rest of the mob picks it up. "Save Bobson. Save Bobson."

Captain Cook says, "This could be trouble."

Bobson steps to the front of the porch and raises his cuffed hands. The chant falls away and becomes a murmur. He calls out, "Brethren, now is the time for peace. Go home."

A voice comes, "We'll save you, Reverend!"

He lifts his gaze to the sky. "I am already saved."

Another voice. "But you say vampires are damned to eternal hell."

Bobson looks like someone has slapped him.

The voice isn't done. "And they say that now you're one of them."

Tom steps in front of Bobson. "It has been alleged that he's a vampire, but there's no proof of that."

"What about all that blood? The evidence is all over him, and it's red."

Ginger Grant turns to Meg. "Ms. Murrow, if you are an actual vampire, haven't you killed innocent people to feed your blood hunger? Aren't you as much a criminal as the Reverend Bobson?" Her question provokes boos from the Rev's flock.

Tom says, "*Alleged* criminal!"

Grant holds out her microphone to Meg.

Meg holds up a hand until the boos stop, and then returns it to scratching Patch's neck. "No, I've never done what they say he did. We have more civilized ways to take care of our needs." She says to the crowd, "We are no danger to you. We just want to live ... er, coexist in peace."

Grant snarls and jabs a finger at Patch. "That ... that ... *vampire* killed my Puffy!"

Captain Cook raises an eyebrow. "Your Puffy? Killed?"

She sobs, and it actually sounds sincere. "Yes." She glares at Patch. "Murderer!"

Meg looks down at Patch. "Murderer?"

Patch licks his chops.

Captain Cook says to Grant, "Come see me at my office. I have to deal with this arrest right now." He takes one of Bobson's arms. "Let's go." He guides him through the crowd to a patrol car. Reporters surge toward cars and vans, noses in the air, following the perfume of disgraced celebrity. Law-abiding vampires running for sheriff, she guesses, aren't quite as interesting as a murderous vampire at the altar of a church. She can hardly blame them.

The cop from the backyard approaches the reverend's mob, waving his arms to shoo them away. The big bearded guy, built like a pro football tackle, holds a wooden stake in one hand and a torch in the other. "But we haven't destroyed the vampires."

The cop says, "There'll be no destroying tonight. Get yourselves home."

Bearded Guy stares at Meg and Patch on the porch. The flickering light from his torch makes his eyes seem to glitter with evil. He stretches out the meaty hand that holds the stake and booms, "You are damned. You will not endure." He raises his stake, turns away, and heads back the way he came. "Follow me," he says to the mob. "We will yet cleanse the night of evil." The flock trails behind him, and soon a double chant rises up as they disappear past the big hedge. "Undo the undead."

"Save Bobson."

"Undo the undead."

"Save Bobson."

Their voices fade, the patrol car with Bobson inside and news vans pull away, and Tom says to Archie and Meg, "Can you handle things here? I really should go along to make sure he's protected from the sun."

Archie says, "I've got to go home and get some sleep. If you want to appear in court for the arraignment tomorrow, I'm going to have to file briefs to make sure it's after dark."

He starts for his car and Tom heads for the garage. Tom says, "I'll be back in an hour or so."

Meg says, "You go ahead. Patch and I will be fine." She looks up at the night sky. It's clear and filled with stars. She gives Patch a scratch behind the ears. "I'm getting a little stir crazy, being cooped up all day and night. What do you say to a walk?"

Patch takes enough of a breath to say "Mrrr."

"Good." She sets him down. "I'll see if Seiko wants to go."

Patch follows Meg inside and gives her a "feed me" meow. She nods. "Sure, one for the road."

He trots ahead of her toward the kitchen. They come across Lester and Seiko at the dining room table, each spooning from bowls of blood.

Lester looks a little sheepish when Meg laughs and says, "So, the wild vampire likes the comforts of home."

Seiko pats Lester's hand, her tiny hand on his big paw like a baby's on an adult's. "Hey, be nice. He's had a busy night."

Lester gives Seiko a sappy-looking smile. Awww. Vampire love.

Meg says, "Sorry. This is the guy who was going to crush Patch, and then kidnapped him. Lester hasn't exactly been on our side."

Lester scowls and stands. "Well, I'm still not. Screw you." But then he turns to Seiko. "Not you."

"Seiko, Patch and I are going for a walk. Want to come?"

Lester holds out a humongous hand to Seiko. "If you want to go out into the night, come with me. Let me show you the true vampire world."

Oh, no. There he goes again. Seiko stands. "All right. But no murdering."

Lester's smile dims, but he says—bravely, Meg thinks—"Of course not."

Five minutes later, Meg ambles along the sidewalk, Patch trotting ahead a few paces. They've left Seiko and Lester finishing their blood.

When they approach the hedge that separates the condo from the apartment house next door, there's a "Shhhhh." When they pass the hedge, she finds the reverend's flock hidden there. Bearded Guy steps in front of them, his torch flaring. The rest, a good twenty angry worshippers, swarm around them until they are surrounded. Bearded Guy says, "And the Lord delivereth the sinners unto us, so that we may cleanse the earth."

The mob says, "Undo the undead!"

Meg says to Bearded Guy, "We mean you no harm. And I'm no more a sinner than you are."

He raises his torch high and booms, "Evil ones! Prepare to meet your maker."

A woman grabs Patch and holds him tight against her chest. Two Bobsians take Meg's arms. Bearded Guy says, "To the park," and strides away.

A chant rises. "Undo the undead. Undo the ..."

27: Meg

The chanting, torch-carrying mob of Bobsians marches through neighborhood streets. Porch lights flick on along the way, people peek out of windows, and then they retreat and lights flick off. Although Meg usually prefers to be left to herself, this is one time she'd love to see a swarm of police cars. But the mob reaches a small park unhindered.

Bearded Guy leads the way to a pair of picnic tables. He points to one. "Put the damned woman there. On her back, so she can see the wrath of the Almighty come upon her."

Meg struggles, but the two beefy men holding her arms have no trouble hoisting her onto the table. She kicks, though, and they have trouble holding her still. Two more extra-large men step forward, grab her ankles, and soon have her pinned, though she still twists and writhes.

She says to Bearded Guy, "This isn't righteous behavior."

"Oh, no?" He sticks his wooden stake in his belt and pulls *The Righteous Hallelujah Gospel* from his hip pocket and holds it in front of her face. "The gospel tells us to rid the earth of evil." He leers. "That's you."

"That doesn't mean you can kill innocent people who have done no harm."

"That's where you're wrong, slattern of Satan. You are not innocent. Nor are your fellow abominations."

He points to the other table. "Secure the beast there."

The woman clutching Patch to her chest carries him to the table. When she tries to pin him down, he struggles and lashes out with his claws. When he digs deep into her hand, she shrieks. But Bearded Guy bellows, "Help thy sister." Three more women surround Patch.

Each takes a leg and stretches it out, and they spread-eagle Patch on his back.

Meg twists uselessly against the creeps holding her. If she had a pulse, it would be pounding.

Bearded Guy hands his torch to a slender, pretty young woman. Well, she would be pretty except for the way her face twists when she looks down at Meg. She gnaws her lip, and she doesn't look like she's all that certain about what she's doing.

He raises his stake in the air and looks toward Patch's table. Darned if the man doesn't smile. "Ready?"

A teenage boy, the kind of kid commonly dubbed Pizza Face, steps forward and holds a sharp stake over Patch. He carries a hammer in his other hand. Meg hopes his acne will go pepperoni on him.

Bearded Guy places the point of his stake on her chest. She says, "Don't I get any last words?"

"You shall not sully our hearts with your unclean ravings." He holds out his *Righteous Hallelujah Gospel* to Pretty Woman, who takes it and hands him a hammer. Bearded Guy looks to the kid with the stake at Patch's table. "Hammer!"

The kid raises his hammer. Bearded Guy does the same over Meg.

Pretty Woman cries out, "We can't do this! The gospel says to love thy neighbor."

Bearded Guy glares at her. "Do your neighbors live in graveyards?"

Technically, he has that wrong. But he doesn't seem concerned about technicalities, especially right and wrong.

The woman says, "It shouldn't matter where they live."

"These are vampires. The undead. The unclean. The unholy." He lifts his gaze to the night sky and intones, "'In this way, you will cleanse this evil from among you, and all will hear about it and be afraid.'" He lifts his hammer higher and focuses on the stake. Pizza Face plants his stake on Patch's chest and does the same.

Meg pulls and kicks and gets nowhere. No! This can't happen.

Bearded Guy says, "On three. One—"

A wild, high-pitched shriek splits the night and Seiko sails through the air out of the darkness to land on Patch's picnic table, her feet straddling him. She crouches and opens her mouth wide; enormous fangs protrude. She hisses at Pizza Face, who drops his hammer and stake and stumbles back. The women holding Patch let go and scurry into the dark. Patch flips onto his feet and looks ready to run.

A roar sounds from the far side of the mob, and Lester races into the torchlight. He holds his hands high, fingers like claws, and he looks ten feet tall. His cape flares behind him, red lining blazing. Blood reddens his chin and drips from his fangs.

He roars, "Fe, fi, fo, fum, I smell the blood of a Bob-si-an."

Bearded Guy yelps and runs. So do the men holding Meg down. Pretty Woman looks up at Lester, drops her torch, and faints. The rest of the mob runs screaming into the darkness.

Meg sits up and grins at Lester, then gives him a big smile. "I never thought I'd be glad to see you."

He points at Seiko. "Thank her."

At the other table, Seiko leans down and gives Patch a scratch. "How you doing, kitty-cat?"

He gives her hand a head-rub.

Meg gets off the picnic table and picks up the torch Pretty Woman dropped. Holding it high, she peers at Seiko. "Fangs? And you can fly?"

Seiko laughs, grips her fangs with her fingers, and pulls them out of her mouth. Lester says, "From last Halloween. Before I got my caps." He wipes at the blood on his chin and licks his finger. "Ketchup."

Jumping down from the table, Seiko stands next to Lester. "As for flying, Lester was all-state in the shot put, and I was into gymnastics." Okay: seven-foot guy and four-foot woman. Meg gets it.

Pretty Woman moans, and Meg helps her get up. When the woman sees Lester, she cringes. Meg says, "We won't hurt you. And thank you for trying to help me."

She says, "I feel like screaming."

Meg laughs. "Me, too. Why don't you go on home?" The woman nods and hurries away. Meg calls after her, "Remember, a vote for me is a vote for equal protection for everyone." Meg shakes her head—she'd sure sounded like a politician.

Meg hands the torch to Seiko and picks Patch up. She hugs him. "Patch, I'm so sorry I got you into this."

A deep voice comes from the darkness. "Not half as sorry as you're going to be."

A familiar female voice jumps on top of the deep one. "This is wrong, Sammy!"

"And who's going to stop me, Vera?" Sammy steps into the torchlight. Vera follows him, and behind her is Bruce, who looks even larger than before, which seems impossible. Sammy glances back at his lumbering henchman and then says to them, "You know, they say that might makes right." He reaches behind his back and produces a pistol. "I agree."

Vera gasps. "You brought a gun?"

He points it at Vera. "How would you like to be tied to a tree and left here for the sunrise?"

She doesn't even flinch. "You don't have a rope."

"God, I hate argumentative women." He shifts his gaze to Meg. "And that includes you. Especially you."

Meg sets Patch on the picnic table. "Oh, so the American Vampire Association is a sexist bunch of leeches?"

Sammy says, "I resent that. Anyway, it doesn't matter to me who is screwing things up for us, I'm going to stop them." He gestures to the beef behind him, and Bruce spreads his arms as if to surround them. Meg knows it seems unlikely that one guy could surround three people and a cat, but he's that big. On the other hand, they have their own big guy. Lester steps next to Bruce, and Bruce gives him nervous little glances. He has to look up to do it.

Meg says, "We're not screwing things up. We're making them better."

"Things were fine before you came along. Now vampires are all over the news, and my people are scared."

"They shouldn't be scared, they should be fighting for their rights. Together, we can do it."

Vera takes a step away from Sammy. "She could be right. What if she is?"

Meg says, "We can regain our birthright to live, er, to exist and have the lives we had before we were mostly killed!"

Sammy shakes his head. "We're not going to give you the chance to find out. We'll just keep you out of sight until the election is over. The press will satisfy their vampire hunger with poor Reverend Bobson. Knowing how competent the cops in this town are, they'll probably march him out into daylight and then all there'll be for them to talk about is holy toast."

Lester leans an elbow on top of Bruce's head and smiles at Sammy. "What if I don't feel like being kept out of sight, munchkin?"

He has something there; Sammy reminds Meg of those officious munchkins in Oz, only a whole lot more dull. Is Patch Toto to her Dorothy?

She shakes off a temptation to wander down that fantasy yellow-brick road. Patch walks to the edge of the table, takes a breath, and hisses at Sammy. The little guy just generally seems to piss her cat off.

Sammy's eyes widen and he takes a step back. He aims the gun at Patch. "Get him."

Bruce's big hand wraps around Patch and lifts. Patch hisses, and Meg is pretty sure he's as tired of being in the clutches of various huge, lethal people as she is.

But Sammy's pistol could mean permanent holes, and she wonders just how functional even a vampire can be if his brains are blown out. Seiko takes a step back. Meg lifts her chin and steps forward.

Patch growls.

He squirms and twists to escape Bruce's grip. Sammy smiles. "Make one move toward me, cat, and you're nothing but a bad memory." He turns to Meg. "You're coming with us, aren't you?" It's more of a statement than a question.

Lester takes his elbow off Bruce's head. "Just say the word, Meg, and these guys will wish they'd never been killed."

Sammy nods to Bruce, and he grips Patch with both hands. "One wrong move and Bruce tears the cat in half."

Bruce looks to Sammy, his mouth gaping, an expression of horror on his face.

Lester roars, "Don't hurt the kitty-cat." He grabs the torch from Meg and throws it at Sammy. It misses by inches, and the smell of burnt hair pollutes the night. Sammy shrieks.

Lester tucks Seiko under one arm and grabs Meg's hand with the other and hauls her into the night.

The torch goes out, and Sammy fires shots in the direction they went.

Bruce holds Patch, poised to tear him in half.

28: Patch

I windmill my legs to hook a claw into Bruce's hand. I can't reach it.

Sammy yells, "Get them!"

Bruce charges forward, his arms wide. He stumbles, blunders into Sammy and wraps him up, the little guy's face to his chest.

Sammy's shout is muffled. "Not me, idiot!"

A beam of light spears us, and a policeman walks up, his flashlight scanning us. "What's going on here?"

Sammy tucks his pistol behind his back, and Vera smiles at the cop. "We were hunting for our kitty-cat." She gestures at me. "And we found him." Waggling her finger at me, she says, "Naughty kitty."

If that finger comes just a few inches closer, I'll give her naughty.

The cop runs his light over Bruce and me. We cringe, but it's only a flashlight, just a little irritating. The officer says, "There were reports of a bunch of people with torches."

"They left, thank goodness."

"I heard shots."

Sammy looks behind him. "Darned kids and their firecrackers. Scared me half to death." I figure the cop can't recognize the irony behind Sammy's grin.

The cop backs up a step. "Wait a minute. You're not some of those vampires, are you? The ones with a vampire kitty-cat?"

I nod, but a quick squeeze from Bruce stops that.

Sammy steps up. "Oh, gosh, no, officer. That's why we're out here, to save our perfectly normal cat from those fiends." He reaches out as if to scratch my head. "Our little Pussykins."

I growl.

Sammy shrugs and flicks a hand signal at Bruce, who steps closer to the policeman, practically stepping on his toes. The cop cranes his neck and looks up. And up. Bruce is the kind of guy who expands the meaning of the word *looming*.

The officer tugs at his collar and swallows. He backs up a step and squeaks, "You people need to move along."

Sammy smiles. "Yessir. You bet. No problem. Happy to." He leads the way toward the street. Vera sticks close to him, and Bruce brings up the rear.

I'm glad to see that Sammy has moved up from his VW Beetle to a big, black SUV. Being scrunched in the back of a Bug with Bruce is something I don't care to imagine. Vera rides in front with Sammy while the muscle takes the back seat. Bruce holds me in his lap, his grip firm but unexpectedly gentle. Then he strokes my head and back. Mmmmm.

After we pull away, Sammy peers into the rearview mirror at us. "Bruce, is that cage on the roof of our building in good shape? I'm thinking that come dawn, we could provide an object lesson for our contrary lady friend."

Bruce says, "Y-y-y-y-y..."

"Good."

While we ride to A.V.A. headquarters, Bruce keeps me clamped to his lap with a hand the size of a catcher's mitt, but lightly. I look up at him to watch for any sign of laxness. Not that I would know what to do if it came.

He's one of those pasty-faced redheads, skin really white, red-orange hair. Bruce's is cropped close, about a claw-length, and thinning at the front. He glances down at me; his eyes, set close together, are an icy cold blue, the kind you see in some Siamese. But Bruce has a surprise for me. He gives me a small smile and uses his other hand to scratch me behind the ears. It's clear that he's been a good associate for a cat in the past, because his touch is expert. Nothing beats a good ear scratch.

However, his grip with his imprisoning hand never lets up. When we get to the A.V.A. building, Bruce carries me while Sammy leads the way up to the top floor and into a big corner office, Vera trailing behind us, her face unhappy. Bruce sits on a couch and holds me in his lap. He also gives me a scratch under the chin. Man, that feels good.

The little man goes behind the desk and plops into a big leather chair. He looks at his watch. "Two hours until dawn. Vera, I want you to call that woman's lawyer and tell them that he has until then to get her here if she cares about her cat."

Vera paces, her brow furrowed by a deep frown. "And what happens if she shows up, Sammy?"

"For the safety of the American Vampire Association and all those we represent, she will be held incommunicado until after the election."

Bruce says a word. "Kitty?"

All heads turn his way—Sammy and Vera gape at him. Sammy says, "I didn't know you could talk."

Bruce nods. I wonder if he's exhausted his vocabulary. But, if he can know only one word, I think *kitty* is a good one.

Sammy shrugs. "The cat is safe as long as he gives us leverage over Meg."

Vera stops pacing. "And when he doesn't?"

"Well, what use is a vampire cat? If we turn it loose, it'll just run around giving a worse name to vampires." One corner of his mouth turns up as he gazes at me. On Meg it would be a wry grin. On Sammy it's a sardonic sneer.

Vera sits in a big chair, but on the edge of the seat. "I said it before, Sammy, this is wrong." I catch just the tiniest of nods from Sammy to Bruce, who moves to stand behind her. "Vampire versus vampire is not what the A.V.A. is supposed to be about."

Sammy's basso profundo voice ups in pitch. "They're against us! Exposing us to the world. Making trouble. That's wrong!"

"But what Meg says makes sense to me. We're still people. We should still have rights, but we never will if we hide." She glances at Bruce. "I hate being cooped up here all the time."

Bruce nods. The man has become a whirlwind of communication.

Sammy snorts. "Cooped up? You don't have to be cooped up. There are plenty of places open at night. Walmart, gas stations, lots of places."

"That is not a life, Sammy."

"Yeah? Well, you don't have one anyway, so what's the problem?"

"I want one! I was a successful file clerk before this happened to me, and proud of it." She stands. "I'll call the lawyer, Sammy, but to tell him to come down and get the cat back. And then I think you should get the A.V.A. board together to support Meg's campaign for sheriff so she can protect us. Isn't that what we really should be about?"

Sammy draws in a breath and sighs. "No, it's not. We're about safety. Security. We're about what I say we are about."

Vera says, "Well, not anymore." She turns to go, but Sammy nods and Bruce grabs her by the neck.

Shaking his head, Sammy stands. "Vera, Vera, Vera. What will we do with you?" He smiles. "I've got it: you'll help the kitty-cat send our message to that woman." He opens a desk drawer, takes out a ring of keys, and strides to the door. "To the roof."

Bruce shifts his grip from Vera's neck to her arm. Sammy peers out the office door. "Now. Nobody's around."

They hurry up a flight of stairs to the roof, me in one of Bruce's hands and Vera towed by the other. The lights of Bloomsburg spread out around us. An iron-barred cage, big enough to hold two people if they sit, is positioned next to an air-conditioning tower. When we get closer to it, I see a skeleton sprawled inside the bars.

Sammy looks down at the bones. "Hello, Gunther. I'm so glad you stopped trying to take over the A.V.A."

Vera says, "Gunther? I thought you said he moved to Cleveland."

"I still can't believe you bought that. Who'd want to move to Cleveland?"

She says, "You can't do this." Now, I've heard victims say those very same words in countless movies when a bad guy is about to do something nasty, and I always thought it was a stupid thing to say because the bad guy has all the power and can do whatever he wants. And usually does, unless a hero comes in the nick of time. Nobody here but the victims and the perps.

However, on this occasion I appreciate her effort.

Protesting doesn't do us any more good than it did the people in the movies, of course. A metallic click sounds when Sammy unlocks a big padlock on the cage. The door

squeaks when he opens it. To Bruce he says, "Put them in."
Bruce flings Vera in, and she rolls to sprawl against the back
bars of the cage. She scurries away from the skeleton and
sits in a corner.

Sammy gestures. "The cat, too."

Bruce hesitates. Sammy clouds up. "You want me to cut
off your blood supply, dummy? Put you back on the street to
sleep in the dirt?"

Bruce says, "Sorry, kitty." And he sets me inside the cage,
careful not to drop me.

Vera picks me up and holds me to her. "Someday, Sammy,
you're going to regret this."

I've heard those words in movies, too. Often, they turn
out to be true, and I hope they are for Sammy. But I don't
think I'll be around to see it happen.

Sammy padlocks the door shut. "I'll be back tomorrow
night to take a few photos of what's left so little Meg will
finally get it: vampires don't belong out in the 'real' world."

After a lot of screaming for help and rattling the bars of our
cage, Vera sits slumped in a corner. The night sky to the east
is not as dark as it was. A few minutes later, my nose and
eyes start to itch.

Vera rouses and stares at the horizon. She grips the bars
and screams, "No! No! Please!"

After a few more hopeless minutes, she turns to me and
holds her arms out. "Come here, Patch."

Curious as usual, I wonder what she wants. I'll do anything
to keep my thoughts away from what is coming. I remember
the agony from the television lights, and I don't want to think
about what might be on the way with real sunlight. I go to her
and she gathers me into her arms. It's comforting.

I find myself wishing for Meg. And hoping that she won't let Sammy get away with this.

The night pales, my eyes and nose burn, and Vera whimpers.

Without warning, she puts me on the floor of the cage and then lies down on top of me. I struggle to get out, but stop when she lifts up and pets my head. "Stay there, Patch. Maybe one of us will get out of this. My dress and ... what's left of me might protect you."

I settle down, and she lowers her body on top of me. It's utterly dark, and the burning stops. There's no danger of suffocating, of course, with no breathing being necessary.

The sun is not over the horizon yet, but there's already way too much sunlight. She moans.

Time goes by. Vera squirms, but she stays on top of me.

The padlock clicks and the cage door squeaks. Vera rises up. I peek out from beneath her.

It's Bruce with a handful of Sammy.

Sammy screams, "No-o-o-o-o ..." as he sails into the cage, bangs off the back wall of bars, and falls to the floor. Then I clamp my eyes shut against the burn of the growing light.

A big hand grips me and pulls me out of the cage. I hear the cage door clang shut and then the padlock clicks, and whoever has me runs. A door slams shut behind us and the sun pain goes away. Someone is gasping. I open my eyes.

We're inside the stairwell that leads to the roof, dimly lit by a single light bulb. Vera leans against a wall. She lets out a long, shuddering breath. "Thank you, Bruce."

I twist and look up. Bruce pulls back a sweatshirt hood and takes off a pair of dark glasses. Gloves protect his hands, and the rest of him is covered. He lowers me to a step. "Kitty okay?"

Thanks to Vera shielding me and the fact that I'm a fur-bearing creature, I'm fine except for a little itching where my skin was most exposed—my nose and ears. I give Bruce a rub against the legs. He says, "Awww."

Vera tugs on her dress to straighten it, then smiles up at him. "I thought my life had ended when I was infected with the vee bug, but now I'm real glad you helped me hold on to what I still have."

I second the motion with another rub against Bruce, and then start down the stairs. Vera follows, and Bruce comes behind her.

Meg's shout cuts into the quiet. "Where is he?!"

When Vera opens the door, I scoot out into the office area. Meg rages along an aisle of cubicles, poking her head into each one. "Patch! Where is Patch?" Tom trails her.

I fill my lungs with air and give a plaintive meow, the one that sounds helpless. It's just one of a cat's repertoire that pushes people's buttons—I'm hungry; feed me; feed me now, dammit; let me out; I agree; and so on. I guess it's the centuries of association. I don't have to think about that, it's just a part of my vocabulary.

The burn of blood hunger ignites in my belly, and I add the "I'm hungry" meow.

Meg steps back from a cubicle, sees me, drops to her knees, and holds out her arms for a hug. I trot to her and am instantly cradled in her arms. "Oh, Patch." She kisses me on top of my head. I don't even begin to mind.

Vera and Bruce step from the stairwell. Meg says, "You bastards!" She looks around. "Where's Sammy? I want a piece of that little worm."

Vera says, "He's in a place where he won't be a bother anymore. And Bruce saved me and Patch from"—she lifts her gaze to the ceiling—"a terminal case of sunburn." She rubs her belly and then looks up at Bruce. "How about a little snack, big guy?"

He nods. Bruce's photo ought to be in the dictionary next to the word *taciturn*.

I give Meg a lick on the wrist. She looks down at me, strokes my head, and of course, I forget what I was about to say. Then the hunger fires up and reminds me. I give her the "feed me" meow.

"Oh, you poor baby." Bless those centuries of mutual conditioning. She turns and leads the bunch of us to the break room, and soon there's warm blood all around.

I finish my bowl of V1 juice and lie on the floor, enjoying the rush. Vera explains what happened—and is happening right now with Sammy—to Meg and the lawyer. She holds Bruce's hand the whole time, and he looks at her like, well, like he looks at me. I'm not jealous, though.

Meg's eyes go round. "Oh, man. We just barely beat the sun into your garage. And I was feeling it, even through the dark windows on the car."

Tom gives me a pat on the back. "Now that we have the cat back, on with our campaign."

Things are pretty hunky-dory.

Tom's cell phone rings. He answers and says, "Archie?" He listens.

Whoop-whoops and wails of police sirens stab into the room. I wonder what a vampire has to do to get a little peace around here. Vera says, "Follow me" and leads the way down the hall. We crowd into a room with a bank of monitors that shows views all around the outside of the building.

I jump up onto a desk to see better. The street in front of the building is packed with police cars and vans, their colored lights flashing and blinking.

A van door opens and big guys in black uniforms, each carrying an assault rifle, trot out and head for the entrance.

Office workers gather behind us and stare at the monitors.

Vera scans the crowd. "Anybody here order a SWAT team?"

29: Meg

Meg points to the big cops with big guns. "How do they know we're here?"

Tom ends his call. "The cops raided my place, looking for Patch after Grant reported the murder of her dog, Puffy. By Patch."

Meg looks into Patch's eyes. "Murder? Puffy?"

Patch gazes back, unperturbed. "Mrow."

"The cops came here because they learned about the A.V.A. from Archie."

On the monitor, the SWAT team forms two lines outside the front door and stands at attention, assault rifles ready. After a pause, a guy with incredibly broad shoulders walks between the lines and stops outside the door. It's Captain Cook, the cop who arrested Bobson. He carries a bullhorn. An equally broad-shouldered woman in a uniform— something gray and not the navy blue of the police—follows him. She carries a thing that looks like a butterfly net.

Behind those two march Ginger Grant and her cameraman, Ernie. When they stop, Captain Cook raises his bullhorn. "This is Captain Cook. I order you to surrender the cat known as Patch."

Ginger Grant signals the cameraman to move around to the side. He does, and aims his lens at the captain. Her voice thin and sharp on the speaker, she says, "Once more for the news, Captain?"

Cook swells his chest. "This is Captain Cook. Surrender the cat."

Meg goes to Patch, pulls him close, and puts an arm around him in a protective way. "They can't have Patch, whatever it's for."

Tom says, "There's something familiar about that cop."

Meg scratches behind Patch's ears. "He's the one who arrested Pat Bobson."

"Yeah, but it's something else."

Meg nods. "The election. He's running for sheriff."

Captain Cook swells up his chest again and says to the camera, "We will not allow our citizens and their pets to be terrorized and murdered by vampire scum."

Vera says, "Well, he just lost my vote."

Turning back to the door, Cook juts his chin out. "Surrender the cat or we're coming in the hard way."

Tom finishes off his V1 juice and gazes at the bottle; a thin film of red slides down the sides and pools in the bottom. "The cops're gonna just love finding cabinets full of blood."

Vera says to Tom, "We can't let them bust in here."

"Is there a way to talk to them?"

She hands him a microphone. "This connects to speakers by the front door." She flicks a switch on the control panel.

Tom says, "Captain Cook, this is Patch's legal counsel speaking. What is the charge?"

The captain opens his mouth, but it's Ginger Grant who provides the answer. She screeches, "Murder most foul!" She sobs, then pauses until the camera swings her way, and then her voice goes quivery. "My baby. My sweet little Puffy." She holds something up toward the news camera.

Vera steps to a television and clicks it on. The picture shows Grant, her face screwed up as if she is crying but with no tears. She holds a picture of her former poodle up to the camera.

Grant turns to the captain. Now her voice shifts into murderous. "Get him, Sheriff." She pauses and her lips move just slightly, as if she's counting one, two, three ... She smiles and bats her eyelashes. "Oh, I'm sorry. That's Captain, isn't it?"

Meg says, "Smarmy bitch."

Cook turns to the baddest-looking SWATTER. "Prepare to break in."

The SWAT guy says, "What do you think, sir? The battering ram or ..." He grins. "Explosives."

The captain says, "Take no chances with these creatures. Blow it."

The cameraman's voice slips in. "Oh boy."

Tom talks into the microphone. "There's no need for that. We're coming down to talk. But the sun is up now, and we can't be exposed to sunlight, so you'll have to come inside. We'll let you in. We are unarmed."

On the television, the picture zooms in on the captain's jutting jaw and courageously stern gaze. "Agreed."

Grant's voiceover whispers, "Imagine stepping into a vampire den. A stunningly brave move by Captain Cook. Will this gutsy man survive this daring raid on vampires to continue his bid for sheriff?"

Meg picks up Patch and holds him to her. She shouts at the TV, "You can't have him!"

Tom says, "We have to talk to them."

Vera turns to Meg and Patch. "If they bust in here, we could all be doomed."

Patch butts Meg's hand with his head.

She looks down at him. "You really want to do this?"
"Mrf."

Tom says to the captain, "I'm sure we can straighten this out. We're on our way down."

Downstairs, Vera and company stand behind a black curtain in the building entrance and she presses a button. A buzzer sounds at the front door, and a monitor shows the captain marching in, followed by the woman with the net. Right behind them come Grant and the cameraman. When the door shuts and daylight is cut off, Vera opens the black curtain.

The cameraman points his lens at Patch.

Tom says, "We have no need for the press, Captain." He indicates the door. "My client should have privacy here."

Keeping his gaze on Patch, Cook says, "Patch the cat, you are under arrest for the murder of Puffy, a sweet little dog."

"On what grounds do you make this ridiculous accusation?"

Grant pushes the cameraman closer. "Show them."

He lowers his camera and gazes at the little viewfinder screen that sticks out to the side while he presses buttons. Then he holds it up for Tom to take a look. Meg leans in enough to see it as well. Grant says, "Got it all on tape."

They watch. Yappy dog sounds go on for too long and then end abruptly. After the yapping stops, Tom steps back. "Well, it's Patch." He gazes at Patch. "Sorry, pal, but your calico markings are distinctive. And you definitely terminated that yappy little dog."

Meg has to admit that he's right. But she's glad he did it. It was clearly self-defense of his ears.

The broad-shouldered woman holds out her net. Tom steps in front of it. "My client is willing to surrender, but to go outside in that sunshine would be the end of him."

Grant snaps, "Poetic justice!"

Captain Cook says, "This creature's problem with daylight is not—"

"I wonder," Meg cuts in. She gazes up at Captain Cook. "I wonder how many cat lovers are voters in Bloomsburg. Seems like I've read that there are even more cats than dogs living with voters." She winks at Patch. "And, as we all know, cats are pretty much in charge."

The captain glowers at her and then says, "As I was saying, this creature's problem with daylight is not going to be used against him." He tells Net Woman, "Get a lightproof container. The creature will be safe indoors at the pound."

At the words *the pound*, Patch wrenches free from Meg's arms and leaps.

But Net Woman is quick. She snares him in the net before he touches down. She lowers it to the floor and turns it over, trapping him.

She says to the captain, "Cover him."

Captain Cook draws a pistol and aims it at Patch.

Net Woman reaches behind her and brings out a sack made of black cloth. With one smooth move, she raises the rim of the net and shoves Patch into the sack.

30: Patch

I can tell you that a day spent in the basement of a city pound is, for my nose, a day in hell. Now that I'm a vampire, I don't really need sleep anymore, so during daylight hours I lapse into a state of rest pretty similar to catnapping, only more conscious. Too bad for my sense of smell.

The stench of feces from the kennels on the floor above settles in the basement and drives me to dreaming of a giant sack of kitty litter opening from the sky and burying the top floor. So I'm more than happy when, the next night, Tom and Meg arrive.

I'm up and pacing behind the bars of my cage, the burn of blood hunger so hot I'm beginning to panic. Meg pours a bottle of V1 juice into a bowl and puts it in the cage, and soon the pain turns into lassitude and purring. While I savor the rush through my body and enjoy feeling the beat of my heart return, Tom says, "Time to go to court, Patch." He places me in a Critter Carrier with a black curtain across the front door and the air vent holes covered with duct tape. No more sacks. I will seek justice with my dignity intact.

When we get to the courtroom, Tom leads Meg to the defense table. There's a fair-sized crowd, and murmurs fill the room when I step out of my carrier. Meg sets me on the tabletop.

A really tall desk dominates the room. I've seen enough TV shows to know that's the judge's perch, but what I didn't expect is a television on a stand off to the side. On the other side of the room, a video camera on a tripod is trained on the courtroom by a tiny blond woman. A man with a microphone sits beside her.

Meg points and says, "Hey, Patch, friends." Vera and Bruce are there, and so is Tom's aide, Archie. He gives me a little wave of his fingers. Seiko sits next to him. No Lester, but, with those fangs of his, I'm not surprised.

My archenemy, newswoman Ginger Grant, sits in the gallery behind the prosecutor's table, which is occupied by a skinny little guy with pale blond hair and ghost-white skin. Captain Cook, looking serious, is in the gallery on that side. Next to him slouches Ernie, Grant's cameraman. His beard looks trimmed, and he has a clean bandanna on his head.

Then I spot Amy. My former associate smiles at me and mouths, "Hi, Spot." Despite the "Spot," the sight of her brings joy into what is so far a crummy day.

We have just gotten settled when the court clerk calls the session to order and people to stand. The clerk says, "This court is now in session, Judge Juanita Escobar presiding," and a small, dark-haired, brown-skinned woman in black robes comes from a door in the back.

She sits behind her big desk and surveys the courtroom. "*Caramba.* Look at all the people." She gestures and says, "Be seated, *por favor.*" Her expression is stern. She looks to the clerk. "What's up, Watson?"

The clerk, a tubby, balding guy with a frizzy combover, says, "First is case 432, Your Honor, the arraignment of Patch the cat for the murder of Puffy, a dog."

Judge Escobar's eyebrows lift, and she turns her gaze on me. I guess she is in her forties. Her big brown eyes are not friendly, and the corners of her mouth turn down.

"Is this some kind of joke? A cat?"

The prosecutor stands. The TV camera points his way, and he turns a little bit sideways, I think so it can catch his profile. "Your Honor, this is the notorious vampire cat, and the state seeks justice for the slaying of Ms. Ginger Grant's beloved poodle."

Notorious? I wonder if I'll get fan mail in jail.

Judge Escobar eyes Grant, and then smiles at the prosecutor. Her smile is a long way south of amiable. "Oh, yes. You're running for district attorney, aren't you, Mr. Povich?"

A look of chagrin flickering on and off, he squeaks, "Yes, Your Honor, but I fail to see what that has to do with this case."

"Yeah, right, you're not looking for a little free press exposure." She glares, and then she shakes her head and sighs. "How am I going to try a cat?"

Tom stands. "Tom Conway, Your Honor, for the defense."

"The cat has a lawyer?"

"Yes, Your Honor." He indicates Meg. "And this is Meg Murrow, his owner."

I start to bristle at the "owner" crack, but then Meg stands beside him and strokes my back. Mmmmm.

Tom says, "I feel confident that she is qualified to speak for her cat."

"Ah, yes, the vampire woman running for sheriff. Is this all a publicity stunt?"

Meg shakes her head. "No, ma'am. This is not our idea, my cat is not guilty, and we would much rather not be here."

It's the judge's turn to bristle. "Something wrong with my courtroom?"

I have to hand it to Tom. Smooth as a Persian's fur, he says, "Absolutely not. Your reputation for fairness and expertise is unmatched in the city."

Tom's sucking up runs aground on the judge's deepening scowl. "So you're pandering now? Because I'm a woman? Because I'm Latina?"

Tom gives as good as he gets. He draws himself up. "Your Honor, as a member of a minority myself, I understand your sensitivity to such possibilities. However, unless you wish to say that you are neither fair nor expert, I believe my statement is accurate."

Her eyes widen and her jaw drops for a moment, then she restores her scowl and scoffs. "Minority? What minority is your Caucasian self a member of?"

"Vampires, Your Honor. And we are the subjects of enormous discrimination. The court will soon be seeing a class action lawsuit seeking relief under the Americans with Disabilities Act."

Judge Escobar opens her mouth as if to speak, but shuts it. The hard, hostile look on her face softens as she gazes at Tom. Then it toughens again. "Have you also heard me referred to as a 'hanging judge'?"

He nods. "I'm in favor of severe penalties myself, Your Honor. My client has no problem with that."

I eye Tom and give him a soft hiss. He winks at me. I do not find it reassuring.

The judge leans forward. "I'm warning you, sir, one hint that you are not sincere and you will be held in contempt."

Tom nods. "And I would deserve it, Your Honor."

She turns to the prosecutor. "Speaking of sincerity, you're bringing a charge of murder against a cat? Please tell me that Ms. Grant's stature as Bloomsburg's top media personality and that you're running for DA have nothing to do with it."

"That's correct, Your Honor. No connection." He tries to trade stares with the judge, but then drops his gaze to his table and shuffles papers. "At the very least, there's cruelty to an animal and dogslaughter, and I believe that Your Honor will see the defendant's actions as murder, pure and simple."

The judge sighs. "All right. Let's hear your evidence, Mr. Povich."

"I call Ernie Bert to the stand."

Grant's cameraman goes to the witness chair. Once he's sworn in, Povich says, "Is it true that you captured this terrible crime in a video?"

"Every bloody second."

31: Meg

Meg's nerves and her grip on Patch's fur tighten up a couple of notches when Povich the prosecutor strides to his table and picks up a DVD case.

Povich says, "Your Honor, the prosecution would like to enter this video into evidence as State Exhibit One." He takes it to the judge to examine. The judge nods, and the prosecutor hands the DVD to Ernie Bert.

He asks Ernie, "Is this a video of the murder of Puffy the poodle?"

Tom stands. "Objection, Your Honor. No crime has yet been established."

"Sustained."

Povich scowls. "Is this a video of the alleged murder of Puffy the poodle?"

Ernie opens the case and examines the disc. "It's the copy I made for you, yessir." He points. "There's my initials right there."

Striding to a TV, Povich inserts the disc into a player. "Once you see this video, Your Honor, there will be no doubt in your mind that a crime has been committed and we should proceed to trial."

He presses a button on the remote control. Meg sees a number of people wince when Puffy does his yappy-dog thing. Then the scene shows Patch charging the dog. He knocks the dog ass over snout and rips open its throat, and the courtroom is filled with sighs at the instant silence. Patch laps at the blood while the poodle twitches and expires. Meg has to admit that it's pretty ugly. But she knows the power of the blood hunger and how it takes over.

Then the scene shows Grant reaching for Patch and him growling at her, blood all over his muzzle. The judge frowns at the screen. It looks like Patch is a goner.

Povich stops the video. "Do you affirm that this recording accurately depicts the events of the night of the killing?"

Ernie cuts his eyes toward Patch for a moment, and then glances at Grant. The reporter sits on the edge of her seat, dabbing at a tear with a hanky and scowling at Ernie at the same time. "Yes."

Meg has a distinct feeling that Ernie has more to say.

Povich says, "No more questions, Your Honor."

The judge looks to Tom. "Your witness."

Tom and Meg exchange glances, and then he says, "No questions at this time, Your Honor."

Patch leaps down from the table and trots toward Ernie. The courtroom guard scrabbles for his pistol, yanks it out, and drops it on the floor. By that time, Patch has made it to Ernie.

He stands on his hind legs, puts his front paws on Ernie's knee, and gazes into his eyes.

Povich shouts, "Objection, Your Honor. This wild, rabid, bloodthirsty monster is trying to intimidate the witness!"

Patch takes a breath and launches a good, loud purr and then turns his built-in kitty-cat smile on the judge. She leans forward and studies him. "Doesn't look like intimidation to me. Do you feel intimidated, Mr. Bert?"

"No, Your Honor. I like cats."

"Objection overruled."

Wondering what Patch is up to, Meg leans forward when Patch turns his gaze back to Ernie and gives him the "big eyes" treatment. She knows how it feels when a cat lets you know he has an urgent communication. Out of the side of her eye, she sees most of the gallery also leaning in.

Patch says, "Mrrr?"

Ernie stares at him, and then reaches down and scratches behind his ears. Patch purrs louder.

Ernie straightens and tells the judge, "There was more on the tape."

Wow. Patch had sensed the same thing Meg had, but he had known what to do about it.

Judge Escobar says, "Well, let's see it."

Povich stands. "Your Honor, I object. There's no precedent for cross-examination by a cat."

"There's no precedent for indicting one for murder, either. Give Mr. Bert the remote."

Like a kid who's been caught swiping a candy bar at the drugstore, Povich surrenders the control.

Ernie hits a button. "I'm going back to the start of the event."

The screen shows Ginger Grant with a black bag in her foyer. She opens the bag and Patch leaps out.

Then the shot widens to take in the poodle, standing between his mistress's legs, yapping. Ernie turns up the sound, and the dog's yapping fills the courtroom. Meg feels like her ears will start bleeding.

The judge claps her hands over her ears, and the rest of the people in the courtroom do the same. Except for Ginger Grant. She smiles adoringly at the TV. There's no explaining some people.

The judge cries, "Cut the sound!"

Ernie hits Mute and then lets the scene run past the attack on Puffy to show Patch's eventual escape.

When it's over, Tom stands. "Your Honor, we demand that Ginger Grant be arrested."

"On what charge, Mr. Conway?"

"First, for harboring a public nuisance."

That has to be the yapping. The judge nods. "I agree."

Tom's voice takes on a dramatic tone and he projects, "And for kidnapping!"

True! Meg likes the sound of that.

The judge looks to Ernie. "Mr. Bert, does this video accurately reflect the events of that evening?"

Grant springs to her feet and screeches, "You're history in this town if you're not careful, Ernie."

Judge Escobar says, "Make a note, Mr. Povich. Intimidating a witness in a murder trial."

Ernie looks down at Patch. He grins, then turns to the judge. "It exactly portrays the kidnapping and harassment of this little kitty-cat."

Grant says, "I object!"

The judge rolls her eyes. "Ms. Grant, if you do not restrain yourself, I will order your immediate arrest for assault, kidnapping, harboring a public nuisance, and intimidation of a witness. Not to mention contempt of court."

Grant puts the back of her hand to her forehead and swoons. She falls across the laps of the people sitting next to her. After a moment, she opens one eye. When she sees that the TV camera is trained on her, the eye shuts and she moans.

Tom says, "Your Honor, I move that we dismiss these proceedings."

"Not so fast, Mr. Conway." She gazes at Patch. "It's still true that the defendant killed that obnoxious dog. The question is, was it justifiable? And is he a menace to others because of his condition?"

Povich says, "I call Patch the cat to the stand."

"Mr. Conway, are you willing to allow your, er, client to testify?"

"We have nothing to hide, Your Honor."

The judge says to Ernie, "You're dismissed, Mr. Bert. Thank you for your service." Ernie gives Patch a wink and leaves the chair.

Meg comes to the witness chair, picks Patch up, and sits with him in her lap. The judge peers at them. "Ms. Murrow, do you feel that you can interpret for your cat?"

"Yes, Your Honor. After all we've been through, I understand him pretty well."

They are sworn in, her hand and his paw on a Bible, and then Povich attacks. "Why did you massacre that poor little puppy?"

Grant, still in her position across laps, moans even louder.

All eyes focus on Patch.

He leans back against Meg, spreads his hind legs, and licks his butt.

Meg giggles, her belly rocking Patch.

Povich steps back and points at Patch. "Your Honor, I object."

"To what, Mr. Povich."

"This creature just told me to kiss his ass!"

Patch looks up at him. Meg thinks the idiot is quicker than she'd thought.

The judge says, "Objection sustained. Please answer the question and avoid the rude gestures."

Tom stands. "My client wishes to invoke the Fifth Amendment, Your Honor."

The judge rolls her eyes and sighs. "Why me, Lord?" To Patch she says, "I need to hear it from the defendant."

Patch shakes his head. "Mrrrah."

Meg gets it. "Patch respectfully declines to answer on the grounds that to do so might incriminate him."

Povich says, "Did you rip open the throat of the dog known as Puffy?"

With the video, there is no denying that. "Mrf."

Meg says, "Yes."

"When did you first plan to murder the dog?"

Meg suspects it was the second his ears were attacked by its yapping. It certainly had been for her. Patch says, "Mrrrah."

"Patch respectfully declines to answer on the grounds that to do so might incriminate him."

Povich turns to the judge. "Your Honor, this is ridiculous."

"I don't think so." She leans forward. "I have questions." She looks at Meg. "Ms. Murrow, remember that you are sworn to tell the truth."

"Yes, ma'am."

"Are you and your kitty-cat truly vampires?"

"Unfortunately, yes."

The judge raises her eyebrows. "You don't want to be?"

"No, ma'am. We were both attacked by hungry vampires, and that's how we became infected." She strokes Patch's back. "No one would want to be a vampire."

Patch adds, "Mrf."

Meg says, "We are also an unrepresented minority, subject to unhampered aggression by the breather majority."

The judge shakes her head. "Are you pandering to my ethnicity?"

Meg lifts her chin. "No, Your Honor, I'm merely trying to illustrate the difficulty of being a minority."

Judge Escobar shrugs. "How can I deny you that?" She pauses. "But you do have advantages that the rest of us don't have. You live—er, exist—forever, right?"

"I don't know. It's not much of an existence yet, because we are so limited in what we can do during the night. Because of our handicap, we don't have access to public services and most businesses."

"You see this as a handicap?"

"Wouldn't you, if you were limited to the hours of darkness to be able to move around in the world?"

"I'll ask the questions here. The video shows the defendant lapping up the blood of that loathsome little dog. Aren't you all killers?"

"No, Your Honor."

"I just watched the defendant kill that awful dog."

"But he didn't do it on purpose. The blood hunger creates ..." She looks to Tom.

He says, "An irresistible impulse."

"Yeah, that."

"But you need blood, correct?"

"Yes. Through the American Vampire Association, we get our nourishment through socially acceptable, perfectly legal means." When the judge raises her eyebrows, Meg adds, "Slaughterhouses."

"There's an American Vampire Association?"

"Yes." Meg shoots a look at the prosecutor. "And we're registered voters. Several hundred of us."

Povich glances at Ginger Grant, still lying back on laps, and then gets a thoughtful expression on his face.

The judge turns to Tom. "Do you have a plea, counselor?"

"Yes, Your Honor. Not guilty on grounds of self-defense. The yapping, and he was surrounded by kidnappers. The case should be dismissed."

"*Caramba*, that yapping." She looks to the prosecutor. "Mr. Povich, do you have any other witnesses?"

"No, Your Honor, nor do I believe any are necessary. The video is clearly a record of a vicious killing. We request that this defendant be detained for trial."

Judge Escobar picks up her gavel. "I rule that there are insufficient grounds to try this defendant for murder." She gazes into Patch's eyes and gives him a stern scowl, then turns and hits Meg with it as well. "But I caution the defendant that he'd better be careful. I don't want to see him in my court again." She whacks her gavel on a wooden pad.

Meg claps with joy. Patch leaps from her lap to the top of the judge's desk and goes to her, offering a loud purr. The judge's scowl doesn't go away, but she does run her hand down his back until he lifts his rear end for the little bit of extra pleasure at the base of his tail. Then she smiles and gives the spot a scratch. Meg can almost hear "Mmmmm" coming from Patch.

On the way out of the courtroom, Povich stops Tom and Meg and Patch. After a smarmy smile, he says, "I hope there's no offense. Just doing my job."

Patch makes a move toward his butt again, but Meg straightens him and says, "Of course, Counselor."

A woman approaches and Patch greets her with a happy-sounding "Mrrowf."

She scratches between his ears. "Hi, Spot. But I guess you're Patch now." She smiles at Meg.

Meg says, "Spot?"

"He used to live with me. I'm Amy." She gazes into Patch's eyes. "I miss you, little partner."

Patch sounds a little sad when he says, "Mrf."

Amy says to Meg, "I understand that he can't be mine anymore, but could I stop by for a visit now and then?"

Meg's answer comes with a smile. "Of course."

Patch gives her a look of thanks. Meg says, "Would you rather be called Spot?"

Patch gives a soft growl, and Meg joins Amy in a laugh. It feels good to be treated like a human being. They head out into the night, Tom behind them with the Critter Carrier.

Outside, a crowd of reporters assaults them with rapid-fire questions. One reporter shoves a mike at Patch. "Did you kill a yappy little dog?"

Patch says, "Mrow!" and a cheer pops out of the crowd. The reporter turns to a camera. "There you have it—good news for the citizens of Bloomsburg courtesy of a vampire kitty-cat."

A woman shouts from the courthouse. "Murderer!"

Would they never be done with Ginger Grant?

Grant races down the steps and bullies through the gaggle of reporters and cameramen who block her way. If her glare were a wooden stake, Patch would be dead and gone. She says, "You monster." She shifts her rage to Meg. "And you, too, enabler of the slaughter of my innocent little Puffykins. I will fight you to the death."

Awash in irony, Meg says, "You're a little late to the party on the death part, Ms. Grant. But I'm so sorry about—"

"Oh, you're not even started with feeling sorry. After I get through with you, no reporter in Bloomsburg will even talk to you, much less report on this sick campaign. It's as dead as you are." Tears spill from her eyes. "As my sweet puppy is."

An armed guard steps next to her, holding a pair of handcuffs. The guy has a wart on the end of his nose the size of a marble. "Judge said to take you in if you cause a ruckus."

She smiles up at him and leans close. "Mmm, what a great face. Have you ever considered acting?"

He grins, exposing a gap where one of his front teeth should be. She whirls and hurries down the courthouse steps.

Back in Meg's apartment, she and Patch have a supper of V1. After she cleans up, she says to him, "I've got something I need to do. Why don't you just stay here and relax?"

Still in the grip of happy lassitude, Patch can only open his mouth. No meow comes out, but the message is clear. She pets him and heads out.

It feels so good to be back in her car that Meg has to resist honking the horn and waving at pedestrians. She loves her little green Miata, especially on a balmy night like tonight when she can put the top down. It gives her a sense of things being right with the world. She hasn't felt much like a person, a real person, a human being, since she was attacked. It's good to have that back. With Patch safe at her apartment, she's in control of her life again.

She smiles. Yeah, good luck with that.

Meg pulls into the parking lot at the cemetery and finds a spot to park. It's good that a bright moon is still out—she doesn't have a flashlight, and it was being here in the dark during her last visit to the graveyard that got her into trouble. Who knew that an innocent mission to check out the ambience of a cemetery to write a Halloween commercial for the local grocery store would be a life and death matter?

A sob from the far corner of the cemetery tells Meg where her quarry is. She wends through grave markers until she comes to an area separated from the main graveyard by a white picket fence barely two feet tall. A post holds a sign that reads "Pet Heaven." Inside are twenty or so small plots. Ginger Grant stands beside a fresh mound of dirt in front of a pink tombstone engraved with ribbons and bows and the words "My Precious Puffy."

The poor woman. Meg steps through the gate and says, "I'm so sorry."

Grant screams and whirls to face Meg. Her expression swaps terror for hate. "You?" She peers behind Meg. "Where is your little killer? Isn't he here to gloat too?"

Meg holds her hands out. "I didn't think he'd be welcome. And I'm here to say I'm sorry, to offer my condolences."

Grant snorts. "Condolences! What the hell does that word even mean?"

"It means—"

"I know what it means. Here's another word for you—get lost!"

"That's two w—"

A huge sob takes Grant's breath away. She seems to crumble, hunching her shoulders. Her hands come to her face and she turns to Puffy's grave. Her moan strikes Meg in the heart. Meg says, "What can I do to—"

"Do?" Grant turns back to Meg. She straightens, and tears wash her cheeks while rage reddens them. "You can put a stake in that criminal cat's heart."

Meg shakes her head. "He's an innocent."

"Ha! As if that poor excuse for a judge had any—"

"You kidnapped Patch, you threw him in a bag." Now Meg is the one scowling, clenching her fists. "He couldn't feed, so the blood hunger took him over." She steps forward and raises her hand to point in accusation. "If it hadn't been for what *you* did to Patch, your little dog would still be alive."

Grant's mouth opens as if to reply, and then she slumps under the weight of Meg's words.

Meg pushes her anger away. The woman is truly hurting. "Still, I'm sorry that it happened. We just want to make what we can of what little is left of our lives."

Grant's sobs resume as Meg heads back to her car.

Somewhere in the darkness, a chant floats through the night.

"Death to vampires."

32: Patch

The next night, the weather is nice enough when we leave Meg's apartment to go to the lawyer's house that Meg doesn't bother with a jacket over her T-shirt and puts the convertible top down. The shirt has a picture of a Siamese cat on it, reminding me of the pussycat I set out to visit before, pardon my French, the shit hit the fan. Even though the cat on the shirt is not a calico, I approve.

After we get going, I decide I like riding in a convertible, the wind whisking through my whiskers, the starry sky above. It's unsettling to be traveling without my feet doing the moving, but I've learned to accept it. Except for the times Amy took me to the vet.

We park in front of the lawyer's condo, and Meg carries me into the study. Tom is at his desk. Archie leans against the fireplace mantel. I'm a little surprised to see Lester occupying most of a couch, with Seiko curled up next to him in what's left of the space. They wear "Vote for Meg & Patch" buttons, even Lester. Nice.

Meg sits in a comfy wingback chair and sets me in her lap, facing her. She strokes my back. "You did it, Patch. You won the case."

Tom says, "I don't know how you picked up the fact that the prosecutor was concealing exculpatory information, but

it was brilliant. I may take you with me to my next trial. I'm
going to need all the help I can get. I've served the city with
a civil suit for equal access to public facilities after dark.
They'll resist, of course."

So maybe I'm into a new career as a legal consultant? I
don't know about that. Besides not wanting to lower myself
from being an animal to a lawyer's level, I much prefer being
petted. Meg's steady stroking sparks a purr. Mmmmm. It
becomes hard to focus on the talk.

Lester says to me, "You're still welcome to come with me,
Patch. Live the life of the wild, free vampire."

I'm not too keen on going there. However, Lester has
turned out to be good to have around at times.

Seiko pats Lester's shoulder. "Let's go to the A.V.A. Vera
offered you a security job there, and they've got plenty of
V1 juice."

I look up at Lester. He scowls, then gazes down at Seiko,
his expression softens, and he nods.

Awww.

A voice I don't like says, "Well, if it isn't the cat that thinks
he's above it all." Papa Gambino steps in from the dining room.
Behind him looms Giles, his hand inside his coat as if ready
to pull out a gun.

Papa sneezes, then glares at me and mutters, "Useless
ball of allergens."

Meg frowns at him. "Hey, that's my cat you're talking
about."

Papa shrugs, and then yawns. "Well, folks, it's past my
bedtime. What say we have our little meeting?"

Seiko stands. "I'm in the mood for a snack." She holds
a hand out to Lester. He grins, gets up, and they leave for
the kitchen.

Meg leans in and strokes my back. I give her my "feed me" meow, and she pulls a roll of Death Savers from her jeans pocket and gives me one. "We'll have breakfast later."

Tom raises a hand. "Ah, we have a new supporter aboard. In here." He gestures toward the dining room, where there are enough chairs for a meeting. He leads the way to where Prophet Pat Bobson sits, the front of his white shirt stained red. Bobson gives us the kind of smile that makes you shudder as if something slimy has touched your mind.

Bobson says, "Welcome, brethren."

Meg gazes at Tom for a long moment. "Really?"

Tom shrugs. "Any port in a storm and all that."

She checks Bobson out. He's relaxed, unworried. "Why aren't you in jail?"

Tom puffs his chest out, which only makes his belly protrude a little more. "Me." He grins. "You should have seen me. Their only witness was the guy who saw Lester and his fangs. All he could talk about. So I said that the unknown giant vampire had killed The Guy Who Had to Pee. And that the blood on the Rev was from him trying to resuscitate the victim."

Bobson smiles even wider. "They let me go, and there was talk of me being a hero."

Tom sits next to Bobson. "And we're going to sue them for wrongful arrest."

Shaking her head, she takes a chair at the head of the table. "You're such a ... such a—"

Tom says, "Genius."

"Lawyer."

Papa Gambino sits across from her, and Tom says to Bobson, "So, Reverend—"

"Prophet."

"Reverend, you say you control how many votes?"

Meg pats her lap. I'm still in need of a good petting, so I oblige her. I sit and face the people around the table while she scratches me behind the ears. Mmmmm.

The "prophet" smiles. "I'm pleased to say that there are now over three hundred Bobsians in my flock, all dedicated to the cause of our earthly paradise. And all their friends and families. Could be a couple thousand by the time I'm done bringing them into the fold."

Tom says, "I think he means turning them into vampires."

Bobson reaches into his shirt pocket and takes out a folded piece of paper. He hands it to Meg. "And here's a check for ten thousand dollars' worth of support."

Papa Gambino rubs his hands together. "Now we're getting somewhere."

Meg studies the check, then sets it on the table in front of her. "What do you want?"

Bobson raises his eyebrows and smiles in an imitation of innocence. "Nothing, my dear."

She waits, her gaze as steady as a cat's.

He shrugs. "Er, we think that justice and human rights will be better served with you as sheriff."

Tom reaches for the check, but Meg stops him with a hand over his. "And by that you mean ..."

Bobson shrugs. "Perhaps this persecution of me and my faithful by the city prosecutor will stop. In the name of religious freedom." He scowls at her. "We are not murderers, just people seeking a new, and higher, form of existence. Nobody dies. Er, completely."

This guy is as bad as Gambino. One wants to exploit vampires for cheap labor, the other to exploit gullible people for their blood and cash. But she thinks we need their backing. Their money may talk, but will she listen to it?

Meg says, "I'm running for sheriff of the county. You're talking about city law enforcement."

Shaking his head, Bobson says, "I've done my research. The sheriff is the primary law enforcement officer in the county and can enforce laws within the entire county. Including the city."

Meg lifts the check and says, "Justice is the heart of my campaign, Reverend."

I look up at her and hiss. Her gaze scurries away. She can't look me in the eyes, which is kind of silly. After all, she's not doing anything wrong. Right?

"We ..." She swallows, and then her mouth tightens and she looks down at me. "We have to get elected, Patch, to do the good that's so badly needed." She places the check on the table. "That's what counts now." Bobson grins.

Papa claps his hands. "We got ourselves a candidate, gentlemen." He grins at Meg. "And lady. I'll get some, er, platform thoughts over to you tomorrow. Maybe something on protecting the rights of entrepreneurs."

Bobson adds, "And I'll give you some ideas on religious freedom."

Meg winces, but then she smiles and says, "I appreciate your input."

Papa says, "Good! You've got my support, all the way to the sheriff's office." He sneezes and wipes his nose with his sleeve.

The hum of a microwave oven in the kitchen sounds, and the red smell of warm blood wafts in. I hop from Meg's lap and trot into the kitchen.

Meg says, "Good idea," and follows me.

In the kitchen, Seiko looks up from putting a bowl of blood on the floor. "I wondered if a snack would get your attention."

Lester lifts a mug in our direction. "Cheers."

Meg joins them for a cup of warm V1. After downing every drop and then sitting for a spell in a flood of pleasure, I've had more than enough *Sturm und Drang* lately and want nothing more than a life(?) of sleeping, eating, licking, petting, and sex. Did I mention licking? Can I still make love?

But where to get that life? Except for her recent corruption, I like Meg. And I'm supposed to be her co-candidate, which sounds like it could mean a continuing supply of the necessities of undead life. She has a great touch for scratching behind my ears, too.

But there are the sleaze and weirdo parts of the equation—Papa Gambino and Prophet Bobson. As with all cats, quality of life comes first, and those two humans have a way of mucking up my day whenever they appear.

They just want a little compromise, though, right? Am I some kind of kitty-cat purist? Well, actually, there's no way to *not* be a purist when you're a cat.

I can become a creature of the night, feeding on whatever I can catch and sleeping in dark places during the day. But that sounds like a lot of work. There wouldn't be any petting, either. I don't think I could take hanging out with Lester and Nasty.

Voices still come from the dining room—after all, this is vampire daytime—so I slip back there to see how it might feel to stay with Meg despite her sleazy political side.

When I walk in, Tom says to the preacher, "How about a glass of V1 juice?"

Bobson shakes his head. "Oh, no, we don't defile ourselves with animal blood. My revelations have made it clear to me that our mission is to purify the blood of sinners through our holy transformation."

I wonder how long he would say that if he woke up in an alley with nothing to feed on other than, let's say, a nearby rat.

The prophet stands. "In fact, I'm due at a gathering of the faithful now. We're meeting on the south side to rustle up some dinn— salvation."

Mmm, no doubt the winos and homeless who hang out on the south side are tasty indeed. This guy gives me four kinds of creeps.

Meg comes in behind me. "Thank you for your contribution, Reverend."

Bobson stops beside her. "Prophet." He opens his arms and reaches for her, but she flinches away from his embrace like a vampire from the sunrise.

His mouth smiles, but his eyes don't. "Take care, woman. My power is growing, I can feel the infusion of grace from the Almighty, and thou shall not deny me." He turns to leave. I scoot around in front of him, stop, and brace myself.

My timing is perfect. My body catches one foot and he falls. The crunch of cartilage when his nose hits the floor is an unexpected bonus.

He scrambles to his feet and glares down at me. "Damned foul beast!"

His nose now skews to the left, not unlike Nasty's. I give him the innocent look and say, "Mrrr?" He storms out and slams the front door behind him.

Meg smiles at me. "You did that on purpose, didn't you?"

In answer, I go to her and rub against her leg. She sits in her chair and slumps. "Oh, Patch, what should I do? I know I can do so much good if I get elected, but I don't know if I can stomach this."

Relief lightens my load. She isn't really corrupt, just doing corrupt things. But, of course, if she keeps doing corrupt things, actual rottenness isn't far behind.

But I hope we can work it out. I leap up onto the table. Bobson's ten-thousand-dollar check is still there. I go to it, position my butt over it, and squat. Nothing comes out—I guess those days are gone forever—but Meg gets the message.

"But we need the money."

Money. There has to be a way. This is one of those few times that not being able to talk is a real problem. Oh, I have more than a hundred meows and chirps and body-language gestures that I can use to communicate my needs, but I have no way to have a dialogue about abstractions like fundraising.

Tom reaches for the check. "Money's not dirty in itself, and we're not either."

Yet. When his fingers touch the check, I extend my claws and put my paw on top of his hand. I give a low growl.

He grabs the scruff of my neck and lifts me off the table. That's the problem with taking on a creature that has hands and is ten times bigger than you. Try it sometime.

I sag, of course, reflexively helpless. Tom says, "Up until now, I've been going along with this cat, but he's getting in the way. And Papa hates him."

Papa says, "You can say that again."

Meg gets to her feet and scowls. "Let him go."

Tom's eyes have a beadiness like Sammy's that I hadn't noticed before. He says, "And if I don't?"

Meg gazes at Tom, and then at me dangling, and then at the check on the table. Next to it is a "Vote for Meg & Patch" button. She taps the button with a fingertip. "Then you don't have this."

Me, I'm getting tired of hanging here. It's okay when your mom carries you around by the scruff of your neck when you're a kitten, but it's darned uncomfortable when you're grown.

Tom says, "We can get new buttons made."

"But this"—she holds up the button—"is a promise I made to Patch."

"Who worries about keeping a promise to a cat?"

People who don't want their beds peed on, that's who.

Meg says, "Isn't there room for integrity in politics?"

When Tom and Papa sober after a fit of giggles, Tom says, "You think the cat will make a difference?" He snorts.

I wonder how long my neck skin will hold out. Will my fur be all crunched and funny-looking forever? It's an impossible spot to reach for licking.

"Besides, this election is about money," Tom says. "They all are."

Meg flips the button onto the table and stares up at Tom. "Well, I'm not about money. You put him down or I'm outta here."

Tom releases me and I drop to the floor.

Meg smiles. "Thanks, I knew you'd understand."

"You're the one who doesn't understand. Don't let the door hit you in the ass on the way out."

Meg picks up the campaign button and Pat Bobson's check. "You'll lose this campaign money."

Tom shakes his head. "I'm thinking I should be the one to run for sheriff." He winks at Papa. "And I have Papa's bucks coming in, thanks to his toxic disposal litigation and his twenty-five-thousand dollars in cash."

Papa chimes in. "It's great to have a talented young abomination, er, lawyer on my team."

Tom smiles. "A sheriff should know the law, and I do. You, however, don't have a clue." He smiles at Papa. "You prefer a cat-free vampire candidate, right?"

Papa nods, and a grin takes shape on his face. "I'm with you a hundred percent." He turns to Meg. "Like my candidate told you, don't let the door hit you in the ass on your way out."

Tom leans forward and snatches Bobson's check.

He's got a real appetite for money.

Papa stands. "Congratulations, Sheriff."

Tom says, "Awww, shucks."

Papa eyes me with a hard look and then says to Giles, "Let's go. I have a little job for you."

After Papa's out the door, Meg says to Tom, "You're a rat."

"No, I'm a lawyer."

What she said.

Seiko appears in the kitchen doorway. "Who's a rat?"

Lester looms behind her. "Yeah, who?"

Meg's face scrunches up, and I wonder if she's going to cloud up and rain the way people do sometimes. If she still can. I go to her and rub against her legs. She bends down and picks me up. "I almost was." She kisses the top of my head. "Thanks, Patch."

She aims a shaky smile at Seiko. "Patch and I have been kicked out of the campaign."

Seiko says, "You're quitting? But what about protecting us from the Devils?"

Meg lifts her chin. "Quitting is something I don't know how to do."

I bump her hand to let her know me too. "Mrow." I'm rewarded with a scratch behind both ears. Mmmmm.

Meg picks up the Patch & Meg button. "Trouble is, I also don't know how to do this, either, moneywise."

Lester clears his throat. "If you need money, I've got a little stash and some jewelry and stuff we could pawn." Seiko looks up at him and gives him big eyes and a bigger smile. He grins.

Hmm, Lester is increasingly showing signs of being a human being.

Meg shakes her head. "I don't know, Lester. It'll cost a whole lot. I've got to think on it."

Tom butts in. "Well, think of it somewhere else. I've got a speech to write. I'm going to get Papa to set up a big rally tomorrow night, with signs and a band."

Seiko says, "Why are you writing a speech?"

"Because I'm the candidate now." He hands Meg a box filled with Patch & Meg buttons. "I won't be needing these." He rubs his hands together, then flutters his fingers at us. "Shoo! Shoo!"

We shuffle out, with the sleaziest lawyer in town, the wealthiest man in the state, and the bloodsuckingest preacher nutjob arrayed against us.

33: Patch

Back home at Meg's apartment, after helpings of V1 juice for
both of us, Meg is a storm of planning how to get back into
her campaign, scribbling notes on a pad and researching on
her laptop when the ringtone of her phone sounds—it's the
chorus of "Don't murder me" from "Dire Wolf" by the Grateful Dead. She sees the caller and answers on speaker. "Hey,
Mom. What's up?" I like her mom, she gives good skritches.

Her mother's voice is bright and excited. "Meg, honey!
I'm going to be just like you. Prophet Bobson is going to
administer his sacrament to me and I'll be a vampire too.
Isn't that great?"

I'm nearly flung into the windshield when Meg slams to a
halt at the curb in front of her parents' house. She scrambles
out of the car and dashes up the sidewalk, then circles back,
still on the run, to snatch me from the car. I don't know why
she needs me. I was perfectly happy to just sit, still basking
in the afterglow of all that V1 juice. But my duty as her associate calls.

She rings the doorbell and then, when nothing happens
immediately, pounds on the door.

Her father swings it open. His face reddens and he yells
at Meg, "You! This is all your fault!"

Behind him, her mom says, "Oh, is that Meg?" She doesn't sound loony, but then, crazy people often seem more sane than most. I think it's because they're completely sure that their nuttiness is the real thing. Cats are utterly sane. Think about it. Ever see a cuckoo cat?

Dad opens the door wide to reveal Meg's mom. She wears a long white gown. Red stains spill down the front. Her hands are pressed together in front of her as if she's praying.

She says, "The truth has been revealed." She spreads her arms wide. "I will be saved." She beams.

Meg cries out. "Oh, Mother, you didn't!"

Dad says, "No, not yet."

Meg sets me down and peers at her mom. Dad stares at me, and his expression is like a pistol aimed at my head.

Her mom claps her hands. "We'll be sisters in salvation!"

Meg says, "Tell me this isn't true." She touches the stain on her mother's robe and then licks her fingertip. "Spaghetti sauce?"

"Well, you know, I had to see if the look worked for me, and it was the only red thing I had in the pantry." She pulls the gown over her head to reveal a black dress underneath. She holds out the gown and examines the stain. "I'll admit it went against my grain to do this, but eternal salvation should be worth a little mess."

Meg leads her mother into the living room. I follow and discover a nice fire in the fireplace. For old times' sake, I curl up on the hearth. The warmth feels good, but I know it won't last. Death sucks.

Mom hands the gown to Dad. "Would you put this in to soak, honey?" He scowls, but takes it and heads down a hall.

Meg sits her mother on a love seat and joins her. "Mom, this isn't like the Save the Marmots club you joined, or even the Mothers for Long Underwear movement."

Her mother laughs and pats her daughter's hand. "Of course not, dear. They didn't promise eternal life, and the prophet does."

"Well, Pat Bobson can't deliver on that promise."

"But his Holiness says he can. He has such a nice face." She leans back and appraises Meg. "Besides, look at you. You look great, you don't have to worry about dying, and you don't have to diet. If it's good for you, it's good for me."

"But it's *not* good for me! I spent my first night of being a vampire hiding in the dirt." She glances at me. "And attacking innocent creatures. It was awful."

I can testify to that.

Her mom laughs. "Oh, how awful can it be, now? You're a politician, and you have a marvelous career in law enforcement ahead of you." She stands. "I'm going to do it."

Her father comes back. He takes Meg's hand. "You've got to stop her." Then he frowns at her hand and drops it. "Clammy."

He looks at Meg's mother and his eyebrows rise. "Will she be clammy too?"

Meg says, "All over."

He frowns. "Wait a minute. Does this mean no more—" He flicks a glance at Meg and then back to Mom. "—no more you-know-what?"

Meg says, "Ewww."

I wonder what he's talking about.

Mom waves his question away. "Oh, I don't think that's such a big deal. Besides, we don't do it much anymore."

Dad says, "There's always hope." He glances at Meg. "While you're alive, that is."

"You can't do this, Mom. Think of how you love to walk on the beach. The sun would destroy you."

Her mother smiles. "Well, moonlight walks will be even more beautiful."

"Your garden? Who'll take care of that?"

"We'll put in lights. No problem."

Her dad grumbles. "The neighbors will love that."

"What about ..." Meg's gaze flicks around the room, searching. "What about chocolate mousse pie?"

Mom smiles. "I'll have an eternity to enjoy it."

Meg's grin is like me pouncing on a mouse. "No, you won't. You won't be able to eat anything but blood."

"Oh, no. Surely that can't be true. An eternal life of nothing but, ugh, blood?"

"Sad to say. Anything else makes you sick."

"What about wine? You know I do like my glass of sherry before bedtime. Or maybe I should switch to red wine, a nice cabernet."

"Nope. Nothing but blood."

Her mother's gaze goes blank for a moment, and then she says, "Maybe I should go add some bleach to my gow—"

The doorbell rings. Mom answers it, Meg on her heels, Dad hovering behind them. Me, I'm perfectly comfortable where I am.

Standing on the porch, dressed in a white robe with red stains down the front, is Bearded Guy from Bobson's Righteous Hallelujah Church, the guy who wanted to drive stakes into Meg and me. Two other white-and-blood-robed guys flank him.

Bearded Guy smiles widely, his horse-like teeth gleaming from within the wiry black bush of his beard. "I'm Brother Alexander, captain of the prophet's God Squad. We're here to help you on your way to eternal life. You can call me Al."

Meg glances back to me, then stands next to her mother. I leave the fire and join them, wondering if Al will call Meg "slattern of Satan" again. It has a Lesterish quality to it.

Al glances at Meg. "Have we met?"

"Yeah. I was on the wrong end of a stake. The other end was in your hand."

Al laughs. "Oh, my, how our past sins haunt us. Luckily, I now have eternity to make amends, Sister." Then he frowns. "You are one of the saved, aren't you? Not one of those wild heathen vampires."

Mom says, "Alexander, I want to thank you and the squad for coming by, but I've changed my mind."

Meg puts an arm around Mom's waist. "Way to go, Mom."

Mom pats Meg's hand and then grimaces. "My, you are clammy."

Al gestures behind him, and his accompanying goons part to reveal a long white limo parked at the curb. "The prophet himself awaits you, in person, ready to begin your journey to Heaven on Earth."

Mom shakes her head. "Oh, I'm so honored, but I think I'll try for Heaven the old-fashioned way."

The limousine's horn honks.

Al scowls. "He's hungry." He pastes his smile back on. "Er, eager to save you. You can't say no to divine deliverance."

"Oh, but I am."

"No, I mean you can't." He swells up, and his voice booms, just like it had when he was going to end our undeaths in the park. "We are on a mission from the Almighty, and we will not be denied!" He steps to the side. "Take her to the car."

When the two goons behind Al step forward, Meg calls, "Dad!" and then stands in front of her mother. "You're not taking her anywhere."

Mom scoots next to Dad. "I don't want to do this anymore." He wraps an arm around her.

Al booms again. "None shall be denied the keys to the kingdom of Heaven on Earth. The prophet has spoken!" More honking from the limo. I start past Al to see if I can see the prophet. I have to tell you, if these are God's people, He—She? It?—works in more than mysterious ways. The word *lunatic* comes to mind.

During long winter nights, curled in front of one fireplace or another, between licking sessions I'd contemplated the notion of humankind being created in the deity's image the way they claim. Looking at all the wackiness in the world, it seems to me that, if true, there is something seriously wrong with the Prototype. Oh, He/She/It did get some things right, such as cats. No wackiness in cats. Illness is the only thing that can interfere with us being soft, beautiful, canny creatures our whole lives. Well, maybe we get a little neurotic now and then, but you can pin that on our human associates.

And then there's this herd instinct people seem to have. No matter how nutty, an idea can attract enough believers to make it a "fact." Even though I don't see Bobson's Heaven-on-Earth idea as having much going for it in reality, good old Al is ready to insist that it's a fact whether you want to believe it or not.

Al glances down at me as I approach, and he scowls. "Is that the animal perversion of our Lord's gift?"

Not in my view. Quite the opposite. I ignore Al, of course, but he doesn't ignore me. He points down at me and cries, "Blasphemy!" Before I can react, he stoops and snatches me up and hands me back toward one of his goons. Not only is Al built like a football player, but he has the quickness too.

The goon holds his hands up and shies back. "Ewww."

"Take it. The prophet will want to dispose of it, and he will cleanse you afterward."

What is it about being a vampire kitty-cat that keeps crap raining down on me? I need to associate with better people.

Goon One takes me, grimacing as if he's accepting a handful of poison ivy. Meg lunges forward, yelling, "Hands off my cat!"

Al clotheslines her with one huge arm, wraps it around her, and crushes her to his body. He gestures at Meg's mom. "Take the volunteer."

Goon Two advances, and Mom backs away. "You don't understand, I'm not volunteering." She hides behind Dad.

Al looks skyward. "Oh, Prophet Bobson, forgive this supplicant her confusion and grant her the peace of eternal life on Earth." He turns to Goon Number Two. "Please help our good sister do as she truly wishes, no matter how much she screams."

When Goon Two reaches for her, she cries, "Franklin!"

Dad steps forward. Goon Two looms over him. "You wanna come to the Lord too?"

Dad, his face pale and sweaty, steps aside. "No, not really, not today." He glances at his watch. "Look at that, way past my bedtime."

Goon Two pulls Mom out the door by the arm, Goon One carries me toward the limo, and Goon Two follows, towing Mom. Al brings up the rear, holding Meg suspended off the ground. She shouts back to Dad, "Call the A.V.A.!"

Dad calls, "Uh, do you have the number?"

Good question. It doesn't seem like a bunch of vampires would be listed in the phone book.

"Go there. Corner of Fourth and Fifth. Call the police!"

Dad redeems himself to some extent by running to the driveway, slamming himself inside his car, and peeling rubber out of there.

When we get to the limo, Goon One opens the door and Pat Bobson steps out. His garb is now a white suit, white shirt, and white tie with red bloodstains down the front, and white shoes. His white teeth show in a saintly smile. He licks his lips, his gaze glued to Meg's mom. He says, "Delicious."

Meg shouts, "You ... you ... creature!"

Bobson frowns at her. "Oh. It's you. What are you doing here?"

Kicking her feet in the air while trying to hit backward and connect with Al's face, she shouts, "Stopping you from hurting my mother!"

Well, maybe slowing down, it doesn't look like "stopping" is on the dance card.

Bobson chuckles, and Al and the Goon Brothers join in. Then Bobson sobers. "You are of no use to me. The lawyer is going to win the primary, and"—his eyes glitter, he spreads his arms wide, and he looks up—"the wave of holy darkness will spread freely throughout Bloomsburg."

Like I say, if these charming folks are like the Prototype, there are some serious design flaws.

Bobson's gaze drops from the night sky to me. "And then there's your little beast."

Seeing as how *beast* means "lower animal," I resent that. I take a breath and hiss. Goon One loosens his grip. I twist, push, and spring free. When I hit the ground, I dash under the limo.

Al shouts, "Get him!"

The prophet says, "Never mind the vermin. Assist our new recruit into the car, and we'll go to the church for the ceremony. And put the other one in the trunk."

Crouching under the car, I watch disembodied feet scurry to do their owners' tasks. The trunk opens and then slams shut, and then car doors do the same.

I'm about to be on my own again, friendless, homeless, Megless.

The car engine starts.

34: Patch

One word simmers in my mind. *Vermin*. That sleaze, that pimple on the butt of humanity, called *me* vermin? I charge out from under the car, hoping to find a door or window open. One good leap and the prophet, with his never-healing undead skin, will have something to remember every time he smiles into a mirror.

But no luck—I bounce off a closed window. Inside the car, Meg's mom spots me and struggles to reach the door, but Al cuffs her back into her seat. Not very religious behavior, to my mind.

I run toward the front of the car: maybe I can hitch a ride on the bumper and tag along. I don't know what I can do if I do. Cats aren't much for planning ahead, preferring to focus on the nicer parts of any given moment, but I want to help Meg, not to mention find a way to wipe the smile off the prophet's face.

The limousine takes off and leaves me behind. Curses, foiled again. When I head for the curb, wondering where my next blood meal is going to come from, headlights turn on down the block and tires squeal. A van hurtles my way.

I leap for safety on the sidewalk, but I'm in no danger. The van steers wide of me and then tires screech when it skids to a halt beside me. It's the KTBC news van. The passenger door opens, and the pointy features of Ginger Grant, ace reporter, look down at me.

In the driver's seat, Ernie, the cameraman, leans to look at me. She says to him, "You missed him. Back up. I want the little murderer flattened."

A blue bandanna holds back Ernie's long hair, and a smile peeks out of his beard. He gives me a little wave. "Are you sure? Seems like there's a story here." When she doesn't answer, he says, "We have a job to do. We're professionals. This is a story, not your life."

Grant shoots him a hard look; if gazes were concrete, he'd have a knot on his forehead. She turns back to me. Her voice is sharp with scorn when she says, "So why did the God Squad leave you behind? Vampire fleas?"

I stick out my tongue and consider plopping down and giving my nether regions a lick to illustrate my feelings.

Ernie says, "Hey, Patch. Want a ride?"

Grant scowls. "That homicidal creature? In here?"

Ernie's eyebrows rise. "He's a part of the story, isn't he? We're following the prophet and his squad, they grab Meg Murrow and that woman, and they leave Patch here. I'm thinking they're on the way to Bobson's church." He reaches down and pulls up a small video camera. Putting his eye to the viewfinder, he focuses on me. "If I was a reporter, I don't think I'd leave a famous part of Bloomsburg's story of the century sitting here." He gives Grant a look. "Or flatten it."

Grant squints at me, and I can almost see the whir of her thoughts. Then her features soften. No, they don't soften, they just become a milder kind of stony. She holds out her hand and says, "Here, kitty, kitty, kitty." The corners of her mouth turn down as if the words taste bad.

But "Here, kitty" is hard to resist. And I do want another shot at Pat Bobson. So I hop into the van, bounce off of Grant, and curl up in Ernie's lap. Grant slams her door shut and then leans as far away from me as possible. I can almost see red streams of hatred beaming out of her eyes.

Ernie puts the camera on the console between the seats, gives me a scratch behind the ears, and hits the gas.

Minutes later, we ease to a stop in front of the Righteous Hallelujah Church. When Ginger opens her door, I leap from lap to lap and out, heading for the church, its doors wide open.

A hymn comes from inside, each line punctuated by the chorus of breaths vees need to take to fill their lungs.

Breath. "This is all my hope and peace—nothing but the blood of Bobson";

Breath. "This is all my righteousness—nothing but the blood of Bobson."

Breath. "O precious is the flow that makes me white as snow";

Breath. "No other fount I know, nothing but the blood of Bobson."

They sure seem to be bloody-minded people. God only knows what they will do with their wacky notion of vampire Heaven on Earth, and She's not telling. I wonder how Bobson's flock does their feeding. Who are their victims? What happens to them? Are they dead, or new vampires?

Behind me, Grant's high heels hit the sidewalk and start after me. The driver's door on the other side slams, and then Grant says, "You're leaving the lights?"

"You know what it does to those, er, people—all that writhing and screaming gives me the creeps."

He's right about that. TV lights hurt like hell.

Grant says, "And it could be too dark inside the church to shoot. We need to be prepared."

Stopping and turning back to them, I attempt a telepathic projection. *Would you get a move on? Meg's in trouble.*

Ernie mutters, "Fine."

It worked? I gotta try that more often.

He opens the side door and gets his camera and a cart that holds a rack of three lights hooked up to a battery.

Screw it, I'm gone.

I take off in a run for the church door, leaving Grant and Ernie behind to hurry after me.

The church is about a third full, everyone standing as they sing. In the chancel in front of the congregation, the Reverend Prophet Pat Bobson, dressed in his bloody white suit, stands behind a waist-high table. On it, Meg's mom struggles against straps that bind her to it. A white gag covers her mouth.

Lined up on the side of the chancel stand a half dozen white-robed vees, including Al, the God Squad leader. They sing and clap along with the rest of the congregation.

Standing beside the table, Meg pulls and wrenches at the grip of Goon One, but her five feet of determination is no match for his six feet of sanctimony and muscle.

The singing ends and the worshippers sit in their pews.

I pad down the aisle past empty rows of pews, swiveling my ears back to make sure Grant and Ernie are behind me. Their footsteps approach.

Bobson raises his hands high and his voice soars, echoing from the high ceiling. "Brethren of the Holy Blood, we are gathered to redeem another lost soul."

Meg's mom produces a muffled, "No-o-o-o-o-o-o-o."

Bobson places a hand over her face, further stifling her voice. He gazes down at her and smiles. "I know, my dear, it's difficult to wait. Soon. Soon." He licks his lips. "Oh, I know how eager you are. But we must take the time to dedicate this holy moment to My gift of Heaven on Earth." He bows his head.

Behind me, Grant whispers, "This is Ginger Grant, KTBC news, bringing you exclusive footage of the savage rites of the new vampire church headed by murder suspect Pat Bobson."

I stop just before the first row that has people in it and glance back. She sits at the end of a pew, leaning into the aisle, holding her microphone close to her lips with one hand shielding it. I have to admit, she's good—even quieter than a commentator at a golf match. None of the Bobsian vees notice. Ernie stands in the aisle beside her, camera on shoulder, recording the scene. On the cart beside him is the rack of lights with a hand grip. Apparently there's enough light without them.

Meg shouts, "No! This is evil!" I whip my focus back to the front.

Bobson raises his head. "Evil?" He laughs. "Impossible. I speak with the voice of the Almighty, and He has blessed Me and given Me guidance in My mission."

Some people who say things like that are locked up and given medication, so why is this nut running around loose? I shake my head. Unlike cats, people aren't entirely coherent much of the time. You have to wonder how they've gotten so far. Probably the opposable thumbs.

Bobson says, "Now is the time to welcome our new sister into the fold."

He leans down, opening his mouth wide, his pitiful canine teeth white against the pink of his mouth.

Meg screams.

Bobson puts a hand on Mom's forehead and stops her from thrashing her head from side to side. He bends down and licks her throat. His smile is hungry.

Behind me, Grant whispers, "This is the first-ever actual look at a vampire feeding on a human victim, brought to you exclusively by KTBC News. Disgusting, but compelling."

Ernie says, "We oughta do something."

"You're already doing it. Keep recording."

"But they're going to kill that woman."

"We're journalists. We watch. We report. That's our journalistic ethic."

It seems a little oxymoronic for a television reporter who tried to frame me for dog murder to use the word *ethic*, especially as she watches a fellow human being about to be snacked upon. I look back. Grant licks her lips and stares ahead. She reminds me of a mouser I once knew, stalking her prey. Ernie glances down at the lights on the cart, but then goes back to his viewfinder and continues videoing the altar action.

Meg screams, "Mommm!" She back-kicks Goon One in a kneecap and tears free. She throws herself onto Bobson's back. He falls onto Mom.

The congregation boos. Someone cries, "Blasphemy!" A clamor of outrage assaults my ears.

Meg's goon grabs her by the arms and rips her off the prophet. He lifts her into the air, slams her feet to the ground, and then wraps his arms around her to hold her tightly against him.

Bobson stands, straightens his suit coat, raises his arms to the congregation, and smiles. The people silence. He says, "My blood brothers and sisters, you have witnessed the rabid violence of the unsaved undead."

He indicates Meg. "Poor child. If only she had been converted by My holy bite."

Meg shouts, "You're not—"

Goon One slaps a big hand over the lower half of her face. It's a good thing she has no need to breathe.

Bobson croons, "Just as the Almighty has granted Me the power to bestow eternal life, It has given Me the power to take life away." He extends an arm toward the side of the altar, where Al and five henchmen stand, Goon Two among them.

Bobson snaps his fingers and holds out his hand, palm up. Al hustles to him, his bloodstained white robe billowing behind him. Al pulls a sharp wooden stake from under his robe, bows his head, and places it in the prophet's hand. Then Al pulls a mallet out and stands at attention, holding it ready.

Although I don't think the stake can actually kill Meg outright, we vees do need our hearts to pump every now and then to get blood to the rest of our bodies. If Bobson puts a hole in her heart, I have a hunch that the terrible pain of blood hunger will end in, well, the end.

I dash back to Ernie and look up at him; he keeps on taping. I stand on my hind legs and put my paws against his leg. He looks down, but then Grant leans out from her pew and bats me away.

At the front of the church, Bobson raises the stake high in the air. "Blessed be this holy instrument of the Almighty." He gazes at the congregation. "I ask you, brothers and sisters, shall we give this unrepentant sinner release from her profane, pitiful existence and grant her the solace of Death's embrace?"

As one voice, the congregation shouts, "Yes!"

How generous—as long as the stake isn't intended for them.

Behind me, Ernie says, "My God, they're going to murder Meg."

"Keep taping or you'll never work in this town again. Besides, she's not exactly alive."

The prophet nods to Al, who nods to Goon One, who nods, lifts Meg, and moves her closer to Bobson. Al hands the mallet to the preacher, takes one of her arms, and stretches it out from her body. Goon One does the same with the other arm, and they hold her prisoner between them, each pulling on an arm.

Meg says, "This isn't a Christian thing to do."

Bobson smiles. "What do I care? I am reborn with the wisdom of the Great Father as His Second Son. Welcome to the new salvation of Bobsianity."

The congregation sings out, "Hallelujah."

He steps in front of Meg, his back to the audience. He glances over his shoulder, then moves to the side to where we can see his face. Holding Meg taut, Al and Goon One sidle around to keep her facing Bobson.

"Any last words, sinner?"

Mom struggles against her bonds and screams, "Nooooo."

Bobson places the point of the stake on Meg's chest, over her heart.

Meg wrenches at the grips on her arms, but she's never going to break them. "Don't do this."

Bobson's smile is beatific, but his eyes are hard. "Oh, I'm sure you'll prefer this to the last method we tried." He shakes his head. "Stoning a vampire just makes an undead mess, and we had to leave him outside for the sun to finish him off."

The congregation says, "Amen."

He raises the mallet.

I launch myself down the aisle. Hurtling toward Bobson full speed, I let out a mighty yowl and leap for his arm. I catch it just as he swings the mallet down. I dig my claws in and sink my fangs deep into Bobson's wrist.

The mallet flies from his hand and hits Al in the eye. Al shrieks and grabs his face, letting Meg go.

Meg twists and kicks Goon One square in the balls. I've seen this maneuver before, and I look forward to him writhing on the floor. But he just looks down and doesn't react. Oh, yeah. Vampire. Not much in the way of sensation without a healthy shot of blood.

A roar goes up from the congregation and then shifts into a cacophony of cries for my blood, ripping me to pieces, and other blessings.

Even though I'm not hurting Bobson, I hamper the hell out of him. He shouts "Beast!" and shakes his arm. Well, *beast* is a promotion from *vermin*, I guess. Still, I'm not letting go.

Meg kicks Goon One in the balls again, and I have to wonder what he will feel the next time blood pumps through his body, activating things.

Fingers grab my skin at the back of my neck and lift. Oh, no. Once again, my body goes limp and I release all my grips, claws and teeth. Whoever has me pulls me off and holds me high in the air. The hand swivels me around. It's Goon Two.

Al takes his hands from his face and grabs Meg's free arm. The eye the mallet struck doesn't track with the other one, but rolls around and seems to be operating on its own. Al and Goon One quickly have Meg spread-eagled again.

Bobson pulls up his sleeve and stares at the deep punctures my teeth left in his arm and then glares at me. If looks could kill—and if I wasn't already mostly dead—I'd be joining the dearly departed right here and now.

But his scowl eases into a beaming smile. He turns to the congregation and raises his hands in the air. His vee groupies respond with immediate silence. "And so you see, the Almighty delivers the infidels and pagans to us."

The congregation answers, "Amen."

Bobson points to the floor. "Hold it there."

Goon Two grabs my dangling hind feet, kneels, and stretches me out on the floor. Bobson steps close and places one big foot on my head, pressing down until I feel the pressure in my bones.

His voice almost a hiss, he says to me, "Let's see how well you fare after I crush your skull and your brains come out of your ears."

He presses harder.

35: Meg

As Meg struggles with the hands holding her, Patch takes a deep breath and lets loose the longest, moaningist, pitifulist help-me meow ever heard.

Bobson laughs, then calls out, "The creature is praying to Satan. A lot of good that will do."

Chuckles and titters from the congregation, along with a couple of amens.

A voice shouts, "Stop!" Ernie?

Ginger Grant says, "You idiot."

Bobson takes his foot off Patch's head and peers into the church. "What have we here? More supplicants at the altar of eternal life?"

"No," Ernie says. "We have videotape of you kidnapping two women and your cruelty to animals."

Bobson laughs. "Hold the cat. I'll come back to it."

Goon Two stands and holds Patch tightly, one big hand gripping his hind legs and the other his front legs. All heads are turned in Ernie's direction. He stands in the aisle, and Ginger Grant scowls up at him from her pew.

Meg cries, "Call the police!"

Bobson calls out, "The doors!"

At the back of the church, two white-clad acolytes step forward and close the doors. The slam echoes through the sanctuary like a boom of doom. Meg flinches at the final sound of it.

"Brothers and sisters," cries the prophet. "Tonight the Almighty has sent us riches. Three to feed our holy needs, three to join the immortal flock of the Righteous Hallelujah Church."

Ginger Grant stands, straightens her shoulders, and looks down her nose at Bobson. "We are accredited members of the press doing our public duty."

Her whisper to Ernie is clear to my kitty-cat hearing. "Pick up your gear and let's get out of here."

So much for duty.

Ernie hangs his camera by a strap from one shoulder and picks up the lights, but he steps forward, not back. "Let the cat and those people go."

"Oh," says the prophet with a smile, "I don't think so." When the Reverend Bobson smiles, he's at his most dangerous.

Ernie lifts his camera. "I've got you assaulting the woman you have strapped to the table."

"Assault? You consider the administration of a holy sacrament to be assault? We have religious freedom in this country!" The smile broadens and the prophet extends his arms, turns his palms up, and raises them. "Brothers and sisters, we need to help these sinners see the light of My Truth."

The congregation stands and faces Ernie and Grant. She says to Ernie, "Maybe you shouldn't have said that."

The prophet Bobson gestures with a lifting motion to the left side of the congregation. "God will not allow you to threaten His holy Servant. Bring them to Me."

The left half of the congregation, at least a hundred righteous vampires, hasn't taken more than one step toward the aisle and the intrepid cameraman and his weasel companion before the lights in Ernie's hand flare.

They aren't aimed at Meg, but hot pain still hits her eyes. That side of the congregation screams and falls back like wheat before a scythe. They scramble over each other and crawl under pews to get away from the light.

Bobson shields his eyes with his arm, but he doesn't yield. He lifts his right fist and roars, "Get them!"

Though Meg's eyes are tearing, she sees the right side of the congregation surge toward the aisle. They howl with fury. Ernie swings the lights and, like a roundhouse punch from a heavyweight boxer, takes out that side too.

When the light passes over Bobson, the Rev screams and drops to the floor. So do the rest of the holy vampires in the chancel.

Goon Two drops Patch and hits the deck, and Patch manages to scramble around behind him and shield himself from the worst of the light. Meg covers her eyes and curls up on the floor behind Al's bulky body. Still, she screams.

Ernie yells, "Ginger, untie the woman and get them out!"

Grant shouts, "Behind you!"

The pain of the light vanishes and Meg peeks over Goon Two. Ernie swings the lights around to nail the two doorkeepers rushing them from behind, and they dive into pews to escape the light.

Ernie yells again, "Untie her!"

Grant says, "I'm outta here."

Meg peeks above Goon Two. He still has his head buried in his arms. Ernie holds the lights aimed at the floor, and although it's uncomfortable to look in that direction, the pain is bearable. The congregation is in various stages of recovery—a bunch huddles on the floor like Goon Two, some struggle back into the pews, and a few sturdy souls stand.

The prophet rouses, and then gets up. "Get them!"

Ernie calls, "We're coming, Meg."

The prophet thunders, "Rise! Rise and face down the hellfire of this spawn of Satan. Do My holy will! Take them!"

More righteous vampires stand and move toward Ernie and Grant from both sides. Ernie swings the lights up, and Meg shuts her eyes. She knows when the light comes because Bobson screams. She opens her eyes a slit and sees him crawl around behind one of the goons to escape the light.

Ernie says, "I'll hold them back while you untie the woman."

"Nope. I'm gone."

"I'll record you rescuing innocents from hundreds of rabid vampires. Think of the ratings."

Silence, and then footsteps running Meg's way on the carpeted aisle. The lights shut down and she opens her eyes.

Grant takes the gag off of Meg's mom, unstraps her, and helps her off the table. Meg slips her hands under Mom's arms and helps her toward the aisle toward Ernie. Grant stops beside Patch and looks down.

Prophet Bobson moans, puts his hands on the floor, and starts to push himself up.

Ernie shouts, "Get the cat."

Meg turns to Grant, who scowls and says, "Never!"

Ernie points to his camera. "You'll be number one with cat lovers! Or, if you decide not to help him, you'll be number zero."

Grant sighs and picks up Patch. She puts a foot in the middle of Bobson's back, pushes him onto his face when she puts her weight on him to step over, and heads for Ernie.

She pastes on a smile that looks like it wouldn't take much to make it fall off.

By the time they reach Ernie, Bobson is yelling, "Kill them! Kill them!" Apparently, he's lost interest in saving sinners. "Stake them! Rend them! Burn them!"

All but a few members of the congregation get to their feet, teeth bared, arms out, hands like claws. They advance on Ernie.

Ernie raises the lights. "The door. Fast." Meg and her mom hustle up the aisle, Grant behind them carrying Patch. Even though the lights face away from her, Meg feels it when they go on, and the congregation screams again.

The two door guards now stand at the door, blocking their way. Grant calls out, "Ernie. The door guards!"

From the side of her eye, Meg follows the light swinging around toward the front doors. She braces for its impact.

The lights dim and then go out.

Ernie says, "Battery's gone."

Behind them, the congregation screeches its blood hunger.

From outside, a bugle sounds "Charge," the good old cavalry call you hear in John Wayne movies. The congregation silences. The bugle sounds again, and then the doors to the church slam open.

A stream of people led by Vera from the A.V.A. and Dad surges through the doors. Vera carries the bugle, and she raises it to her lips to deliver another charge. It hurts Meg's ears, but she's not about to object. The two parishioners who'd been guarding the doors flee down the aisle and join the congregation.

Dad rushes to Mom and takes her in his arms. Meg sags, but Vera arrives and steadies her. Vera wears a bandolier of bullets diagonally across her chest, and a big cowboy pistol in a holster on her hip.

Maybe thirty vampires come behind them and spread in a line across the back of the church. The silence is enormous.

Mom, her voice muffled with her face pressed into Dad's chest, says, "I'll never join anything again."

Dad squeezes her in a hug. "Well, I signed you up for the A.V.A."

She lifts her head. "The A.V.A.?"

"American Vampire Association. I thought you might be one by the time we got here."

Ernie taps Vera's bugle. "Nice touch."

She smiles in an embarrassed way. "I'm a big fan of the Duke's westerns, and I always wanted to do this."

"Behold!"

Oh, no. Twenty feet down the aisle, the prophet is back.

Bobson spreads his arms wide. "Behold the perversion of the Almighty's gift of eternal life."

Eternal disease is more like it. But there is no telling the good Prophet Bobson.

He clenches his fists. "We shall crush the abominations."

Ah, Meg is back to being an abomination. She thinks this is the dog calling the fence post stupid.

Meg goes to Grant and takes Patch. Holding him tight, she faces Bobson. Ernie raises his camera to his shoulder. A little red light starts blinking on the front, and then he aims it her way.

Bobson strides toward them. His flock follows, filling the aisle behind him. He raises a hand and points a finger at Grant and Ernie. "I feel the Holy Hunger."

The congregation calls, "Amen."

Come to think of it, Meg has a little belly-burn too.

"You shall not deprive the Saved of the sacrament of blood."

"Hallelujah," shout the Saved.

Meg calls out, "You're the abomination, Bobson."

"Boo," go his followers. Bobson smiles.

"You say you're saving people, but you're nothing more than a new Typhoid Mary, spreading a horrible disease. You're not giving eternal life, you're robbing people of good lives."

From the side comes Ginger Grant's voice, doing the at-the-golf-match murmur. "KTBC brings you exclusive footage of what could be a bloody confrontation, considering that we're looking at a bunch of wacky vampires."

Bobson's slow march up the aisle continues, and his soft voice drips menace. "Blasphemy." His voice rises, his brows dive into a scowl. "You question the Word of Bob?" He raises his arms high. "I have spoken Holy Truth!"

Meg widens her stance like a fighter about to go into battle. "Well, *I'm* talking now." She strokes Patch's head.

She sends her gaze across the congregation behind Bobson. "You people who follow this wingnut, doesn't it bother you that you've lost your lives?"

Bobson booms, "Nonsense! They've gained eternal life."

Meg shakes her head. "We are the *'undead,'* not alive. We have lost the sun and our freedom. We are prisoners of death and blood hunger."

Someone in the A.V.A. crowd behind her mutters, "Amen."

Patch squirms. He could do with a little blood right now. But the only nearby blood is Mom, Dad, Grant, and Ernie. Can't go there.

Well, maybe Grant.

A murmur bubbles up from the congregation. People exchange glances. A number of them rub their stomachs.

Bobson turns to face his people. "We have gained the night, the holy hours when the Blessed of the Blood shall rule."

He takes three strides toward the congregation; those in front press back. He roars, "Deny Me and you will be damned!"

He spins and points at Patch and Meg. "Strike down the blasphemers!" He starts for them, and his followers follow.

Vera shouts at the people lined up across the back of the church. "Ready!"

From behind come rustling sounds. Meg peers back at the A.V.A. members. They're taking something from their pockets.

Vera cries, "Aim!"

The A.V.A. vees get ready to throw the stuff in their hands, their faces grim. Meg catches a faint whiff of blood.

Vera yells, "Blood!"

They throw, and blood-red rings rain upon the congregation. Death Savers!

The mob breaks into hungry pieces, catching Death Savers out of the air, dropping to all fours to scrabble for them on the floor.

Bobson shouts, "No! Do not contaminate your holy state with animal blood!"

What does he think people are? Fish? Death Savers still fly through the air, and Patch leaps to the floor.

A Death Saver hits in front of him and he pounces. He catches the little ring of blood with his front paws, flips onto his back while tossing the Death Saver up, and it drops into his mouth.

Ernie has the camera aimed Patch's way. "Cool." He winks and then swings the camera to take in the congregation.

Vera offers candies to Meg. She pops them into her mouth. The growing pain fades.

Patch gets to his feet, scarfs up two more Death Savers, and then sits, no doubt feeling the same pleasure rush that spreads through Meg. She shakes her head to clear it. Not a good idea to be drowsing off with a killer mob bearing down on you.

Goon One, whose gonads had experienced a couple of severe taps from Meg's foot, pops a handful of Death Savers into his mouth and swallows. He smiles. Then he frowns. Then he grips his privates, howls, and falls to the floor.

Meg pumps her fist.

Bobson dashes from follower to follower, pounding on one and slapping another. "No! No!"

But the faithful ignore him and settle onto pews, relaxing with the blood rush Meg is resisting.

He comes to Al, the God Squad leader. "Attack!" Al gives him a sleepy smile and shakes his head.

Bobson plunges his hand into Al's robe and takes out a two-foot, sharpened wooden stake. He turns to face up the aisle, and he focuses on Meg. He charges, the stake held out in front of him like a lance.

36: Patch

Vera pulls out her cowboy pistol, cocks the hammer, and aims it at Bobson. "Stop or I'll shoot!" She glances at Ernie, who shifts his camera from me to aim her way. "Always wanted to say that."

Bobson slows, and his mouth twists as if he were snarling. Somehow it seems to be a better fit for him than his constant smile. "I am on a holy mission!" He lunges ahead, the stake ready to spear Meg.

I see Vera's finger tighten on the trigger and wish I had hands I could put over my ears.

Bobson is only three feet away when the gun goes off, and he's blown off his feet to sprawl on his back in the aisle. The stake leaves his hand and clatters onto a pew, where it slides to the floor. There's a small black hole in his white suit, right where his heart is. He just lies there. No blood appears.

Meg says, "You killed him?"

Vera blows smoke from the muzzle of her gun. "You're forgetting what we are."

Bobson stirs, and then gets to his feet.

Meg takes a step back. "We're zombies?"

Vera cocks her pistol and holds it at the ready. "No, with zombies a hole or two doesn't matter. Besides, zombies are fictional. Most holes in a vee don't matter much either, but I think I got him right in the ticker."

Bobson rubs his belly, takes a breath and moans. The blood hunger is on him. He steps forward, his gaze locked on Meg's mom. He licks his lips.

Raising the pistol, Vera aims at his head. "You're not going to be much of a preacher without a face."

The hole in his heart didn't stop him, but her threat does. Vera digs into a pocket and then tosses him a roll of Death Savers. His hands shake as he rips open the roll of blood rings and downs them all. He relaxes.

Vera says, "Watch this."

A spurt of blood bubbles from the hole in the prophet's white suit and runs red down his front. He looks down and touches the blood with a fingertip, and his face twists with pain. Blood spurts again with the rhythm of a heartbeat.

He needs a plumber, badly.

He grips his stomach and doubles over. "It hurts!" He looks up at the ceiling. "Why Me, Lord?"

I think maybe it has something to do with the fact that he's an asshole.

With a silent scream, he falls to the floor and writhes. I know that pain and almost feel sorry for him. I have no idea how this will end, but it has to be nasty.

Bobson cries out. "This isn't right!"

I don't know much about the God thing, being more in the Mother Nature camp myself, but I think Bobson has this one wrong.

Vera turns to Meg and me. "This isn't going to be pretty. If he doesn't get blood into his system, which isn't going to happen with that hole in his heart, the vee bug will consume his flesh before it dies out."

Grant says to Ernie, "Get this. You gotta get this."

Bobson cries out, "I'm coming to the Almighty!"

Most of the congregation sits in pews, enjoying the rush after eating their Death Savers, a few of them searching the floor for more. A voice says, "Amen."

Another voice adds, "So long."

Bobson cries, "I don't want to go!"

Meg says, "Patch, what do you say to getting out of here?"

"Mrrr!"

Vera holsters her pistol. "Come on back to the A.V.A. with me. You'll be safe there."

Judging from recent experience, I don't think there's safety anywhere. I've been attacked and nearly mutilated at the A.V.A., although there's been worse since then. But, now that Sammy is ashes, I'm willing to give it a try.

Bobson now jitters on the floor with major convulsions, and I think I glimpse a hole open in one cheek before he flops onto his face. Wisps of vapor come from his sleeves.

When Meg and Vera start up the aisle, Grant goes to Ernie. "Did you get plenty of writhing and feasting on blood?"

"Oh, yeah. In fact, I'm a little disgusted. But I could cut together something that looks like it came straight from *Buffy the Vampire Slayer*."

Grant calls out, "Miss Murrow! How about an interview?"

Meg stops and turns back. "All right. But outside."

Bobson has stopped writhing. His suit collapses as his body suffers things I don't want to think about.

Outside on the church steps, Ernie gets in front of us and holds up a hand to stop us. "That's good." He glances up at a streetlight. "Got enough light."

The vampires from the A.V.A. file out of the church and create a little audience on the steps below us. A half dozen of the former prophet's followers join them, and more crowd in behind us.

Grant steps next to Meg and says into her microphone, "Ginger Grant here, speaking to Meg Murrow and her cat Patch, vampire candidates for sheriff."

Meg says, "I thought you didn't think we're real."

Grant sneers. "Please. I'm a professional observer, and I know what I see." She turns to the camera. "We've just left the stunning, apparent demise of the Reverend Pat Bobson, accused murderer and self-proclaimed prophet of the Righteous Hallelujah Church. Any comment, Meg Murrow?"

She thrusts the microphone at Meg. It hovers just above my face.

Meg shrugs. "What goes around comes around."

I add a "Mrrr." Cats have a special appreciation for poetic justice.

"Tell me, Ms. Murrow, what are your campaign plans now that your fellow vampire, Tom Conway, has entered the primary race for sheriff?"

Meg squares her shoulders and lifts her chin. "I'm going to fight every way I can. Too many Bloomsburg citizens are denied protection, and I'm not just talking about vampires." She glances down at me, gives me a scratch behind the ears, and looks back to the camera. "For example, what about cats? They can be snatched off the street and put to death. Don't they have a right to protection from murder?"

You go, girl!

Grant says, "But wasn't your cat—"

"Patch is his name."

Well, technically speaking, it isn't. But I like it as my *nom de plume.*

"Wasn't Patch arrested for murdering a certain innocent little poodle?"

Darned if I don't see a tear well in one of Grant's eyes. I'll never understand people who love yappy little dogs. But I respect their right to do so.

Actually, no, I don't.

"It was self-defense, and the court said so. It was a rare instance of a cat receiving the due process of law." She raises her voice. "I intend to see that justice is no longer a rarity for the minorities of Bloomsburg!"

Applause and whistles erupt from the crowd, and Ernie swings his camera to take it in. It looks like we have the vampire vote, and this interview will be great exposure for Meg. Maybe we have a chance. Maybe my associate will be able to provide me with the life, so to speak, I deserve.

Tires squeal on the pavement, and a black Hummer limousine pulls up to the curb. Papa Gambino's toady, Giles, gets out of the shotgun seat and opens the rear door. He helps Papa out, and then Papa points at us and says something.

Giles trots up the steps, pulling a pistol from under his suit coat as he comes. He stops beside Ernie and puts the muzzle of the gun to Ernie's temple. "Stop."

Ernie lowers his camera until it hangs by his side. I notice that the little red light in front still glows, and that the camera lens tilts up, pointed our way.

Looking like a tall bulldog, Papa Gambino makes his way up the steps. When he reaches us, he takes a cigar from his inside coat pocket and lights up. He smiles at Meg, but his eyes have a nasty squint to them. He blows smoke in our faces. Who'd have thought there was a benefit to not breathing? He says, "Y'all wouldn't be talking to the press about running for sheriff, would you?"

"I am. Unless I'm mistaken, we still have free speech around here."

Papa glances at Giles, his pistol still at Ernie's temple. I get the feeling Papa thinks that she's mistaken.

He turns to Ginger Grant. "You're wasting your time with her. She won't be running for sheriff anymore, the way I see it. I'm backing the best vampire candidate." He taps an ash from his cigar. I'm glad I'm not breathing—the smell of cigar smoke is one of the planet's most noxious odors, as far as cats are concerned. The idea of carrying around a little fire and inhaling smoke that causes a fatal disease has always seemed, well, less than intelligent to me.

Grant says, "So who should I be interviewing?"

"Tom Conway, naturally."

Meg protests. "You promised to back me! Where's your integrity?"

Even Ernie, with a gun at his head, laughs at that one.

Papa holds his hand out toward Ernie. "I'll take that video."

Ernie shakes his head. "Can't do that."

The lens is aimed at Papa, and the red light still shines. Papa says, "Giles, what caliber is that pistol you're holding to this idiot's head?"

"Nine-millimeter."

"And what will it do if it, er, accidentally goes off?"

"Pretty much blow his brains out."

Ernie swallows hard. But he doesn't give up the camera.

Vera says, "Hey, Papa, how would you like to become a vampire?"

He snorts cigar smoke and laughs. "Are you kidding? I've got a great life."

She signals to the A.V.A. members to come closer, and they move up the steps. "Well, I'm thinking that we have a life-for-a-life thing going here. Your goon puts the gun away, or we give you a new look at life from another side—the graveside."

Papa's eyes widen and he glances at the vampires crowding close. Hey, there's 7-Eleven George. He licks his lips and smiles at Papa. The smile looks hungry.

Papa turns back to Vera, and then his face relaxes into a smug grin. "How about you and all your members are blackballed from getting any jobs in Bloomsburg?"

"You can do that?"

He blows a smoke ring in answer.

Vera holds up a hand, and the vampires stop. She glances at Meg and then shrugs.

Papa says, "Give me the video."

Cats, being live-and-let-live creatures, hate bullies. This guy needs to be taken down a notch or five, and Vera's threat gives me an idea. I twist in Meg's arms, brace my hind feet against her belly, and leap for Papa's shoulder.

I pride myself on my leaps, and for good reason—I land lightly, brace myself with one paw across the back of his neck, and lean in. I place my fangs against his throat with enough pressure for him to feel it but not to break the skin.

He swings a hand at me; Meg shouts, "Freeze or you're dead."

He freezes.

"I mean, undead. If Patch's fangs break your skin, the vee bug will enter your bloodstream, and then it's goodbye heartbeat."

I wonder if that is all it will really take, but it sounds convincing to me. And Sammy said a kiss would do it. Meg projects a certain authority when she wants to. Papa lowers his threatening hand to his side.

Vera steps close to Giles. "The gun."

Giles looks at Papa and raises his eyebrows. I tighten my jaws. Papa nods, and Giles hands her the gun. Ernie lets out a long sigh and raises his camera to keep recording.

Vera tucks the pistol into her waistband and draws her own. "I think you folks had better be moving on."

Papa sneezes. "Get this thing off me."

Thing? I'm tempted to prick him with a fang just to see what happens. But I give his neck a nuzzle with my nose instead.

He shrieks and I leap down. I scamper back to Meg's side while Papa points to his neck and gibbers at Giles, "Am I bleeding? Did he do it?"

Giles peers and shakes his head. Papa says to Meg and Vera, "All right, we're leaving. But you show that interview and you're out of work forever."

Ginger Grant says, "It's KTBC's video, and you can't stop them from airing it."

Gambino grins. "How do you think your boss will feel when all local advertising is yanked from your two-bit station?"

Grant asks Ernie, "Get that?"

"Got it." He points the camera at Ginger.

She lifts her microphone. "This is KTBC reporter Ginger Grant, bringing you exclusive footage of leading citizen and businessman Papa Gambino attempting to blackmail a candidate and threatening assault with a deadly weapon—"

Papa holds up his hands. "All right, all right. But you don't play that video. That's blackmail."

Grant continues, "And attempting to stop us from reporting his crimes with his vile"—she grins at Papa—"blackmail."

Like Meg says, what goes around comes around.

Papa and Giles retreat to their limo and leave.

Meg turns to Grant. "You guys saved us. I thought you hated us."

"Not you. You were nice to me after Puffy ..." She scowls and points at me. "I hate him." She sighs. "But together you're a great story."

"Well, thanks anyway."

Vera says to the crowd of A.V.A. vampires, "Thank you all for your help. Free blood on the house back at headquarters." They split up, heading for cars. The Bobsians just stand, expressions of confusion on their faces. "You, too, if you'll be good." They brighten and take off into the dark.

Vera starts for the street. "Come on," she says, and she leads Meg and me to, of all things, Sammy's old Volkswagen Bug.

Ginger and Ernie head for the KTBC van.

When we pull up to the four-story building that houses the A.V.A., a crowd mills around in front of the first-floor garage doors. Vera punches a remote control and the doors begin to open.

But before she can pull in, the crowd floods into the opening. The headlights reveal tattered clothing and dirty faces. They look a lot like Meg did when she was in the cemetery.

They surround the car and rock it. Then they chant. "Traitor! Traitor! Stake the traitor! Traitor. Traitor. Stake the traitor!"

37: Meg

Meg's gaze meets those of enraged vampires, their dirt-streaked faces plastered against the car's windows. Maybe a half dozen carry pointy stakes. They open their mouths wide as they scream their chant. They don't have fangs, but it sure feels to Meg like they do.

"Traitor! Traitor! Stake the traitor! Traitor. Traitor. Stake the trait—"

Vera volunteers, "It looks like you've picked up a fan club, Meg." She turns to her. "I like you, honey, but Sammy was right when he said there would be trouble if you outed us." She looks at the mob. "Only I didn't expect it to come from vees."

"But what have they got against me?"

Meg's car door jerks open and grubby, claw-like hands grab her arm and pull. She grips Patch to her chest.

Sucking in gasps of air, the mob members ululate victory cries. When Meg and Patch are wrenched from the car, the mob leaves Vera where she is, punching numbers on her cell phone.

Two vampires grip Meg's arms and haul her through the crowd, which parts to let them pass and closes in behind them. One arm is in the clutches of a muscular-looking Black woman in dirt-streaked, light-blue pajama-like clothes that make Meg think of the surgeons she's seen in medical dramas. A young man who is prettier than he is handsome, dressed in nothing but the briefest of briefs, grips the other. His wide-open eyes roll and flare, and the word *mindless* comes to mind.

"Traitor! Traitor! Stake the traitor!"

Headlights swing across the crowd and then turn off. Grant and Ernie emerge from the KTBC van with their microphone and camera.

Meg's captors push through the throng to the brick side of the building, then turn her around and pin her to the wall, facing out. The vampires mill in front of them and brandish their stakes, but none step forward.

"Why?!" Meg draws a breath and screams, "Why me?!"

A voice comes from the other side of the vampires facing her.

"Because you're taking away their way of life."

The mob quiets as only a bunch of people who don't have to breathe can.

Tom?

The mob parts and Tom strides through. His suit is dirty, and he sports smudges on his face, but his hair is clean and neat, and the clothing isn't wrinkled and tattered like the others'. Since he doesn't need to be dirty, Meg figures it's an act.

Ernie and Grant follow in his wake and join the front ranks of the vampires. She wonders if they know how much danger they are in. They only know about the tame, civilized A.V.A. vampires. The wild kind now surrounding them will have no problem turning them into a banquet if they get hungry.

Tom stops in front of Meg. "Although ruining their lives is bad enough for them, even worse for me is that you might win. Can't have that."

"You were my ally. My defender. My lawyer."

Tom shrugs. "All true."

Young Guy shakes Meg. "Are we gonna stake 'em?"

"But why?"

Tom gives a shrug. "Because I want to win. That's what lawyers are all about."

Meg strains against the hands that hold her. "But what about justice?"

"Not nearly as important as winning."

"It's the money, isn't it? It's Papa Gambino and his big bucks."

Tom raises his eyebrows. "Heaven forfend. What do you think I am?"

In a word, a *lawyer*.

Meg turns to Young Guy. "Can't you see that he's using you?"

"He's not the one who exposed us. You are."

The doctor-type holding Meg's other arm says, "Right. And now that people and the cops know about us, it isn't safe to be a vampire."

As if it ever was?

Meg says, "But you *can* have your old life back. You can be people again if you help me get elected. I'll protect your rights."

Young Guy snorts. "People like me didn't really have rights before. For a long time, we couldn't even marry each other."

Meg protests. "But you can now! That shows you laws can be changed."

Doc shakes her head. "Besides, we like following the Dark Path, spreading terror and drinking blood in the depths of the night."

Shades of Lester. The old Lester, that is, before Seiko came along.

Young Guy says, "And you're taking all that away."

Meg tilts her head toward Tom. "But this guy is campaigning, too. He'll expose you even more. *He's a vampire!*"

Doc says, "You've already let the cat out of the bag."

Patch squirms in her arms. "Mrf." Was that because she mentioned a cat or because of the cliché?

Doc continues. "And Tom promises he'll get the cops to leave us alone after he's elected."

"You're trusting a lawyer's promise?"

"You've got a point there," says Young Guy.

Tom raises his hands. "That's enough of this. Of course I'll keep my promise." He reaches for Patch. "I'll take Patch with me. I'll say I rescued him. Good sympathy vote."

Patch takes a breath, hisses, and raises both front paws, claws extended. Tom stops.

"On the other hand, I don't want to go around for the rest of my death with wounds that won't heal. Patch will just have to take the stake too."

Young Guy says, "Hey, not the kitty-cat."

Meg is warming to Young Guy. Patch gives him his wide-eyed look. For good measure, he adds a questioning, "Mrrr?"

Doc says, "Yeah. The kitty-cat didn't out us."

Tom's voice has a hint of desperation in it. "What's the matter with you people? I thought you liked ravaging the innocent."

"People, sure. But not kitty-cats."

Patch would think that was the right priority.

Tom shakes his head. "Why couldn't I have found dog-lover vampires?"

Young Guy smiles at Patch. "Doc, you hold her and I'll take care of Patch."

Doc reaches around and grips Meg's other arm. Young Guy lets go and puts his hands around Patch's chest.

Meg looks down at him. "Go with them, Patch. You'll be okay."

Young Guy pulls at Patch, but he digs all four sets of claws into Meg's shirt and hangs on. Young Guy tugs, and then releases him. "He doesn't want to go. Now what?"

Tom smiles. "The stake."

A grandpa holds a stake out to Tom.

He takes it, stands next to Patch and Meg, holds it in the air.

Tom says, "Who wants to be the first to stake this traitor?"

Dead silence.

Tom says, "Well, it's not going to be me. I'm no barbarian."

Doc scowls. "You're saying we are?"

"No, no, of course not. You're my friends and voters. I've just never used actual violence. I'm more like management. I delegate."

Doc says, "Well, this time, since you're the guy who got us all riled up, I think you need to do your part." A little old lady holds a hammer out to Tom.

Tom shrugs. "Well, a lawyer's gotta do what a lawyer's gotta do." He takes the hammer and places the point of the stake over Meg's heart.

Ernie steps closer, and it's so quiet that Meg hears the small sound of his camera lens zooming in for a close-up.

A big voice calls from the far side of the crowd. "Hold!"

Young Guy looks up. "Lestat?"

Yes!

As heads turn, Seiko sails through the air and lands between Tom and Meg. She grabs the hammer from Tom and hits his stake-holding hand with it, knocking the stake out of his grip.

Lester says, "Make way," and the vampires part, leaving a clear path between Meg and a magnificent, seven-foot, black-clad savior. Vera stands a step behind him, packing her cowboy pistol.

Greetings pepper Lester as they stride toward Meg and Patch.

"Yo, Lestat."

"Master!"

"You're back!"

Just a step behind him, Vera evokes hisses and boos, but the feral vees keep their distance when the barrel of her gun swings their way. Seiko says, "We're going to get you out of this."

Meg can't help but smile down at her optimistic friend. Then she looks up at Lester. He actually gives her real hope of surviving.

The crowd fills in behind them.

Young Guy grins and says, "Welcome back, Lestat."

But Doc looks grim. "You back on the wild side? Or still copping out with"—she nods at Vera—"turncoats to the true way."

Lester looms in the way only he can loom, like a bipedal skyscraper. "You are calling me a traitor?"

To give Doc credit, she hardly cowers. "You're the guy who isn't around anymore. You're the one who's clean."

Meg says, "Who's the traitor? Aren't you a traitor to yourself?"

Doc stiffens. "I follow the vampire way."

"You're the same person you were before you got bitten." Meg's voice hardens. "You weren't living in the dirt, running around attacking people and drinking blood. You were *healing* people. That's who you are. So who's the traitor?"

Lester nods. "What she says." He wraps an arm around Seiko and pulls her close. "Seiko made me realize that I'm still a man, and there's a life for me beyond childish play in the dirt."

Young Guy brushes at a smudge on his chest, and Meg catches other vampires looking each other over, tidying their clothing, swiping at dirt streaks. Young Guy says, "Yeah. I still like kitty-cats."

Meg turns to Doc. "What about you? Don't you still like medicine?"

She chews on her lip and gazes into the distance, then looks to Meg and nods. "Sure. But what's there for me to do? I can't work on breathers for fear I'll contaminate them, and vees sure don't need group health."

Lester points to the furrows of raw flesh on his neck, the parallel rows Patch ripped into him with his claws. "What about these? Maybe you could figure out a way for us to do some healing? Or at least cover up wounds."

Not a bad idea. After all, the initial bite wound heals, it's just later that healing is a problem.

Doc's gaze focuses on Lester's neck. She frowns. "Hmm. I wonder ..." She releases Meg's arms and says to Vera, "Will the A.V.A. set me up with a place to work?"

"With pleasure."

Young Guy gives Patch a stroke on his back. "I think maybe I could get my old night shift job back at the Bloomsburg Turkish Baths."

Lively conversation, a rare item in a crowd of people who don't inhale all that much, breaks out among the vees. They split up and begin to wander off in groups of two or three. Meg sees a lot of smiles. "I can't thank you enough, Lester, Seiko."

He shrugs. "Let's just get you elected."

Tom says, "Well, time for me to hit the campaign trail." He starts off, but Lester grips his neck with one major hand and lifts Tom off the ground.

"Behold, traitor, one little twist and you'll be dropping out of the race." He grins. "Voters don't like people who won't look them in the eye."

Seiko frowns. "You're not."

"Aw, come on, Seiko. This jerk tried to get Meg and Patch staked."

Seiko turns to Meg. "Meg?"

Patch gives a bright meow that can only mean "do it."

"I know how you feel, Patch." She shakes her head. "But it's gotta be fair and square."

Lester drops Tom, who says, "Ha! Loser." He turns to what's left of the crowd. "A vote for me is a vote for jobs!"

A huge gasp comes when, as one, the gathered vampires take in a breath. Meg grins when that's followed by a sustained "BOOOOOOOOOOOO."

Tom pushes his way through them, arms up, shielding his head as stakes bounce off of him.

Followed by Ernie, Ginger cuts through the crowd to Meg. Meg holds up her hands. "If you want an interview, can we make it later? I'm beat."

"That's okay. We got footage for a great vampires-versus-vampires' story." She starts to turn away, but then turns back to Meg, "By the way, we heard on the radio on the way here that you've really dropped in the polls. Papa has already flooded TV with commercials praising the lawyer as a vampire savior and a true law-and-order candidate. Your pitiful lack of name recognition alone is going to kill you. So to speak."

No money. No backers. Steamrollered in the media by Papa. Nowhere in the polls. Can it get worse?

She can't imagine how.

38: Meg

Meg sets Patch down on her sofa, relieved to be back home safe and sound, and heads for the bathroom. A shower is priority number one. As steam fills the bathroom, even though sensation is dulled this long after feeding, the hot water still feels great.

She towels off, pulls on jeans and a T-shirt with "Do not inter" on it, and goes to the kitchen. A deep ache of blood hunger simmers in her belly.

She ends up searching the apartment and finds only two leftover Death Savers. Damn. She gives one to Patch and then picks him up. "We need to stock up on V1 so we can just curl up on the couch and take a time-out. I want some peace and quiet. Want to go with?"

Patch headbutts her. She grabs her purse and they're off.

Meg turns the corner onto the street that goes to the A.V.A. building and cries out when a wooden stake bounces off of her windshield. Maybe twenty people march on the sidewalk across from the A.V.A. building, carrying tiki torches. They wave wooden stakes and chant, "Death to vampires!" And her top is down. A second stake flies through the air toward them and bounces off the back of Patch's seat.

The garage doors into the parking in the basement of the building are open, two beefy guys flanking the entrance.

She swervesand the hits the accelerator, They hurtle into the underground parking.

The mob stays across the street, still yelling and shaking fists and stakes at them.

She parks, gives Patch a stroke down his back, and then pries his front claws out of the passenger seat. Even though she's got the shakes a little herself, she manages to say, "Hey, we're okay, partner."

Patch lets out a low growl.

Meg says, "Me, too." She goes around to the passenger door, takes a handful of Meg & Patch campaign buttons from the box Tom gave her, puts them in her purse, and picks Patch up. "Let's go see Vera. And then get a supply of V1."

The elevator doors close and cut off the mob's chant.

On the top floor, a worker directs Meg to a corner office, and she finds Vera's name on a brass plate that declares "Director" on the wall beside the door. It looks new.

Inside, Vera is at a desk, watching a big-screen TV on a wall opposite her. It shows the vampire mob scene from the A.V.A.

Ginger's voiceover tops the crowd noise as the image shows Tom holding the wooden stake against Meg's chest. "Today vampire candidate Tom Conway explored a unique way to eliminate his vampire competition."

Meg says, "Ugh."

Vera turns to her, shuts off the television, and smiles big. "Hey, Meg. You, too, Patch. C'mere and give me a purr."

Patch obliges when Vera scratches behind his ears. She says to Meg, "Did the crazies out there give you any trouble?"

Meg sits in a chair facing the desk, settling Patch in her lap. "A little, but they stayed across the street. I guess they're my fault." Remembering the flying stakes, alarm jolts her. "Tell me nobody's been hurt!"

"Not yet. We've hired breather guards for during the day, and at night most of the nutjobs give up at dinnertime." She chuckles. "Around midnight, a bunch of us runs at whoever's left, yelling 'Blood. Blood. Blood.' Man, do they ever skedaddle."

Meg shakes her head. "I'm so sorry. I sure didn't anticipate anything like those—"

"Comes with the territory, I guess. We just have to live ... er ... get through it."

Meg takes in the spaciousness of the office. "So you got promoted?"

Vera shrugs. "What with all the uproar since we were outed, nobody else would take the job."

"Congratulations ... I think." Meg fishes her campaign buttons out of her purse and puts them on the desk. "Uh, would you consider handing these out?"

"Sure." Vera pins one to her blouse. "We here at the A.V.A. are totally behind you. How's the campaign going for you and our favorite vampire kitty-cat?" She skritches his chin.

"With no money, I don't have any idea how to get the word out, much less run a commercial." She squares her shoulders and lifts her chin. "But we're still going to beat them."

"I'll pass the hat here, but that won't amount to much. We'll do our best, and we'll vote."

"You're a friend, Vera." Meg stands. "I also need to buy some V1 juice."

"We'll make a case our first donation to your campaign." She gets up and goes to her office door. "Bruce! Can use a little help here." She turns to Meg. "He'll carry it down to your car for you."

When Bruce arrives, he smiles at Patch and reaches out to run a humongous hand down his back. "Kitty."

Patch gives him a big purr.

In the garage, Bruce sets the case of V1 in the trunk of Meg's car and Vera puts Patch on the passenger seat. She goes to Meg, glances out at the mob noise coming from the street, and gives her a hug. "Stay safe. Lock up."

"You bet." Meg puts the top up on her car. After a goodbye wave to Vera and Bruce in the elevator, she gets in, rolls up her windows, and locks the doors before she starts her car. But when she exits the parking garage, the Devils across the street rush her. She turns down the street, but a half dozen protesters get in front of her. She can't run people down, so she stops.

The mob surrounds her, chanting "Death to vampires." They rock the car, and she grabs Patch and clutches him to her.

A wooden stake stabs through her convertible top and misses her face by an inch. She honks her horn and tries to ease forward, but more people crowd in front of her.

A protester hammers on her door window with a stake. It's safety glass, so it won't shatter, right?

Four bulky protesters squat down on her side of the car and start to lift. Her little Miata tips up, and up, and up—

A big black Hummer rolls up beside her, knocking the protesters away, some falling to the pavement, one sliding across her hood. Her car drops to the pavement, and the fallen men get up and join the chanters as they form a circle around the Hummer. Their shouts are deafening. Meg holds Patch even tighter.

The Hummer's front passenger door opens, and a very big man gets out and stands between her car and his. It's

Giles. He pulls a gun from inside his suit coat and fires a shot into the air.

The crowd noise drops to zero. Even with her window closed, she can hear Giles say, "The next bullet goes into whoever is still standing here by the time I count to five. One ..."

As if all of them were controlled by the same brain—not that she thinks any of them have one—the crowd races away, except for three of the lifters, who limp away.

Meg takes a deep breath and sighs. Thank goodness for big guys with guns. At least in this case.

Giles raps on her car window with his knuckles. She rolls it down and says, "Oh, thank you, Giles."

"Get out."

That doesn't seem like a good idea with crazed mobs and a gun around. "Thanks, but no thanks, I've got to get me and Patch home." She starts to roll the window up, but he reaches in, hits the door lock knob to unlock the door, and yanks it open.

Giles grabs her arm and hauls her and Patch out. "Stay calm and I won't have to hurt you." He opens the rear door of the Hummer and calls out to a little guy in the driver's seat, "Get ready to lock up, Miles. We have guests."

Miles and Giles? What are the odds?

Miles turns and watches, his eyes too close together in a narrow face, his gaze cold and nasty.

Giles shoves her into the car with such force that she slides across to the other side. She drops Patch on the seat before Giles can get the door shut and shouts, "Run, Patch!"

He glances at the open door, then stands beside her. Giles slams the door shut and gets into the front seat. Locks snick closed. Meg tries the door handle, but nothing happens.

Damned child safety locks.

Giles turns to face her and Meg lunges forward, lashing at him with her fists. She stops when he aims his pistol at her heart. "Papa said to make you disappear until after the election. It's up to you whether you survive until then or end it here and now." He shifts his aim to Patch, who now stands on the far side of the rear seat. "I wouldn't mind getting rid of Hairball immediately if you don't cooperate."

She settles back. "Okay. I'm cooperating."

"Put your seat belt on."

She obliges.

"Now hold your hands out."

She does that.

He snaps handcuffs on her wrists and then says to Miles, "That should hold her until we get to the house." He opens his door. "I'll follow you in her car." He looks back at her. "Don't want no missing vampire reports going out, do we?" Giles gets out and Miles sends a sneer Meg's way.

She pets Patch as well as she can with handcuffed hands. "Oh, Patch, you should have run."

He butts his head against her arm and says, "Mrrowf." Then he curls up in her lap.

The Hummer moves forward, taking them to their disappearance.

39: Patch and Meg

Meg clutches me to her as Giles pulls her out of the back seat of the Hummer. We've stopped in a circular drive that curls in front of a huge house with four colonial columns. Meg's little green car is parked behind the Hummer. Miles comes around and leads the way inside, and Giles tows Meg and me by her arm.

Meg twists and looks back at her car and then says to Giles, "We need our, er, food. It's in my trunk."

Hauling them into a foyer that's so big their footsteps on the marble floor echo-echo-echo, Giles says, "Don't worry about that, we'll order some pizza in."

I growl loud enough to get his attention. He smirks at me. "What, you don't like pizza? You more like Garfield the cat and his love for lasagna?"

Miles sniggers at that.

Meg says, "We can't eat solid food."

"Oh, yeah. You're supposed to be vampires." He peers at her. "Are you guys really vampires? Don't see no fangs."

I hiss, big-time. Miles flinches back.

"Okay, now I see fangs."

Giles hauls Meg and me down a hall that goes to the back of the house. We stop at a door with a ten-inch window in it, and there's a latch and a padlock on the outside.

Giles raps on the door with his knuckles and grins at us. "Steel." He taps the window. "Shatterproof. Papa thinks of everything."

He opens the door and flings us inside. An old-fashioned wooden rocker, a small table and chair, and a bed are all there is for furniture. A window has bars on it. Miles goes to the window and closes the curtains.

Giles says, "You keep quiet and you'll be fine."

"This is kidnapping."

Catnapping, too, and not the sleepy variety. I hop down from Meg's arms. Giles mostly blocks the doorway, so I'm not going to get out just yet.

Meg holds her hands out. "Take these off? Please?"

He shakes his head. "Nope, Boss said to take no chances with you."

"But ... our food!"

"So you'll lose a little weight."

No, we'll lose a little everything. I shudder at the memory of the prophet Bobson's disgusting demise.

Meg says, "No, you don't under—"

Giles slams the door shut behind him.

She sits in the rocker. "Oh, Patch. What have I gotten us into?"

There's only one possible answer to that.

Deep shit.

It's maybe an hour later when Patch jumps from Meg's lap and starts pacing. She's surprised by him ending a petting session voluntarily. But the surprise fades when the beginning of blood hunger kindles in her belly. The Death Savers are wearing off. That's why he can't sit still. "Oh, no."

She hurries to the door and pounds on it. "Help! Help!"

Her hammering and cries stop when Giles's voice comes from outside. "Quit the racket. We're having lunch."

"We need food!"

"You like pepperoni?"

"No. I mean yes, I do, I did, but we can't. Get the special food that's in my car. Without it, we'll go—"

"Maybe later—we're busy."

She hammers and hollers until the door is shoved open, sending her staggering back to land on the bed.

Giles comes in, scowling and aiming his gun at her. "You be quiet and quit this crap or we're gonna tie you up and stuff a gag in your mouth."

Patch hisses at him. The gun swings his way and Giles says, "Same goes for you. I'd do you right now, but my pizza's getting cold."

Meg shouts, "You'll kill us!"

Giles chuckles. "I thought you were sorta dead already. So what's the big deal?"

Papa's voice comes from down the hall. "Hey now, what's all the yellin'?" He appears in the doorway and then steps in front of Giles. "Are y'all taking good care of our guests? They've been all over the news since that interview, gettin' a lot of positive comments." He chuckles. "Especially from people who hate yappy dogs."

Meg says, "He won't give us our food."

"Food? You mean blood?"

She hates to admit that she's blood-dependent, but she has to say yes. She rubs her belly. The pain is rising, but she's still in control. Patch paces, but that's all. So far.

Papa puffs on his cigar. "You know, it's not too late to switch horses, considering how well pretty little y'all and that cat go over with voters. I could still get behind you. Conway

will drop out if I threaten to cut off my lawyerin' business."
He chuckles. "Which I might do anyway if he doesn't win the
election—never cottoned to that man. He's a double-crosser,
can't be trusted. So, are y'all ready to go along and let me
help you with your campaign?"

She shakes her head. "We're not for sale."

Patch rubs against Papa's legs.

Papa kicks, but Patch is too quick and is instantly across
the room. Papa sneezes. His face turns red as he says, "I'll
leave you be for now because I think I might need that mangy
cat in case y'all change your mind, but the second I don't ..."
He trails off and sends a new cloud of smoke at Meg.

Meg raises her cuffed hands. "Please. Let me out of these
and give us the V1 that's in my car."

"Did I hear right? You might, as they say, expire without
it?"

"Most horribly."

"When? How long's it take?"

Meg's shoulders slump. He's not going to go along. "I
don't know. I'm new at this."

Papa smiles. "Well now, I think that's somethin' worth
knowing. We'll just let y'all stew a while and see what
happens."

"But why? We can't hurt you."

"This could give me leverage over a vampire night shift
at the factory. I'll promise them free blood and then lock 'em
in and hold it back to make sure they're working as hard as
they can."

Meg swings her cuffed hands at Papa, but Giles reaches
past him and grabs her fists with one huge hand. She says
to Papa, "You monster." Giles shoves. She stumbles back and
lands on the bed. Patch comes to her and she cuddles him.

Papa chuckles. "Monster? Oh, no. According to our dear departed friend Prophet Bobson, it's y'all who are the monsters. What is it he called you? Abominations?" He backs out of the room and tells Giles, "No food for now. Check every hour and see what happens. Call me if anything changes, I'll be upstairs in my study."

Giles scowls. "And if they, ah, die?"

Papa shrugs. "Who will ever know? We'll just add their remains to the backyard. We've got lots of room left." He checks his watch and studies Meg. He says to Giles, "If it looks like they're going to ... I guess *die* isn't the right word. If they're gonna turn into puddles or something, give them their food."

"What if we don't get 'em their stuff in time?"

"Just make sure you note the time so we'll know how long it takes."

They leave and the door closes. A pain stabs her gut, Patch yowls, and she hugs him to her.

They don't have long.

Meg says to me, "Oh, Patch, I'm so sorry." Yeah, she should be sorry, her being the sole reason my belly hurts and I'm about to disintegrate. The best she can do is *sorry*? I hiss at her and squirm out of her grip and jump to the floor. She says, "You're right."

I pace, walking to keep the throbbing and burning of blood hunger under control. I don't know what will happen if I don't feed soon, but what I saw the lack of blood do to Bobson suggests that it will be unpleasant and highly terminal.

She wraps her arms around herself, her eyes wide as she scans the blank walls. Her voice quivers when she says to Patch, "I'm so scared."

Dang. She's hurting, and I don't like that. After all, she did save my tail, literally. I hop back up on the bed and give her a headbutt.

"Oh, Patch, I don't know how much longer I can stand the pain. I want to scream, but I don't want to give them an advantage over us."

Give them an advantage? They already have it.

Motion at the door catches my eye—Giles looks in the little window. I stop my pacing and growl.

He holds up a bottle of V1 juice and taps it on the window. "Hey, looky what I found."

Meg hurtles to the door and shouts, "Give us that!"

Giles shakes his head. "Don't think so."

She pounds on the door. Where she hits, the metal door dents. She grabs her stomach and doubles over in pain. A loud moan escapes her, a sound not far from being a scream.

Giles smiles.

I leap at the window. Ordinarily I wouldn't be able to get there from across a room, but I don't care, I'm pissed. I zoom through the air and slam into the door, my front paws hitting the window.

The inside pane cracks, and Giles falls back, loosing a loud yelp. I drop to the floor and stare at the window. He peers in again and I crouch. He gives me the finger and vanishes.

Meg feels the crack in the glass. "Wow. Look what you did." Then she slides her hand over the dent she made in the door.

She grabs the doorknob and yanks. It rips out of the door, screws and parts scattering across the floor.

She gapes at the doorknob in her hand. Her eyes widen, then she smiles. "Patch, remember what Sammy told us about getting stronger when the blood hunger hits?"

I do. We have a superpower? But only when we're about to self-destruct? That's messed up.

Meg says, "I think I'm there." She puts her fingers to the cracked window glass. "You, too."

She holds up her hands and gazes at the handcuffs, then scans the room. Going to the bed, she yanks the mattress off, revealing a metal frame. She grins. "That might work." Meg slips the handcuffs under one of the legs and then pulls them up so that they rest against the frame. She puts a foot on it, braces herself, and yanks the cuffs up. "Ow."

Meg yanks once more, even harder this time, and one of the links in the chain breaks and she staggers back.

With her hands now free, she faces the door. She shifts her foot back. Then she kicks it high in the air in front of her. Then she does it again. This is no time to be dancing. I say, "Mrrrow!"

She gives me a glance. "That's the Krav Maga front kick. Get ready, Patch, we're going to rock and roll!"

She steps closer to the door, rears back, and kicks it.

The door slams open into the hallway. Meg's glad the door is metal; otherwise, she would be standing there with her foot stuck through it. Her wrists hurt from the handcuffs, but she ignores it. Being really, really pissed helps.

She charges out and turns down the hall toward the front. A tricolored flash, Patch races past her. She calls out, "Don't bite anybody!" Not that Patch listens to her, but she doesn't want any new bad-guy vampires running around.

When she gets to the dining room. Giles and Miles are just standing up from the table, a large pepperoni pizza in the middle missing half its pieces. Her case of V1 juice sits next to the pizza box, along with her phone and her car keys.

Patch runs up the front of Giles's body to the top of his head, spins, and then digs all four sets of claws into his scalp. Giles roars and reaches for Patch.

Miles is quicker than Giles, and he yanks out a gun from a shoulder holster. Here's hoping all that Krav Maga training in disarming a shooter works.

He straightens his arm and points the pistol right at Meg. It's in his right hand.

Perfect.

It's like he's moving in slow motion and she's not.

She swings her left hand and puts her fingers on the side of the gun. She pushes it to the right, bringing her left shoulder forward.

Then she closes her hand around the pistol, her weight now directly over it. She pushes it down and away.

Stepping in with her left foot, she moves the gun farther away from herself and traps it and Miles's hand between their bodies. With her right hand, she punches Miles in the nose.

When his head jerks back, she adds her right hand to her grip on the gun, twists it even farther away. His finger is in the trigger guard, and she feels the snap of a bone. Miles screams.

She yanks the gun free, steps back, doubles her fist, and delivers a roundhouse hammer blow to Miles's temple. He drops to the floor and doesn't move.

Meg whirls and finds Giles prancing in pain, trying to pull Patch off of his head. He yowls in pain when he rips Patch off and throws him away. Patch flips, lands on his feet, and then charges. He leaps at Giles and sinks his four sets of claws into Giles's crotch.

Giles screams and doubles over, which puts his head in a perfect position for Meg to deliver a punch to his temple. Just as Miles did, he drops and sprawls on his back.

Man, that temple punch sure works, although she's a little surprised that they'd actually had enough brains to bounce around in their skulls and cause them to black out. They should be down for plenty of time to get away. She drops Miles's pistol on the table. Fishing through Giles's pockets, she finds the handcuff key and gets the cuffs off her wrists. God, she'd hated the trapped and helpless feeling they'd given her.

The blood hunger pain, forgotten in the rush of action, roars back. Patch has to be feeling the same, since he jumps onto Giles's chest and lunges for his throat, fangs ready.

Meg shouts, "No!" and grabs him. She bowls him into the kitchen with her superstrength, and he zooms all the way to the far end. He bounces off the wall and immediately scrambles to run back, but his clawed feet slip on the tile.

She snatches a bottle of V1 from the case, wrenches the top off, and pours a pancake-sized pool on the kitchen floor just as Patch gets to her. He slides to a stop and starts lapping the blood up. Meg takes a big gulp from the bottle.

The cabinets have glass-front doors, and it takes seconds to find a bowl, put it on the floor beside Patch, and pour V1 into it. Relief from her first drink begins easing the pain, and she chugs the rest of the bottle. With a sigh, she ruffles Patch's back. "Sorry about grabbing you, partner, but we don't need any more huge, nasty vampires running around."

Patch looks up, says "Mrf," and continues lapping.

Meg sits at the dining-room table while post-blood lassitude settles in, and she wallows in the pleasure of it while smirking down at unconscious Miles and dead-to-the world Giles.

Papa thought he was going to stop her? Ha.

Papa Gambino's voice comes from upstairs. "Hey, what's all the ruckus down there? Giles?"

She shakes off her lethargy and picks up the pistol. She calls out, "Just having a little lunch."

Footsteps clatter down stairs and Papa bursts into the dining room. "What're you doin' outta your room?"

Patch leaps onto the table, and she runs her hand down his back. He butts her forearm, and she smiles. "I'm giving serious thought to escaping."

Papa scans his men, out cold, then turns to Meg. "Did you hurt my boys?"

"I sure hope so."

He raises his hands and starts for her, his stare fixed on her neck. "Why, you little—"

Meg stands and puts the barrel of the gun on his forehead. He drops his hands, then backs up a couple of steps.

"Little what?"

He gestures to Giles and Miles. "How about hellcat?"

"I like the sound of that." She puts her phone and keys into her pockets, then lifts the box of V1 juice. Umph, it's heavy. Apparently, the superstrength from blood hunger doesn't last. She wiggles the gun that she still holds aimed at Papa. "Get the door."

He nudges Giles with his foot. "Get up and help the little lady out." Giles just moans. Papa shrugs and opens the front door.

Meg says, "Come on, Patch, we've got an election to win." Patch hops down from the table and trots out ahead of her.

As she follows, Papa says, "I just got a new poll this morning. My man is way ahead of you and closing in on the cop candidate. Y'all are dead in the water." He chuckles at his witticism.

The door slams behind her as she and Patch head for her car.

"Patch, we're gonna go down fighting." She turns and glares at Papa's big house. "And that son of a bitch isn't going to get away with this."

40: Meg

After they settle in her car, Meg searches her phone for the Mallan County sheriff's office on her phone. It's after ten p.m., but the law ought to be there. She scrolls down until she finds ...

Hours
Monday–Friday
8:30 am–4:30 pm

"Great. So you're out of luck if you're kidnapped and assaulted any other time." She searches for the Bloomsburg police department's hours and at the top of the search results page is ...

Open 24 hours

That's more like it. She gets the address and soon they're on their way to accuse the town's most prominent citizen of felony crimes. What could go wrong?

The front of police headquarters is all glass, with two big glass doors as the entrance. Floodlights make the outside look like daytime with black-and-whites parked out front, the sidewalk and cars exposed by the light, and uniformed cops stream in and out of the front doors. It makes sense that the police would be open 24/7. Maybe it would be a good place for vees to work.

When she is sheriff, she'll be ready to help people 24/7, and she'll hire vee deputies for the night shift.

When she gets closer, her view of the entrance is blocked by a cluster of people carrying "Cook for Sheriff" signs. Well, that's okay, it's a free country. She just has to change their minds.

When she drives past them, looking for a parking place, the Cook supporters are chanting "Death to vampires."

She gives Patch a look. He's staring out his window at them. It's almost as if he understands what they're doing.

He turns to face her and hits her with a low growl.

Apparently, they're on the same page. She likes that about Patch.

Meg finds a parking place on the street and digs her sunglasses out of the glove compartment. She's always thought that people who wear sunglasses indoors are weird. Not so much anymore. And, with what looks like vampire hunters in front of the station, she sure doesn't want to be recognized, what with her being on TV a lot.

She digs through laundry in the back seat that hasn't made it to the laundromat yet—hey, she's been busy being killed and kidnapped and stuff—and finds her favorite hoodie, black with a Heart logo on it in silver and a big pouch on the front.

She pulls it on over her head and gets out. Patch puts his paws up on the window and meows. What the heck, she can stuff most of him into the pouch of her sweatshirt.

Patch resists until she lulls him with a scratch session under his chin. He's chilled out enough to get all but his head and tail into the pouch.

Her head down, her hood up, and her sunglasses on, she steps through the crowd of Cook supporters.

"Death to vampires."

Patch flexes his claws, and they poke her tummy. She pats him on the outside of the pouch, and he eases up on the claws.

There's something familiar about a curly haired woman ahead who holds a sign that says "Captain Cook. My Hero."

The woman focuses on Meg as she nears her, and then her gaze drops down. She points and says, "Hey, isn't that the cat? The vampire cat?"

It's the woman from the 7-Eleven that Patch chased out of the store.

Meg covers the distinctive markings on Patch's face with her hand and hurries, lengthening her strides and shouldering past the woman.

The woman points and shouts, "That's her! It's the vampires!"

The crowd surges toward Meg, but she hits the front door and is quickly inside. The crowd pulls up outside. The woman's voice comes. "We'll be here all night. See you later."

She and the others go back to milling in front of the station. Their chant is softened by the closed door, but "Death to vampires" still comes through.

Going straight to the big desk with an officer behind it, Meg says, "I want to report a kidnapping and an assault with a deadly weapon."

The guy doesn't react, his eyes dulled as if his brain is on vacation. He points at Patch. "Animals are not allowed."

"This is my service cat. When I have an anxiety attack, his purr helps me." She leans forward. "Like it did when I was *kidnapped!*"

That finally gets the guy's attention. His eyes widen, and he picks up a pencil and poises it over a pad of paper. "I'm Sergeant Anderson. Tell me, who was kidnapped? Who was assaulted?"

"I was. Meg Murrow." She eases Patch out of the pouch and supports him with one arm. "And my cat, too. Patch."

Patch adds, "Mrrow!"

The sergeant says, "How can you be kidnapped if you're standing here?"

This should be obvious, but she keeps the sarcasm out of her voice. "I escaped."

He nods. "Mm-hmm. And who—"

"Papa Gambino."

The sergeant's eyes widen again, and he puts the pencil down. He sighs. "I see. Mister Gambino, who happens to contribute heavily to the Policemen's Benevolent and Protective Association?"

This is not going well. She swallows, but stands up as straight as she can, shoulders back. "That's the one. His men threatened me with a gun, too."

The sergeant glances at a group of people off to the side of the big lobby. Captain Cook is visible as he faces a handheld CNN video camera.

The sergeant points at Meg. "Wait a minute. You're the alleged vampire running for sheriff."

She nods. "Me and my cat. We were kidnapped to take us out of the primary so Papa's candidate will win."

The sergeant proves to be a master of mockery. "I'm sure he did just that." He steps out from the desk and says, "If you'll just wait here a minute."

He goes to Captain Cook and interrupts the interview. Cook looks her way and smiles. It has all the warmth of a pit viper.

Just Meg's luck he's on duty tonight. She says, "Damn."

Patch growls.

The CNN cameraman turns to face them, and she's surprised to see Ernie focusing on her and Patch. The reporter turns as well, and it's Ginger Grant. Her mike has a CNN logo on it.

Trailing the sergeant, Ginger, and Ernie, Captain Cook come to Meg and Patch. Once again, the captain towers over her. She gets so weary of the size advantage that most men have over her. That and their tendency to think that makes them the more powerful.

Captain Cook shows his teeth. "Well, Miz Murrow and her famous kitty-cat." He reaches out to scratch Patch's back. "Spot, isn't it?"

Patch shoots out a paw, claws fully extended. The captain yanks his hand back. He levels a sharp-bladed gaze at Meg. "I'm tempted to call Animal Control on it. He is clearly dangerous and hostile."

Patch retracts his claws but keeps his paw ready to strike. He adds a growl, and Cook eases back a half step.

Meg says, "I'm not here about politics, Captain, I'm here to report a kidnapping and assault with a deadly weapon."

He glances at the sergeant, who nods. "By Papa Gambino?"

"Well, he didn't do the actual kidnapping and assaulting. His man, Giles, did the dirty work. But Gambino was there! He told them to lock me—us—up in a room with bars in the window."

A buzz of voices comes from the front of the lobby as Papa Gambino enters, his man Giles right behind him. Captain Cook gives a wave, and Papa comes to them. Ernie tracks his progress with his camera. Giles has a bruise on one temple and a glare for Meg.

Gambino sticks out his hand, and the captain shakes it. Ginger holds the mike close to them.

Cook says, "So good to see you, sir. And many thanks for your generous donation to my campaign."

It's Meg's turn to sigh. Her shoulders slump.

Papa turns his nasty gaze on her. He points with a stubby finger. "This ... this *person* and her animal invaded my home tonight and threatened me. I want her arrested."

The captain gazes at the CNN camera, a mute witness to the goings-on, including Meg's accusations. He turns to Papa. "That is a serious charge, Mr. Gambino. But she has accused you of kidnapping her. And her cat."

Papa's face reddens, but he keeps his voice calm. "That's absurd. Arrest them."

The captain checks the camera again, and it's still aimed at him. He nods to Papa and says, "I sympathize with you, Mr. Gambino, but at this point it looks like a case of he-said she-said. I promise you I will investigate this with the full force of my office when I am elected sheriff."

Meg says, "But he—"

Cook holds up a palm to her face. "We are not going to politicize your crimes." He spins and marches away, going through a door at the rear and disappearing down a hallway.

When the door closes behind him, Papa leans close to Meg. Ernie steps closer. Papa shoves the camera away and whispers, "I will ruin you."

He turns and leaves, Giles running interference as they go out the front door. "Death to vampires" slips through before the door closes. The crowd has grown, and it surrounds the exit.

41: Patch

Meg strokes my head. "Don't worry, we're gonna get him." She looks to Ginger. "CNN? Congratulations. I thought you'd lost your job."

"Oh, KTBC fired us right after Papa Gambino bought the station." With a smile something like the one a cat gets when it figures out how to open the canary's cage, Grant says, "CNN caught my broadcast of Bobson's, er, demise, and now I'm their expert reporter on vampires."

Ernie clears his throat. Grant glances at him. Her smile drops away. "Okay, *we're* the experts on vampires."

He looks at Meg and grins, then raises his hand for a high five. "We're national now. Gambino can't stop you from getting your message out."

Meg gives him the five and then tells Grant, "I'm ready. Let's find a place to talk." She holds me to her chest, cradled just the way I like. "Patch, we're on our way."

I like the sound of that. And with national press coverage, what could go wrong?

"Death to vampires."

But first, we have to get out of here. As Meg stares at the crowd beyond the glass doors, Ginger says, "Maybe there's a back door."

Sounds like a great idea to me.

But Meg shakes her head. "I'm not going to be pushed around anymore. We're going out the front door."

Ernie, bless him, says, "No, no, you should escape out the back."

"Escape? I'm a citizen, and I have every right to come and go at *my* police station. Come on, Patch."

Temptation to leap from her arms has me tensing. It's feeling like a good time for an escape. She tightens her grip as if she knows what I'm thinking.

Grant says to Ernie, "Let's get out front, then. This'll make the national news tomorrow."

Ernie leads the way, Grant shoving him from behind. Her expression is like that of a cat with its eyes on a fat mouse. Meg follows, but then stops when they exit. I figure she's giving them time to get into position.

I guess the publicity will be helpful. If we survive, that is. As much as I like having a camera focused on me, my preference is survival. Somewhere here there's a rear exit that would save my furry hide.

But no, Meg tightens her grip on me again and heads for the front door.

She says to me, "Patch, we're done with mobs and threats. We're going to threaten them right back."

I have to admit I like the sound of that. I extend my front paws and release my claws.

Meg says, "Yes! You've got the idea, buddy. I'm going to hold you up in front of me and we're going to show them your claws and our fangs."

Okay, I have fangs. But what's she going to use?

The Cook crowd backs away as we come out the door, but they still encircle us. Some of them wave long, sharp stakes in the air.

Ernie and Grant record from the side. Her lips move, but I can't make out what she's saying. Probably something about an exclusive on the murder of a vampire kitty-cat.

Meg calls out to the crowd, "Your stakes are lethal to me and my friend—"

"Death to vampires," the crowd roars. A couple of them take a step forward.

"But have you ever considered that my bite and my partner's fangs are lethal to you?"

Murmurs rise in the crowd.

Meg raises me above her head and holds me facing the crowd, her fingers around my chest just under my front legs. "Well, you're about to find out!"

She charges them, holding me out front, screaming, "YAAAAAAHHHHHH ..."

I extend my claws, open my mouth wide, and add a YOWLLLLL to her YAAAAAAHHHHHH ...

Moses didn't have anything on Meg for parting things.

42: Patch

The next night, after spending a comfortable day recuperating in Meg's apartment, Meg and I go to Vera's office at the A.V.A. Vera wears a "Vote for Meg & Patch" campaign button.

Meg points at it. "That's kind of useless now, isn't it?"

Vera shakes her head. "Not unless you're quitting."

Meg shrugs and points at a newspaper on Vera's desk. "Anything in there about me?"

I say, "Mrf?"

She scratches me behind the ears and sets me on the desk. "I mean, us."

Much better.

"You're included, but Captain Cook is in the lead. Your lawyer pal is in second place."

Meg's face saddens, and her mouth turns down at the corners. "It's probably that name-recognition issue. We're just not out there."

"Well, you've got my vote, and everybody in the A.V.A." She turns to her computer. "Let's see what's online."

I get to my feet, pad across the desk, and nudge Meg's hand with my nose. Sometimes people just need to know that somebody cares. Cats are the same way. Maybe not as frequently as people, but it happens.

When I look up, she smiles down at me. "Hey, Patch. You just don't give up, do you?"

For a cat, giving up isn't really an option. The only choices are to live or not live. Well, admittedly in my case, I am in a creepy middle ground. But the point is that cats aren't equipped to give up on living. If we wanted to surrender, what would we do? Put a gun to our heads? Down a bottle of pills? Yeah, we could run in front of a truck, but seeking out pain and suffering is anathema to a cat.

So I give her a lick on the hand, and she scratches the top of my head, one of my favorite spots. Meg says, "Me neither. We've got two days to get out the vote."

There's a knock on the door. It's Bruce. He smiles when he sees me. "K-k-kitty." He holds a newspaper and takes it to Vera's desk, then stops by to give me a couple of strokes before he goes.

Vera opens the paper and reads, and then a fat smile blossoms on her face. "Hey, a new poll, and you're dead even with Captain Cook, and Tom is in single digits."

Meg's eyebrows arch upward. "I thought I was the one in the pits."

"Two things. This poll includes people they talked to after dark."

Ah. The Night Shift. Us.

"So they weren't including the vampire vote before?"

"Nope. I'm thinking that seeing Tom setting up to pound a stake into you didn't go over too well, even with breathers. The votes he lost mostly went to you. And you were right about the name-recognition problem."

"But I haven't done anything to improve it. We couldn't run commercials."

"Ah, but you were all over the news, especially after the trial. The second thing that happened is they changed the question to ask about Meg Murrow and Patch the kitty-cat. Your numbers shot up."

Hey. How cool is that?

Vera hands Meg the paper and adds a scratch behind my ears to the stroking Meg is giving my back. Nice. Double nice.

Meg reads. "Listen to this, Patch. When they asked about the two of us, people say, 'Oh, yeah, the vampire kitty-cat.'" She scans some more, forgetting to stroke my back. But that's okay, because we're talking about me.

She laughs. "Your approval ratings are very high with people who hate yappy dogs."

I begin to think there is hope for rationality in the human race. It's faint, but there it is.

I can testify that a political campaign, even for a mostly dead cat, is wearing. Sure, all I have to do is smile and look good, all of which comes naturally to me and takes little effort, but when you're furry you're a target for a lot of petting by amateurs. Even dog lovers pound me on the back, and small children pull out bits of fur that will never grow back. Luckily, there are only two days left before the election.

With Lester as chauffeur and bodyguard, Meg and I visit all the late-night places she can think of—the gas stations and convenience stores, any business with a night shift, any place with lights on. Vera puts the A.V.A. to work going door-to-door all night long with flyers that say stuff like, "Safety for all! A vote for Meg and Patch is a vote for freedom and prosperity."

That seems a tad overblown, but we have to come on strong to overcome the slight revulsion—or, frequently, the screaming horror—people feel about vampires walking around and talking to them and pursuing our vampire agenda.

Ginger Grant and Ernie follow us in a CNN van, and her reports raise our visibility with breathers during the day. The last poll of the day includes the Night Shift, and we're actually leading Captain Cook. Tom drops out of the race.

I'd best get to work on my victory meow.

43: Patch

It's afternoon of Election Day and still daylight when Meg and I get ready for her to vote. She dresses in a natty blue suit and gives me a good brushing. As I admire myself in a mirror, she says, "We want to look our best when we vote tonight."

Her apartment doorbell rings, and Meg goes to the door. "Who is it?"

"CNN. Ginger Grant here." There's a mutter, and she adds, "And Ernie Bert."

Meg opens the door to admit them.

Grant eyes Meg. "My, don't you look lively." She says, "We want to get you casting your vote. This could be historic."

Meg smiles. "I hope so."

Since it will make her happy, I do too.

Ernie glances at his watch. "We need to get moving. The polls close at seven, and it's six forty-five now."

"They close at seven?" She turns to the black curtains over her living room window. The itch of sunshine leaks through. "Oh, no."

Grant gets it right away. "Uh-oh."

Meg whips her phone out and does a quick search. Her shoulders sag. "This time of year, the sun doesn't set until a quarter after seven."

Grant holds her microphone out and Ernie starts taping. "Ginger Grant here with vampire candidate Meg Murrow—"

I give her a meow.

Her brows almost furrow into a frown, then she pastes on a smile. "And her most unusual co-candidate, a murderous vampire cat."

Meg picks me up. I give her a dose of purr in hopes that will make her feel better.

Grant goes on. "Local polls, which ended yesterday, showed Meg Murrow and her co-candidate leading in the primary race for sheriff."

She gives the camera a smile. Is she enjoying this? "However, Miss Murrow has just learned that she and, I presume, her fellow vampires, will not be able to vote because the polls close before sunset." She holds the mike out to Meg's face. "What do you say about that?"

"Shit."

About ten o'clock that evening, I'm curled up in Meg's lap when the local news channel goes to their Election Central set. Mom and Dad are with us, wearing their Meg & Patch buttons. A display behind the news anchor shows candidate names and vote counts. Tom Conway got 4 votes, Captain Cook got 3,674 votes, and we got 3,067. Footage of Captain Cook comes up as the announcer says, "KTBC is calling the sheriff primary election for Captain Cook."

Every vote counts ... but only if you can vote. Vampire votes vanished into the light.

Meg slumps, and I'm sure she would have let out a long sigh if she'd been breathing. She does take a breath and says, "I don't know what to do next. I don't have a job, and I'll lose my apartment."

Mom pats her hand. "You can stay with us, honey."

Dad says, "For a while."

Meg strokes me. "I have to figure out a way to get on with my, er, life. But Papa Gambino has me totally blocked in Bloomsburg, even with the A.V.A." She pets my head and looks down at me. "Maybe Aunt Betty in Peoria can help us get started there."

I don't like the idea of having to learn a new neighborhood. It isn't that I'm lazy—I think of it as "easygoing." But I do want to stick with Meg. So I give her an approving "Mrf."

The doorbell rings. Meg says, "I'll get it. It's probably Ginger Grant, wanting to interview the loser, which she will no doubt enjoy. Come on, Patch."

I join her at the door, but when she opens it, it isn't the news folks. It's a man holding a single white rose.

She says, "Clive?"

He holds the rose out to Meg. One look at her shows me a face that makes me think of a thunderstorm rolling in.

Clive says, "I owe you an apology."

The thunderstorm hits and lightning strikes, and, even though Meg's voice is low and even, it's like a fist ready to throw a punch. "You don't owe me anything."

She swings the door to close it but he blocks it with a hand. "But I want to get back to—"

"Together? To do what? Be my boyfriend? What I needed when this happened to me was a *friend*. Where were you?"

Even I can feel the force behind her question. He steps back. "But I was afrai—"

"You don't know the meaning of afraid when sunlight begins to burn you, when idiots want to stab you with a stake, when mammoth goons kidnap you."

"But you look so okay on televi—"

She slams the door. After a long, silent moment, her father applauds and her mom comes to her and embraces Meg's shoulders.

Meg sniffles. "Like Dad says, what kind of a name is Clive?" Her grin is shallow, but it's there. That's my partner.

Another knock on the door sounds. Meg yanks it open and says, "I want you to get ... "

It's not Clive or Ginger Grant. It's a chubby fellow in a suit. He wears a tie with a picture of a cartoon mouse on it.

I like mice. Much better than rats. Fun to play with, and they have a savory aftertaste.

The man holds out a business card. "Can we talk?" His gaze shifts to me and he smiles. "I'm with Disney."

Dear Reader

 A thousand thanks for reading my book—it is to purr. If you enjoyed my story, please consider telling your friends and posting a review on your blog or at Amazon.com.

And my typist, Ray Rhamey, would be glad to talk with book clubs about my tale. He seems to think that there are themes in it, stuff like prejudice, bigotry, greed, and being an outsider. Whatever. You can contact him at ray@rayrhamey.com.

And read my next adventure, *The Hollywood Unmurders*. It's a sequel packed with crimes and dangerous times in La La Land for me and Meg. And you'll meet a handsome but tough detective who is also a werecoyote. Find it at Amazon.

Patch

About my typist

My typist, Ray Rhamey, asked me to tell you a little about him. Since he's been a good associate, what with the catnip and typing up my story and all, I'm happy to oblige.

Ray is quite catlike, independent as hell and really loves to have his back scratched. I think he was purring when this picture was taken.

His wife, Sarah, reminds me of a Siamese cat—elegant and beautiful. Ray has four fine offspring, too: Abby, Molly, Becky, and Dan. They're also catlike, especially on the independence part.

He has made his living with this writer thing he does for quite a while now. He did a long turn in advertising as a copywriter and then a creative director. I hear that his sense of humor bubbled up in a lot of his creative work, which was capped by the droll Budweiser TasteBuds commercials he did that people saw on *Saturday Night Live* back in the Eighties.

But he left advertising and did screenwriting for a while—kids enjoy his television adaptation of *The Little Engine that Could*. Then he moved on from that.

Here's where Ray is less like a cat than, say, a cat—he doesn't sleep most of the day. No, he keeps trying stuff.

He's invented a board game that he says is more fun than Scrabble.

He makes me tired. I want a catnap.

Ray tells me that he's always been drawn to storytelling. It was only natural that he turned to writing novels after his screenwriting period. He has read a couple of them to me, and they're darned good—they were the primary reason I agreed to let him help me with telling my story. If you get a chance to read one, you won't be disappointed, even though they're not funny. There's one—*Gundown*—that really makes you think, if you're into that kind of thing (thinking, that is).

Digging into the craft of writing novels to tell his own stories led him to doing freelance editing of book-length fiction, and that led him to create his blog on writing compelling fiction, *Flogging the Quill*. I'll be honest, some of the things I learned from him helped me do this book . . . okay, that's a plug, but, hey, I'm biased. Full disclosure.

Anyway, his blog led to him teaching writing workshops at writers' conferences and publishing his book, *Mastering the Craft of Compelling Storytelling*. Even though he lives in the Pacific Northwest, he's got fans all over the world, and I can see how much he enjoys being a member of the writing community and helping other writers. But I don't hold it against him as long as I get my full share of his time.

Speaking of which, now he's doing editing and book design full time at crrreative.com. He designed my book.

I wonder what's going to happen next. Stay tuned.

Keep on purrin'.
Patch

Novels by me I think you will enjoy

The old vampire saying, "Life doesn't get any easier after you're dead," nails it for vampire kitty-cat Patch when Meg, his vampire partner, is arrested for murder. When the sun comes up, innocent Meg, locked in a jail cell, will be toast.

Worse, her incarceration means curtains for Patch. Trapped in their apartment, he can't open the refrigerator to get to their V1 Juice (blood), much less open the bottles.

Opposable thumbs are so handy.

Meg begs Nick, the cop who nabbed her, to help Patch, but he's down on cats. Reciprocally, Meg hates Nick for sending them to their doom.

And Nick is the only one who can save them.

Paperback books and Kindle ebooks are available on Amazon.com. A search that includes my last name will find them. Paperback and Kindle available on Amazon.

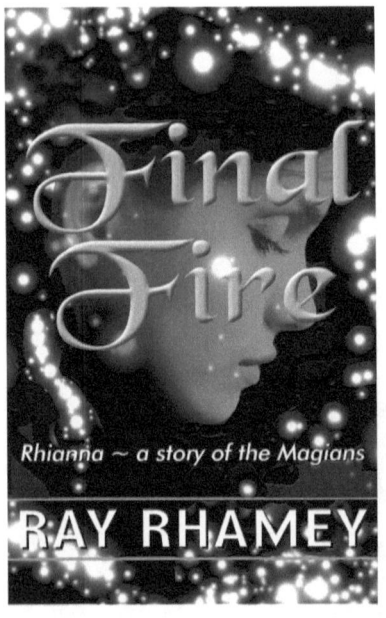

Rhianna ~ a story of the Magians

RAY RHAMEY

Final Fire is the story of a woman, a healer, who loves deeply ... and has lost.

Of a man whose beloved child is deeply troubled ... and he doesn't know how to help her.

Of a child lost in a whirlwind of psychic abilities.

Of a people with an ability to heal, to extend life, or to kill without a touch.

Of a madman who creates a plague to destroy the human race to avenge the death of his son.

Of a Homeland Security agent whose rabid hatred of terrorists leads her to despicable acts.

The Magians are amidst us. A mutation gives them control over natural life energy to extend their lives, to heal ... or to kill. Their kin have been burned at the stake as witches, so they live apart from the rest of humanity in small scattered clans. But their genes course through the populace, and many of us unknowingly share their heritage.

Homeland Security is pursuing Rhianna, a Magian healer, because they see terrorism in the manifestation of her ability. On the run, she learns that Drago, a Magian clanmaster, will launch a fatal plague that will wipe out "ordinary" people, billions of us, as vengeance for the murder of his son.

And battle is joined ...

Paperback and Kindle available on Amazon.

The air was as still as it was hot—only the whir of a grasshopper's flight troubled the quiet. Jesse felt like an overcooked chicken, his meat darn near ready to fall off his bones. Mouth so dry he didn't have enough spit left to swallow, Jesse croaked, "That guy tryin' to kill us?"

Turns out the answer is "Not yet." A ranch hand is murdered and bad things start happening to Jesse, just an average kid working on a ranch the summer of 1958.

And then there's Lola . . . the boss's daughter is a firecracker of a girl, and her bold ways send death their way.

It will take all of their heart and courage to survive.

Paperback and Kindle available on Amazon.

In the time it takes an average person to read this novel, three Americans will die from a handgun bullet.

In today's America there is no hope of preventing those killings. Dealing with gun violence is mired in a cultural logjam—as things are, nothing will change.

But what if gun makers could make billions if states made lethal firearms illegal? They'd make it happen.

And what if we had a way to defend ourselves without using lethal firearms? We'd make it happen.

In *Gundown*, guns are still everyday killers. Ordinary people have no defense—except in Oregon, where reforms have self-defense on the rise and guns that kill are banned.

But gun advocates fear losing their rights. Hank Soldado, Army veteran and ex-cop, is a good guy with a gun. He accepts an assignment to stop the gun-reform leader.

Going undercover to get close to his target—the closer he gets the more he's drawn to the man's vision for a way to turn America's murderous gun impasse into gun-free self-defense, security, and safety.

Then treachery strikes to destroy that vision, and Hank becomes the only one who can save it—a man who has a lifetime of guns in his blood.

Paperback and Kindle editions of these novels are available on Amazon and through your local bookstore. I hope you'll give them a look.

And I'd appreciate it if you could post a review of *Support Your Local Vampire Kitty-Cat* on Amazon.

Thanks for reading.

www.ingramcontent.com/pod-product-compliance
Lightning Source LLC
Chambersburg PA
CBHW030751060526
44539CB00043B/887